THE TEMPLAR HERESY

James Becker

BANTAM BOOKS

LONDON • TORONTO • SYDNEY • AUCKLAND • JOHANNESBURG

TRANSWORLD PUBLISHERS
61–63 Uxbridge Road, London W5 5SA
www.penguin.co.uk

Transworld is part of the Penguin Random House group of companies
whose addresses can be found at global.penguinrandomhouse.com

Penguin
Random House
UK

First published in Great Britain in 2017 by Bantam
an imprint of Transworld Publishers

A CIP catalogue record for this book
is available from the British Library.

ISBN
9780857502308

Typeset in 11/14pt Sabon by Falcon Oast Graphic Art Ltd.
Printed and bound by Clays Ltd, Bungay, Suffolk.

Penguin Random House is committed to a sustainable future for our
business, our readers and our planet. This book is made from Forest
Stewardship Council® certified paper.

MIX
Paper from
responsible sources
FSC® C018179

3 5 7 9 10 8 6 4

To Sally, as always and for everything

Prologue

'The Lord Antipas wishes this event to be performed with dignity, and with a minimum of suffering,' the chamberlain said, 'so make sure it takes only a single blow.'

The executioner nodded and walked over to the guards to give them their instructions. Then he stepped back and watched as they led the condemned man forward to the centre of the cleared area, the ground under his tattered leather sandals beaten flat by the passage of innumerable feet and stained dark brown, a silent reminder of countless previous executions performed on the same spot. The victim looked around him calmly, gazing without apparent curiosity at the circle of spectators, people who had been drawn to the palace courtyard by the spectacle of his imminent death. Some fifty or sixty men, and just a handful of women, had assembled to witness this final act at the end of the day's judicial proceedings. A gentle susurration was clearly audible, a muttering of conversation that had grown in volume as the condemned man was led into position by two soldiers.

The courtyard was bounded on all sides by high walls, constructed from blocks of light-coloured stone. One formed a part of the fabric of the palace, pierced by a wide doorway that led to the building's interior. A number of palace officials were standing in that opening, also watching the proceedings. Two of the other walls were solid, while the third was fitted with a pair of heavy wooden gates, their tops marked by rows of metal spikes, which stood open to allow the populace to enter freely.

Above the palace, the sky was an almost unbroken palette of solid blue, marred only by a handful of small white clouds. And beyond the courtyard, a fitful breeze drove grey-brown clouds of dust into the open space, lifting and flapping the loose garments worn by the majority of the spectators.

The two soldiers leading the man glanced towards the executioner, waiting for his signal. When he nodded, they gestured to the prisoner to get down on to his knees. In one swift movement, they each took hold of one of his arms and pulled them back so that his head and neck were thrust forward.

The executioner drew his sword from its scabbard and tested the blade against the ball of his thumb. The single-edged blade was longer, wider and heavier than a sword designed for combat, but was very efficient when used for its proper purpose.

He stepped forward, the blade hanging loosely at his side, and bent down to talk quietly to the condemned prisoner.

'Stretch out your neck and try to look up,' he said. 'If you do that, I will only need to strike you once. If you don't, this will be very unpleasant for both of us. It's the most I can do for you.'

The prisoner spoke for the first time.

'I understand.'

The executioner took a half pace back, checked that the guards were holding the man in the right position, then stepped forward again and moved the prisoner's long dark hair from his neck. Bearing in mind the man's function at the court, his action showed a surprising and unexpected degree of compassion. Then he stood beside the kneeling figure and lifted the sword above his head.

The crowd now ceased its muttering; their sense of anticipation was almost palpable, their concentration absolute. The executioner waited for a second or two, until the man had done as he'd been asked, pushing his head out and away from his body and tensing the muscles of his neck. Then he swept the blade down in a lethal, glittering arc. The crunch as it met the bones of the man's neck was clearly audible, but the sound was instantly drowned out by a collective inhalation, a sharp intake of breath from the spectators as the head of the prophet hit the ground and rolled gently from his instantly lifeless body. And almost immediately the crowd began to disperse. The deed they had assembled to witness, for whatever reason, was done; the spectacle was over.

The chamberlain stepped forward, taking care to avoid the spreading pool of blood on the ground, then bent down, picked up the head by its long black hair, and placed it on a silver salver.

He paused briefly to instruct the guards to dispose of the body, then retreated inside the hall to show the head to his master, Herod Antipas.

'It is done, my lord,' he said, somewhat unnecessarily in view of the object he held aloft on the platter. 'I have ordered that the body be disposed of in secret. They will bury it deep in the desert, where no one will ever stumble upon the remains by accident, so the man's followers will have no relic to venerate. As you ordered, we can retain the head here, where we can keep it under our control, for the same reason.'

Antipas nodded, then stood up and left the hall, followed by his retinue. The day's business was over.

Two of the men in the crowd outside in the courtyard had watched the execution closely. The event was what they had feared from the moment the prophet had been seized, and although there was nothing they could now do for the dead man – their friend and charismatic leader – there was at least some hope that they could keep his movement going. But only if they succeeded in the next phase of their plan – a plan that they acknowledged had been born of desperation rather than hope.

They left the palace and returned to their village, a walk of about half an hour. A small group, perhaps a little over a dozen men in all, was waiting for them.

The news they conveyed was not unexpected, but the confirmation of their leader's demise brought sorrowful gasps from the assembled company.

'And his death?' one man asked.

'The beheading was swift. And, as we thought, they will be burying his body somewhere where we'll never find it, but the head will be staying under Herod's control. So that at least gives us a chance. A chance to continue our leader's great work.'

'So we steal it?' the same man asked.

The two men who had been at the palace shook their heads simultaneously.

'That wouldn't work,' one of them said. 'If it goes missing, they will know what's happened and hunt us down. We must take it without them realizing that it has gone. There is only one way that can be achieved.'

He turned slightly and looked at another man in the group, a tall, thin man with long black hair and an even longer beard.

The crowd fell silent as if in response to some kind of signal, and they all looked at that one still figure.

'I will do it,' he said, his voice clouded with barely supressed emotion, 'because I believe absolutely in the man who died today. When?'

'For this to work, it must be as soon as possible.'

'Very well. My family have been prepared for this, and I am resigned to what must happen. I will take just a little time to make my farewells.'

A short while later, the man returned to the group and they all followed the two leaders out of the village and into the undergrowth. They halted in a small clearing, where the tall man with the long hair and beard spent a few short moments with each of his companions before walking to the centre of the clearing and kneeling down. With an air of great solemnity, one of the leaders produced a short but heavy sword and stepped over to the kneeling man. He gave him a reassuring press on the shoulder and took a pace back. Then he inhaled deeply, did his best to compose himself and, with a single heavy blow, decapitated his friend. He shuddered and turned away, unable to look at what he had just done.

'Let us hope this works,' he said thickly, as his companion picked up the head and slid it into a heavy linen sack half-full of rags to soak up the blood. 'If it doesn't our brother will have given his life – and I will have become a murderer – for nothing.'

An hour later, in the fading light of early evening, the two men once again walked into the palace courtyard. Perhaps surprisingly, there were still twenty or so spectators there, wandering about under the watchful gaze of two guards. Most of them were looking at the body of a man who had been stoned to death, a killer convicted out of his own mouth earlier that day.

The moment they entered the courtyard the two men separated, one joining the largest group of civilians, while the other, the linen bag slung over his shoulder, moved over to the opposite side of the courtyard, and loitered near the doors that led into the hall.

Moments later, a scuffle broke out amongst the group of spectators, a dispute deliberately instigated by the new arrival, and which almost immediately turned violent. Raised voices and the sound of blows filled the courtyard, and within seconds both of the watching guards had stepped forward to intervene, lashing out with the wooden shafts of their spears to separate the fighting civilians.

The moment the guards had begun to move, the second man had pulled open the door to the hall just wide enough to allow him to slip through the gap, and disappeared from sight.

Inside, half a dozen flickering oil lamps provided barely enough illumination to see from one end of the hall to the other. But it was sufficient to clearly show the silver salver placed upon a table by the wall opposite the throne, on which the uneven outline of the decapitated head of the prophet was visible.

The man hurried over to the table and bowed his head in a brief prayer. Then, looking with sadness and reverence at the features that were as familiar to him as his own, he reached out to seize the hair of the decapitated head. But the gaze of the half-closed eyes seemed to accuse him even in death, and he changed his mind. The prophet deserved better from him.

Instead, he gripped the head with both hands, lifted it off the salver and placed it gently on the floor. It was heavier than he had expected and awkward to manoeuvre. He opened the linen sack, removed the second head – the head of another man he'd also been pleased to call a friend – and placed it on the silver dish. He took precious extra moments to arrange the hair and beard on the salver so that the replacement looked as much like the original as possible.

He gently transferred the head of the prophet to the linen sack, took a deep breath to steady himself and then strode back to the partially open door. Outside the guards were still trying to restore order, and the man could see another two guards approaching the mêlée from outside the courtyard. And then behind him, from inside the hall, he heard the sound of running feet. And then an angry voice rose in challenge.

The man didn't hesitate. The guards would kill him on sight without waiting to question why he was there. He simply took to his heels, pushing open the door and running out into the courtyard, heading for the wide arched entrance. All of the guards, he knew, would be encumbered with weapons and would be unable to catch him, though obviously a well-thrown spear would bring him down.

And even as that thought crossed his mind, he felt a glancing blow on his shoulder and a spear slammed into the open wooden door a few feet to his right. He touched his shoulder. No blood. The blow must have been from the shaft of the weapon, not from the point.

He began jinking from side to side, but no other missiles came anywhere near him. Within a couple of minutes he slowed down to a walk, and before long his companion rejoined him. Together, they retraced their steps, heading back to the village with their gruesome but invaluable prize: the severed head of their leader, the teacher and prophet they had followed for the last decade.

1

Kuwait

When Chris Bronson stepped outside the arrivals building at Kuwait International Airport the humid heat hit him like a hot sodden blanket. It actually stopped him in his tracks, and for a few seconds it almost hurt to breathe. His aviator-style sunglasses instantly fogged up, so the heat had rendered him not only immobile but also unable to see.

'Dear God,' he muttered, putting down his two small bags at his feet. He only had a cabin bag containing his weekend stuff, a couple of books, washing kit and clothes, and a small leather computer bag that held his netbook and tablet. He pulled a handkerchief out of his pocket, took off his sunglasses, squinting against the hard glare of the morning sun, and wiped the lenses. At least then he would be able to see what was in front of him, even if he had no idea at that moment where he should be heading.

He looked around hopefully, trying to take shallow breaths as his body began to acclimatize to the radical change in temperature and humidity. The air-conditioned aircraft, air-conditioned walkway and air-conditioned terminal building had left him woefully unprepared for the blistering-hot reality of the world outside.

'Chris!'

He spun round and saw that a sand-coloured 4x4 vehicle had just come to a halt on the access road in front of him, and through the open window a woman was waving enthusiastically at him.

He grinned broadly and waved back, then picked up his bags and walked the short distance across the pavement to the vehicle, opening his arms for a hug as the woman climbed out of the vehicle.

But she shook her head and simply extended her hand for him to shake.

'No, not here, Chris,' she said. 'They're very touchy about public displays of affection, even between married couples. And we're not even that any more.'

Bronson took her hand firmly and pulled her towards him, bumping shoulders as he met her eyes.

'That, Angela, is the biggest regret of my life,' he said with a wide smile, 'and I'd be very happy to walk you down the aisle again. All you have to do is say the word.'

'I do know that,' she replied, taking a step backwards and looking up at the face of her former husband. 'And I do kind of miss being Mrs Angela Bronson. It has a nice ring to it, but we had our reasons, Chris, you know that. Anyway, it's good to see you again. You look well.'

'So do you,' Bronson said, his gaze running up and down her body, which was entirely covered apart from her face. 'What I can see of you, that is.'

'It's practical, my dear,' she said. 'It's cooler to wear white or light-coloured clothes out here, and local sensibilities mean I need to cover up.'

'And the scarf?' Bronson pointed at her head. 'You haven't fully embraced Islam, have you?'

'Of course not. I don't have to wear the hijab, but I prefer to, especially in the city. And being blonde always attracts attention in this region. It's just easier to cover up to avoid being stared at. It makes me feel more comfortable.'

Bronson looked into the back of the vehicle, saw that it was loaded with boxes and packets, and pulled open the rear door, placed his bags on the floor behind the driver's seat, then walked round and climbed into the front passenger seat.

His ex-wife and still his best friend got in beside him and then, shielded by the tinted windows of the Toyota, leaned over and kissed him firmly on the lips. Bronson grasped her hand and smiled at her, and for a few moments they remained almost motionless, relishing each other's presence after too long apart.

'That's a better hello,' Angela said, returning his smile. She put the Toyota into gear and pulled away as Bronson buckled his seat belt.

'Tell me this jeep has got air-conditioning,' he said

with a groan, feeling the sweat already starting to dampen his shirt. 'It's like a bloody oven out there.'

'Actually,' Angela said brightly, 'it hasn't. But what it has got is climate control, which is much better, so if you just sit there and stop complaining about the heat, you'll cool down in a few seconds.'

Bronson shook his head and adjusted the dashboard vents so that the stream of ice-cold air was directed towards his face and chest.

'Sorry,' he replied, as the cool air started to have an effect. 'The heat was a bit of a shock. I was expecting it, obviously, but it still kind of took me by surprise. How on earth do you manage to work in it?'

Angela shrugged her shoulders. 'You get used to it, at least to some extent, and we do what we can to keep the sun off our backs at the excavation site. Ideally we'd live somewhere here in the city, but we don't really have any option,' she continued. 'The site is too far away for us to commute there on a daily basis from anywhere half-civilized, and being on site all the time means that we can get a lot of work done first thing in the morning before the sun gets too high in the sky, and carry on late into the evening until the light finally goes. We each spend at least two nights in a hotel in Kuwait every fort-night, just to wash off the dust and dirt. Showering in the desert isn't the easiest thing to do.'

'Isn't it a hassle going back and forth across the border between Kuwait and Iraq so often?'

'We do have to cross the border, obviously, but there's absolutely no indication apart from the GPS' – she pointed at a unit attached to the windscreen with a suction cup – 'and possibly a couple of border guards patrolling the area in a 4x4 to tell you where you are and when you've crossed into Iraq. I can promise you that the desert in Kuwait is absolutely identical to the desert in Iraq. The dig is in a kind of empty quarter, so that's why we need a professional standard GPS to navigate by lat and long. There are only a handful of roads out there.'

'Makes sense,' Bronson said. 'So we're heading straight out there, are we? I saw you've already got all the gear in the back of the truck.'

'We are, yes, but we've got to stop and pick up somebody before we leave Kuwait City. Stephen Taverner – another archaeologist from the British Museum. I gave him a lift here a couple of days ago for an appointment and it's easier for us to all go back together.'

'So you didn't just drive down to meet me?'

Angela nodded.

'Well, sort of. The main reason I drove down was to collect you, obviously, but one of our vehicles does a supply run at least once a week, and we also had to deliver some of the relics we've uncovered to the museum in Kuwait. The staff there are collating what we've found, and they'll then arrange to transport everything up to Baghdad.

'Normally, of course, we'd expect to take the stuff straight to the museum that authorized or sponsored the dig, but Baghdad is just too far away to make that feasible in this case. Where we're digging is about three hundred miles from Baghdad as the crow flies, and probably over four hundred by road – not that there are many of them, or not proper roads anyway. But Kuwait City is only about sixty miles away in a straight line, and a bit over one hundred on the route we drive. And don't forget that this is a joint expedition. We have both Iraqi and Kuwaiti archaeologists involved in the dig, plus the three of us from the British Museum and a couple of French experts from a Paris museum, so it really does make sense to use Kuwait City as our base.'

Bronson switched his gaze from Angela's profile to the view through the windscreen. It was the first time he'd been to Kuwait, though he had on occasion visited Dubai and Muscat, albeit briefly, and he could immediately see the similarities. The skyline in front of them was dominated by skyscrapers and there were signs of recent construction everywhere; the roads were wide and in good condition, most of the vehicles looked quite new, and the driving was universally awful, vehicles swapping lanes at random and without the use of indicators or mirrors, and all driving far too close to one another, and far too fast.

'The driving doesn't bother you?' he asked, looking at a car moving alongside them.

'It terrified me at first, but after a week or so I got used to it.' She broke off and hit the horn hard as a white Nissan saloon dived across two lanes of traffic and pulled in front of them with only inches to spare, before swinging off on to an exit slip road.

Bronson lifted his foot from the imaginary brake that

he had applied as the car appeared, and shook his head.

'I thought Cairo was bad,' he muttered, 'but this is probably worse, and everything's moving a hell of a lot faster.'

'We won't be in it for very long,' Angela said, slowing down slightly as the vehicles ahead began bunching up, brake lights flaring into life. 'Once we've collected Stephen we'll be heading out of town, and the roads should be fairly empty.'

About fifteen minutes later she pulled the Toyota to a stop directly outside a hotel on a side street and tooted the horn briefly.

Almost immediately, a tall, thin man with sandy hair and what looked to Bronson like three days' growth of beard walked out of the hotel and over to the Land Cruiser. He'd actually stretched out his hand to the front passenger door handle before he registered the fact that the seat was already occupied. Instead, he opened the rear door and pulled himself into the back seat, a gust of hot damp air accompanying him.

'Sorry, I didn't see you there. I'm Stephen Taverner,' he said, and extended his hand for Bronson to shake.

'Nice to meet you. I'm Chris. I'm Angela's former other half, if you can call me that.'

'Oh, of course, Chris Bronson. She's told us all about you.'

'Nothing good, I expect,' Bronson said.

'No, not really,' Stephen replied, deadpan. Then he grinned, but immediately grimaced and put the palm of his hand against the side of his face. 'This blasted tooth,' he said. 'The dentist hacked out the old filling and put in a new one, but it's still giving me gyp. No, actually, Angela was quite complimentary about you, given the fact that you've been divorced for so long. Absence makes the heart grow fonder, maybe?'

'Not in my case,' Angela piped up, swinging the Land Cruiser around a corner to head back the way they'd come. She gave Bronson a wry smile. 'But Chris can be useful, especially in a tight corner.'

'So if you're not here for some kind of reconciliation with the fair Angela,' Stephen asked, 'why are you out here at all?'

'I had a couple of weeks' leave due, and I thought I needed a change of scene from rural Kent, so when Angela suggested I come out to see what she was up to in Iraq, I booked a flight and packed my shorts. I would have packed a bucket and spade, but she told me not to bother.'

Stephen nodded. 'Quite right too. Archaeologists almost never use anything as crude as a spade. Our tool of choice is usually a brush or, if something is particularly reluctant to come back into the light of day, a small trowel.' He paused for a moment, then added: 'So are you looking forward to seeing the temple?'

'Temple?' Bronson demanded, his interest piqued. 'What temple?'

2

Vicinity of Al Muthanna, Iraq

The tailgates of the lorries slammed down almost simultaneously, sounding like two ragged gunshots, and from the back of each vehicle a group of about a dozen men jumped down to the ground and began walking steadily towards the encampment. They were clad in a wide variety of clothing, everything from classic but rather grubby Arabian jellabas up to military-style camouflage clothing.

But the new arrivals shared one characteristic: they were all carrying Kalashnikov assault rifles. Many of them also wore shoulder or belt holsters containing pistols of various types, and a couple were hefting rocket-propelled grenade launchers.

As the men approached the encampment in two straggly lines, the members of the archaeology team stood and watched, frozen to the spot, the expressions on their faces ranging from merely puzzled to frankly terrified.

Suddenly, one of the younger Iraqi archaeologists turned on his heels and ran towards the small vehicle park at one side of the encampment.

He didn't get far.

A shouted command came from somewhere in the line of men approaching from the east, and two of the figures dropped to their knees, aimed their Kalashnikovs at the fleeing figure, and opened fire.

Two sudden flares of blood discoloured the man's clothing, one on his left leg and the other on his back. He took another couple of steps, probably driven by nothing more than momentum, and then collapsed in an untidy tangle of limbs on the desert sand. For the briefest of instants there was silence, and then the fallen man began screaming as he tried to crawl away. One of the approaching men walked unhurriedly over to where he lay, took a pistol from a holster and fired two shots into the fallen man's legs. He began screaming even more loudly, and the sound only stopped when the terrorist bent over him, took a large knife from his belt and slowly, methodically, sawed through the man's throat. Blood pumped out of the ragged wound as the major arteries in the neck were severed and for a few seconds the only sound in the camp was the scrape of steel on bone as the knife was worked through the Iraqi's vertebrae. Once he'd finished, the killer wiped the blood from his blade on the dead man's clothing, then picked up the severed head by the hair and placed it in the middle of the corpse's back.

If there had been the slightest doubt before about the intentions of the approaching men, the casual and almost incidental but still ritualized murder of the young archaeologist comprehensively removed it. These people were clearly terrorists, perhaps a splinter of the Islamic State, the ruthlessly murderous group that had risen to prominence as ISIS or ISL a few years earlier and which had terrified members of all the nations in the Middle East, including those that followed Islam.

But that really didn't make sense. The Islamic State was a political entity, determined to impose Islam on every nation it could, the choice being offered to people simply comprising an option: 'follow Islam or we will kill you'. The group had left a trail of bodies, thousands of them, across the Middle East, a mute testimony to their implacable resolve and total ruthlessness.

This, however, didn't seem to have a political motivation. Taking over a village and insisting that the inhabitants converted to Islam was one thing, but surrounding a dozen or so people involved in an archaeological dig tens of miles from anywhere seemed completely pointless. There had to be some other reason, some overriding objective, for these men to have driven so far out into the desert.

The two lines of approaching men stopped, now completely surrounding the group of archaeologists. Two of them had fallen to their knees and were visibly quaking, while most of the others were just staring wide-eyed at the intruders, trying to make sense of what had happened just seconds before.

One of the newcomers, a young man with a thick black beard and wearing a military-style camouflage uniform, stepped forward and looked at the group of unarmed men they had encircled.

'Who is in charge here?' he asked softly in English, his voice educated and the tone almost conversational.

Nobody responded, and with a deceptively casual gesture the newcomer pointed at an archaeologist standing to one side of the group, a brush and trowel held forgotten in his hands.

The man standing on the right of the apparent leader of the newcomers raised his Kalashnikov and fired three rounds straight at the archaeologist at virtually point-blank range. The impact of the bullets slammed his body backwards, knocking him off his feet, and he was dead before he even hit the ground. A chorus of ragged screams rang out as the terrified archaeologists stared in fascinated horror at his broken body and the slowly expanding pool of blood around him.

'I'll ask you once again,' the bearded man said, just as quietly as before. 'Who is in charge here?'

For about a second, nobody spoke, but several people in the group looked straight at the man in their centre. Then one of the archaeologists pointed at him.

'He is,' he said, an obvious tremor in his voice. 'His name is Mohammed. Please don't shoot me. Please.'

Mohammed nodded, took a half step forward and slowly raised his left hand.

'Good. Now, that wasn't too difficult, was it?' The bearded man smiled slightly. 'We have been told that you have discovered a hidden temple. An important hidden temple. I would like to see it. Now.'

Mohammed shook his head.

'It's just an empty room,' he said, his voice sounding bewildered. 'There's nothing in it. Well, almost nothing. But of course you can see it,' he added hurriedly, desperate not to antagonize the young man. 'It's this way.'

He turned and pointed towards one of the trenches that ran arrow straight across the irregular rocky ground of the desert. It was marked by flags at regular intervals, and its vertical sides also bore markings to indicate both the excavated depth and the areas where particular artefacts had been discovered. At the far end of the trench, one of the sides displayed a large bulge, a kind of semicircular shape, out of which the top of an aluminium ladder protruded.

Mohammed started nervously across the rock towards the ladder and then stopped right beside it.

'It's down there,' he said. 'Do you want me to go down first?'

The bearded man shook his head.

'That will not be necessary. I know what I'm looking for. Do you have lights down there?'

Mohammed swallowed and nodded.

'We do,' he replied, 'but only when the generator's running. I can have it started for you, if you wish.'

'No. I have a torch.'

The man checked that the base of the ladder was firm, then swiftly climbed down it.

Mohammed peered nervously down into the opening, seeing the flickering light as the torch beam swept around the interior of the abandoned cave they had uncovered just four days earlier.

He glanced around, wondering if there was any possibility of him reaching one of the vehicles and making his escape, but when he looked more closely at the two parked trucks he realized that to do anything of that sort would simply hasten his own death. He had assumed that the two lorries had been abandoned by the armed men, but now he saw that this was not the case. In the back of each vehicle, standing in the loading area but directly behind the cab, he could see a single figure, and beside each person was the unmistakable shape of a mounted heavy machine gun. With those weapons, even if he somehow managed to reach one of the 4x4s, get it started and drive it away, they could still cut him to pieces from half a mile away.

Mohammed's mind raced and he started to shake as he accepted the inevitability of what was likely to happen. They couldn't hide, they couldn't run and they couldn't fight: the fate of everyone in the group rested entirely on the whims of the armed men who had invaded the camp. All they could do was exactly what they were told, and just hope that some of them would still be alive when the terrorists finally left.

He didn't dare to move and, after about a minute, the ladder began to vibrate as the man started to climb up it again to emerge from the opening.

He glanced at Mohammed as he stepped back on to the ground.

'Wait here,' he ordered, and strode away, heading

towards the jeep that had accompanied the two lorries and was still parked some distance away. As he approached it, the vehicle began to move towards him, closing the distance between them, and then came to a halt again.

Mohammed hadn't moved an inch from his position beside the entrance to the temple, and he watched closely as the armed man held a brief conversation with somebody inside the vehicle. Then the back door of the jeep opened and the man climbed inside.

As soon as the door closed, the jeep started to move once again, circling around both the group of terrified archaeologists and the armed men surrounding them, and headed over towards the excavation where Mohammed was standing.

The jeep stopped a few yards away, and the driver – his face virtually invisible because of the tinted windscreen and side windows – switched off the engine. The two doors on the driver's side opened simultaneously and two men climbed out, both wearing shoulder holsters over their military-style clothing and each carrying a Kalashnikov assault rifle. They looked at Mohammed and then scanned the entire area, presumably checking for any sign of danger. Apparently satisfied, the driver turned back towards the vehicle and nodded. Only then did the other two doors open.

The young bearded man climbed out and walked over to Mohammed. He was followed by a man in late middle age who was wearing a somewhat crumpled white linen suit, and who immediately began mopping the sweat from his forehead with a large red handkerchief.

Mohammed stared at the man in disbelief, forgetting his state of terror for an instant.

'You,' he said, his voice quivering with emotion. 'You're involved with these people? Why?'

The man in the suit looked at him with a dismissive expression and shook his head.

'You mean you haven't worked it out yet? Never mind. It's too late for you anyway. I don't think we need your services any further.'

He turned slightly and issued a brief instruction to the driver.

Mohammed didn't hear what he said, but there was no mistaking the meaning of his order.

As the driver began raising his Kalashnikov, Mohammed started to run. He had always been built for comfort rather than speed, and he'd only covered about ten yards before the driver pulled the trigger.

The man wearing the suit nodded in satisfaction as he watched the senior archaeologist's body tumble clumsily to the ground and lie still.

'Tell your men to get rid of the others, Farooq,' he said. 'No word of this must be allowed to get out.'

And as he began to climb down the aluminium ladder into the temple, he heard the sound of the Kalashnikovs opening up.

3

Kuwait

'So tell me about this temple,' Bronson said, as Angela steered the Land Cruiser along the highway that headed south-west away from the city and towards the border – not in fact the border with Iraq, but the one between Kuwait and Saudi Arabia.

'Well,' she said, 'the first thing you need to understand is that we don't really know whether or not it *is* a temple. We've been calling it that ever since we found it, but really only because it's a convenient name. We could be quite wrong about what it was used for.'

'Agreed,' Stephen said from the back seat, 'but the signs are that it was some kind of a place of worship or veneration. Why don't you tell Chris exactly how we found it?'

Bronson looked at his ex-wife, and she glanced at him and smiled, then returned her attention to the road in front.

'OK,' she said. 'There are more potential sites dotted around the world than there are archaeologists to investigate them. This particular area of southern Iraq was identified as being of interest perhaps twenty years ago because the Marsh Arabs lived there, and not a huge amount was known about their early history. This was also the height of Saddam Hussein's regime so for several reasons – mainly political – nobody did anything about it. And as he seemed to be determined to wipe out the Marsh Arabs there was no way any expedition could possibly be mounted while he was in power. And then, of course, there was the turmoil after he'd been deposed, when it still wasn't safe to travel or work there.'

'So what's the site?' Bronson asked. 'A Marsh Arab village or something?'

'It might have been,' Stephen interjected, 'but we really aren't sure what it is. The initial reports had only stated that there were signs of habitation there, and clear physical evidence in the form of pottery fragments on the ground. The assumption was that it was probably the site of a settlement that had been abandoned some considerable time ago. That deduction was based on the type of pottery people had picked up there, none of which appeared to have been made within the last couple of hundred years or so, and the absence of any recent artefacts. No plastic or metal objects, I mean.'

'Anyway,' Angela continued, 'when the situation in Iraq seemed to be a bit more stable, the Baghdad Museum decided it was worth sending a team down to do a test excavation, and because the location is so close to the Kuwaiti border they invited the corresponding museum in Kuwait City to take part, and also asked for a handful of Western specialists to join the group. The British Museum sent Stephen and me, and a chap called George who you'll meet at the dig.

'It really didn't look all that promising when we got there, but that's the thing about archaeology. Until you get below the surface you genuinely have no idea what you're likely to find. The site is a fairly level area, but when we set up our tents and stuff I couldn't see any obvious signs that there had been a village there. No outlines on the ground or anything like that, but there were quite a few bits of pottery lying around, all quite ancient.'

'Of course, we are talking about a desert here,' Stephen said, 'and that particular area is a mixture of sand, rock and earth, so it's quite conceivable that there could have been a substantial village there, but after only a few months drifting sand could have completely buried it. Or, and this might be more likely, the people who built the settlement there might have decided for whatever reason – better grazing for their animals, their normal water source drying up or something of that sort – to dismantle everything and move somewhere else.'

'So you pitched your tents and started digging?'

'Basically, yes. And in fact, what we found was pretty much what we had expected to find. Quite a lot of pottery, the dates consistent with what we had anticipated, a few ritual ornaments and the like, and clear indication of the remains of a building in one trench – rotted sections of cut timber, that kind of thing. But nothing exciting until a few days ago. And then, at the very end of one trench, we found something different: worked stone.

'It was just a right-angled piece of rock on the left-hand side of the trench, and we thought at first it was the base of an individual object, a stone carving or something of that sort, but when we shifted more of the earth from around it, we realized it was nothing of the sort. It was actually a step carved into the bedrock that ran beside the trench. Even before we'd fully exposed that length of stone, we did the obvious and checked to see if there was another step below it. There was, and there was a third one under that. What we were looking at was the beginning of a rough-hewn staircase that descended below the desert floor.

'As you can imagine, that changed the mood on the team quite dramatically. What we'd expected to be nothing more than a perfectly routine excavation of a long-abandoned village had suddenly turned into a treasure hunt. We had no idea what might be waiting for us at the bottom of that stone staircase. We did it properly, though, documenting and photographing each phase of this unexpected turn the excavation had taken, but we were all caught up in the excitement of the moment, and I think that most of us believed we might have stumbled upon something of real importance. After all, it was a buried stone staircase that had led Howard Carter to the untouched tomb of

Tutankhamun in the Valley of the Kings in Egypt.'

'But I presume it wasn't a tomb?' asked Bronson.

'Patience,' Angela said, with a faint smile. 'We excavated the length of the staircase, which went down to about twelve feet below the desert floor. It finished at a small square stone platform, surrounded on two sides by vertical slabs of bedrock. On the third side, directly in front of the staircase, there were half a dozen lengths of roughly shaped wood that formed a kind of door, or that's what it looked like initially. It turned out that they were just individual planks of timber, positioned there to cover an opening in the rock.'

'And?' Bronson asked impatiently. 'What did you find?'

'That was the disappointing bit,' Angela replied. 'There was a large opening, an archway about seven feet tall and four feet wide that had been carved out of the rock. Beyond it was an open space that was clearly a natural geological feature, a small cave, which had been used in the past by some group of people. It seemed fairly obvious to us that the wood had been positioned to keep the dust and sand out of the cave when the decision had been taken to fill in the staircase. And it had worked well. When we cleared away the lengths of timber, we found only the equivalent of a couple of buckets of debris had penetrated behind it.

'So that opened up the entrance and Mohammed – he's the senior Iraqi archaeologist on the team, from the Baghdad Museum – took a look inside first.'

'Rank has its privileges, in archaeology, just like every other job,' Stephen mused.

'Exactly. Anyway, as soon as the lights were working, we went down there in groups of four to have a look.'

'And it wasn't quite what we'd expected,' Stephen said. 'It was just an empty room, and there were no treasures of any sort down there. I don't just mean no gold or anything like that, but I was certainly hoping that it might have been a burial vault or something of that sort, and we might at least have recovered a few bones and maybe some grave goods as well. But there was nothing. It looked as if at some point, maybe a few centuries ago, the people who had used the space had changed their mind, taken out everything that was movable, covered the entrance with the lengths of timber and then filled in the stone staircase leading down to it. And in fact that did sort of tie up with our first deduction that the settlement had been deliberately abandoned for some reason.'

'But you said right at the start that it was a temple,' Bronson objected, 'so it can't just have been a completely empty room, otherwise you would probably have thought it was a storeroom for grain or something.'

'Quite right,' Angela agreed. 'In fact, once we had the lights burning and could examine every inch of the place, we found exactly three artefacts, and one or perhaps two of them did suggest that the cave might originally have been a temple.

'The most obvious of these was a small stone altar – well, actually it's little more than an oblong slab of stone positioned on two shorter vertical stone pillars. But we called it an altar because that's what it looked like more

38

than anything else, though in reality it could have been a stone seat. But the main indicator that the space might have been some kind of a temple was an image carved into the wall directly behind the "altar". That image is a human face. It's not very clear, and the carving is fairly basic – I suppose you could call it primitive – but it appears to be the face of a bearded man with long hair.'

'You mean it's a kind of graven image?' Bronson said. 'I thought a lot of religions forbade images of human beings or animals? Judaism and Islam, for example?'

'You're absolutely right,' Stephen said. 'The technical term is aniconism, and that's basically a prohibition against depicting any kind of living creature, and especially not a religious figure, as an image to be worshipped. It's an important character of the Jewish, Islamic and Byzantine artistic traditions, but it's also worth saying that there are a few grey areas. Public buildings in Islamic states were often allowed to have such images on them as decoration, and back in 1932 a third-century Jewish synagogue was discovered in Syria with its interior walls almost completely covered in paintings showing priests and religious events like the consecration of the Tabernacle. So although you're right in principle, the fact that we have a graven image in this particular structure doesn't mean that it wasn't a temple, and it also doesn't mean we can rule out any particular religion, though I suppose we could probably suggest that the cave was unlikely to have been used by either Jewish or Islamic worshippers.'

'And I suppose the image itself wouldn't help to date it?' Bronson asked.

'No, not really,' Angela said. 'Men shaving their faces and having their hair cut is actually a comparatively recent innovation. For quite literally centuries, going back to the very dawn of recorded history, men wore beards and had long hair as a matter of course. You can see this in all the old paintings and images, everyone from Moses and Solomon to Jesus Christ. So the way the face had been carved was no real help in dating the temple. Unfortunately, radiocarbon dating the wood isn't all that likely to give us a definitive answer either. What we will know when the tests have been completed is the date of the wood. We'll be able to say with certainty that the entrance to the structure must have been covered after that date, but we have no obvious way of proving when the temple itself was created. The cave might have been opened up and used for some kind of religious services for only a year or two before it was shut up. Equally, it could have been used for a millennium, and then abandoned. At the moment, we simply have no way of telling.'

'You didn't find any organic matter inside the cave, then?'

'No, nothing,' Angela replied. 'It was as if the place had been swept clean before they boarded up the entrance.'

'Right, so you have the carving of a face on the wall, and what might have been a kind of altar right in front of it. You said there were three things in there, so what was the third?'

'You can see why he's a detective, can't you, Stephen? The third relic, for want of a better word, was an inscription carved into the wall of the cave at the opposite end to the altar. And that, we hope, might provide us with sufficient information to identify the period and the function of the cave.'

'You mean you haven't translated it yet?' This time it was Bronson who sounded surprised.

'It's not that simple,' Angela said. 'It looks like Latin but it isn't. In fact, let me just clarify that. I'm pretty sure that it *is* Latin, but some kind of encryption has been applied to it – maybe Atbash or something similar – because at the moment it just reads like gibberish.'

'If you can't read any of the text, why do you think that it's written in Latin?'

'It's the character set,' Angela replied. 'You speak fluent Italian and more than enough French to get by, so if somebody handed you a piece of paper with meaningless words written on it, but you saw an acute or grave accent over a letter "e", or a cedilla under a "c", you'd probably guess that it was written in French, even if the words themselves were encrypted. This is pretty much the same thing, though we're not looking at diacritical marks but the actual script itself. We're guessing that this temple or whatever it is dates from at least five hundred years ago because of the known history of the region, and so we would expect an inscription from that period to almost certainly be written in Arabic and probably in what's known as Kufic script. And if it wasn't written in Arabic, then other common options would be one of the other North Arabian languages like Safaitic or Talmudic, which are quite similar to Arabic. But what we wouldn't expect would be to find an inscription written in the Latin alphabet, the same alphabet that we use today, pretty much.'

'Latin changed over time,' Stephen Taverner explained, 'like all languages. The classical Latin alphabet had only twenty-three letters, and all but two of those were derived from the earlier Etruscan alphabet, but during the Middle Ages the letters "j", "u" and "w" were added, and that gave us the same twenty-six letters that are used today in English and form the basis of most other European languages. We have no idea if this inscription contains the full character set, because not one of those letters is carved into the rock, so if it *is* written in Latin, we have no idea of the approximate date. If there had been a "w", for example, that would have told us it had to be late mediaeval.'

'So what do you think the encryption is?' Bronson said.

'Perhaps Atbash – it's a really early form of cipher, allegedly used by Julius Caesar. Basically, you just write out the letters of the alphabet in a horizontal line, then write out the reversed alphabet directly below it, so that "z" is under "a" and "y" is under "b", and so on. In order to encrypt your message, all you do is write down the plaintext and then substitute the letters from the reversed alphabet. The obvious problem is that you always end up with nonsense, so it's immediately apparent to anyone seeing it that the message must be encrypted. The other problem is that if you apply frequency analysis to the message – there are certain letters that occur much more frequently than others in every language – you can probably work out some of the plaintext letters fairly quickly.'

'But if everybody knows that Atbash just uses the reversed alphabet, then presumably anybody could translate the message about two minutes after they'd realized that it was enciphered. Or am I missing something?' Bronson sounded puzzled.

'You are,' Stephen said, 'but not a lot. That's basic Atbash, but there were refinements, most of which involved picking a different letter of the alphabet underneath which you would start the reversed alphabet, so that instead of "z" going under "a", for example, it might appear under "m" or "p". And of course, the second alphabet need not necessarily be reversed, or perhaps the person encrypting the message could reverse only half the alphabet. The result would still be gibberish, the ciphertext, I mean, but fiddling about with the cipher like that would create a huge range of different possibilities for the decoding.'

'Right, I understand all that,' Bronson said, 'but you haven't answered the other obvious question.'

Neither Stephen nor Angela responded, so he ploughed on.

'If you're assuming that the people who wrote that inscription were Marsh Arabs or a similar group that lived way out in the bundu at the southern end of Iraq about half a millennium ago, why did they use

Latin? Presumably they would have spoken Arabic or some local language. So why did they use Latin for this inscription? Was it a kind of lingua franca in those days? Or at least a written lingua franca?'

'Now that,' Angela said slowly, 'is a very good question. Their lingua franca, most probably, would actually have been Arabic, and I wouldn't have expected very many people in that part of the world to be able to either read or speak Latin during the time period that we're talking about. So I have no idea why whoever carved the inscription chose that language.'

'You're right,' Stephen said. 'It really doesn't make any sense.'

Bronson switched his gaze from Angela to the man in the back seat and then to Angela again.

'Well, it does make sense in one context,' he said.

'What context?' Angela asked.

'The message contained in the inscription has got to be important. Or, to be absolutely accurate, it must have been important when it was written, although it might be completely meaningless now, of course. If it wasn't important, there would have been no point in encrypting it, obviously.'

'Yes, obviously.' Angela sounded rather testy. 'I thought we'd already established that. What's your point?'

'The point, as I see it, is that you have a mysterious inscription not only written in Latin – or at least that's what you think – but in encrypted Latin and hidden away under the desert in Iraq. From what you've told

44

me, it's quite likely that almost nobody who used that temple, not even the priest, would have been able to read it. So it seems to be fairly obvious that the inscription wasn't meant to be understood by the people who worshipped in the temple. Perhaps it was intended to be read by somebody else entirely.'

4

Vicinity of Al Muthanna, Iraq

'Is this what you expected, Khaled?' Farooq asked.

He and the man in the white suit were standing side by side in the underground chamber, the powerful arc lights switched on and casting a pitiless white light that illuminated every corner of the space. Faintly, in the background, they could hear the throb of the petrol generator that was supplying the power.

Khaled stared at the carved inscription, nodding slowly. 'We will need to decipher this, but I have no doubt at all it will provide the information we need to track down the relic.'

'But you can't know that for certain,' Farooq pointed out reasonably, 'until you have decoded the inscription.'

In Farooq's case, appearances were more than slightly deceptive. He looked and dressed like the leader of a gang of terrorists, which to all intents and purposes he was, but he was also a highly educated man, possessing two separate degrees from a Middle Eastern university. And he was, just like Osama bin Laden – the man who had first inspired him to take up arms in the service of radical Islam – the product of a wealthy and respected Saudi Arabian family. Khaled, who also had two degrees – and a doctorate – was by no stretch of the imagination a man of violence, though he was more than capable of ordering it when necessary. As such he treated Farooq as an equal.

'This is my business, Farooq, and I have been waiting for something like this to be discovered somewhere in this area for the last two decades. I know that we can't read the inscription – yet – but the fact that the inscription exists at all, and in such close proximity to that face' – he pointed at the carving above the altar at the other end of the room – 'tells me that I'm right.'

He reached into his pocket and took out a compact but high-resolution camera. He aimed it at the carved inscription and snapped about a dozen photographs, checking each image in the camera's viewing screen after he had taken it.

Then he and Farooq climbed up the aluminium ladder back to the surface. Khaled strode over to the jeep in which he'd arrived, opened the rear door and sat down on the seat. Positioned right in the middle of the rear bench seat was a leather computer case, which he unzipped. He took out a slim laptop computer, opened it and pressed the power button. While he was waiting for the operating system to load, he slid open the memory card slot on the camera and pulled out the data card. He slid the card into the card reader on the laptop and examined the photographs that he had taken. He was only interested in the clarity of the images, and checked each one carefully to make sure that every piece, every single letter, of the inscription was clearly visible.

He copied the images on to the laptop's hard disk, but didn't delete them from the camera's data card, and then made a further backup copy on to a separate memory stick that he put in one of the pockets of his jacket. That gave him three separate and identical copies of the images, so even if some catastrophe resulted in both the computer and the camera being lost or destroyed, he would still have one copy left.

He shut the lid of the laptop and slid it back into the case, then climbed back out of the jeep and rejoined Farooq by the ladder.

'The pictures are good enough?' the younger man asked.

'They're very clear. So now we just need to get rid of it. This is our information, and I'm not willing to risk sharing it.'

Farooq nodded, and waved to one of his men, who immediately jogged over. Farooq murmured his instructions, and the man pulled a broad-bladed cold steel chisel and a hammer from a fabric bag he had slung over his shoulder.

The man glanced at Khaled, apparently seeking final confirmation for what he was going to do and then, as Khaled nodded, he strode over to the aluminium ladder and descended into the underground temple.

Farooq issued another instruction, and the generator sprang back into life, illuminating the lights inside the chamber.

Within seconds, the sound of steel on stone became clearly audible as Farooq's man began carefully chipping every last vestige of the inscription off the wall. It wasn't a particularly long inscription, and within about a quarter of an hour he had completed the task and emerged from the temple.

Both Khaled and Farooq climbed down again to inspect what he had done. The section of the wall where the letters had been carved was now completely blank and featureless, with no indication at all – apart from a few barely visible chisel marks – that there had ever been anything displayed there.

Khaled glanced down at the small pile of stone chippings that lay on the floor of the temple underneath that section of the wall.

'One last thing,' he said. 'Get somebody to sweep up all those and then dump them.'

'You really think that's necessary?' Farooq asked. 'I doubt anybody could reconstruct the carving from those few bits of stone.'

'It's not worth taking the chance. I want the evidence gone. And have your men go through every tent in this camp to collect all the computers, cameras, disks and memory sticks, just in case any of the archaeologists took photographs in the underground chamber. Tell them to put them all in the back of my jeep.'

Ten minutes later, the stone chippings had been

collected and then scattered at random around the site, joining a myriad other small pieces of stone, and every piece of electronic equipment in the place had been collected. Now they were all ready to leave. Farooq ordered his men to climb up into their trucks, and then those two vehicles started up and drove slowly away from the encampment.

Khaled waited until his driver started the engine – and hence the air-conditioning – of his 4x4 vehicle before he climbed into the back. Once seated, and with the temperature inside the vehicle dropping steadily, he opened the computer bag, took out the laptop and began studying the pictures that he had taken.

The driver turned the jeep around and drove back out of the encampment the same way they had arrived. He looked incuriously at the bullet-ridden corpses, their clothes blotched with starlet stains, that lay scattered about the area.

But Khaled, sitting in the back seat, didn't so much as glance at the bodies. He was entirely focused on the images on his computer screen.

5

Western Kuwait

'I see where you're going with this idea,' Angela said, 'but I just don't know whether or not you're right.'

They were now well clear of Kuwait City and were driving out into the largely empty desert, heading south-west along the Atraf Road, Highway 70. Traffic was even lighter, with only a few cars; the majority of vehicles on the road were lorries of one size or another. The sun was blazing down from an entirely cloudless sky, and Bronson was not looking forward to the moment when they would finally come to a stop and he would have to get out of the Toyota.

'Look, I'm no archaeologist,' he said, 'but this doesn't really seem to me to be an archaeological matter. We have a situation where the residents of the village, and probably everybody else within a few hundred miles of that location, all spoke Arabic, or perhaps a similar but related language. In fact, whatever language they spoke, we can be sure that it wasn't Latin.'

'Yes, that *is* a fact,' Stephen agreed.

'Right. So that inscription couldn't have been read by, or meant for, any of the locals. It must have been aimed at somebody else. The big question, obviously, is who.'

'Any ideas?' Angela asked.

'Not a clue,' Bronson said. 'That's very definitely your field, my dear, not mine. What I know about this area is basically what you've told me since I got into this car. I have no idea what other tribes or peoples were wandering about round here five hundred years ago or even earlier. But I did have another idea that might help explain the inscription, although you might think it's a bit of a stretch.'

'Try me,' she said.

Bronson turned slightly in his seat so that he could see both Angela and Stephen.

'For people who have religious faith it's based on belief: they believe what they're told and accept, or turn a blind eye to, all the obvious inconsistencies. And they sometimes take on rights and traditions without asking what they mean. Take an obvious example: saying grace. People do it because it's something they do before eating a meal, but I'm prepared to lay you money that almost none of them know why they do it, or where the practice comes from.'

'Did you know Chris was an atheist, Stephen?' Angela asked, with a wide smile.

'I think I might have guessed that, actually. Do carry on.'

'Right. So if we take it as a given that most people

will just accept all the various trappings of their religion without questioning their relevance, then perhaps that carving on the wall of the temple might be a symbol of what they believe. A kind of carved relic that their priests told them dated from the earliest times. If that were the case, then they might not only accept it, but also worship it. It would be a kind of inscribed reminder of something that happened centuries earlier, maybe. Perhaps the followers of this religion had a copy of that inscription in all their temples, just as every Christian church displays a cross, a symbol of execution. Maybe it was some kind of an ancient talisman that they absorbed into their religion over the centuries and worshipped without having any idea at all about what it was or what it was supposed to mean.'

Both Angela and Stephen looked somewhat doubtful at this suggestion.

'That's an interesting idea,' Stephen said, 'but it's rather improbable. We do know a bit about the likely religion the people of this area would have followed. They were almost certainly Mandaeans, and we don't know too much about the origins of this particular belief system. It was a gnostic sect, and some researchers believe that it most probably originated in Palestine or Syria in about the first or second century AD, and then migrated to southern Iraq and parts of Iran, more or less the area that used to be called Mesopotamia. There's another theory that it began in Mesopotamia itself but, whichever is true, we do know that it was an established religion by the third century. In fact, it's still followed by about sixty-five thousand people worldwide, and today it's an important religion here in south-west Iraq.'

'I know Stephen won't necessarily agree with me, but I'm fairly certain that the temple we found was Mandaean.'

'I'm not saying that you're wrong, Angela, but I am saying that your case is really not proven. Your evidence is circumstantial at best, and liable to other interpretations.'

'What evidence is that?' Bronson asked.

'Three things,' she replied, 'and I do agree that not one of them is actually compelling. But I just think that the obvious thing to do is follow William of Occam and apply Occam's Razor, so we should assume that the simplest explanation is the correct one until we find information that proves it isn't. So, first, the Mandaean religion was the dominant faith in this area at the time we think the temple was probably in use, which is basically the Middle Ages, so on the basis of probability it's most likely to have been used by people following this faith.

'Second, Mandaeans followed the Johannite heresy, meaning that they revered John the Baptist and rejected Jesus Christ, because of an obvious logical inconsistency in the Bible. If Jesus genuinely was the son of God, then how could John have baptized him? By what authority could he have done that? So if John did baptize Him, then almost by definition John had to be his superior. So the Mandaeans claimed that John the Baptist should be worshipped, and that Christ was a usurper. And,' she finished, 'that carving on the wall of the temple could represent John the Baptist. It's not that dissimilar to some early representations of him.'

'Yes,' Stephen replied, 'and it could also be a representation of Jesus Christ, of any one of the apostles, of the local priest who officiated in the temple, or the local water seller. Okay, the last is a slight exaggeration, but you take my point. It's unattributed, generic in concept and primitive in its execution, and realistically could be almost anybody. Well, any adult male, at any rate.'

'I don't dispute that,' Angela said. 'I just think that if the temple was used by the Mandaeans, there's at least a possibility that the face they carved on the wall might have been intended to represent the person they worshipped. To me, that makes sense.'

'And to me,' Bronson said.

'The third point is rather less convincing. We know that the Mandaeans were very keen on baptism as a way of absolving themselves of their sins. In one corner of that room is a fairly shallow depression in the stone floor. To me, it doesn't look natural, and I think you can see chisel marks in it. If so, if it was a deliberately created structure, it could have been a bath. Obviously it wasn't a bath you could lie down in because it's only about three or four inches deep, but bearing in mind how precious water is, especially in this part of the world, that might have been their baptismal font or whatever they called it. They could have put a couple of pints of water in there, and then used a cup or something to pour it over the head of a member of the congregation standing in it. That would have worked.'

She glanced at Stephen's sceptical expression in the rear-view mirror.

'I know you're not convinced, Stephen,' she said, 'but I hope you'll agree that it's at least a possibility.'

He nodded, perhaps a trifle reluctantly.

'It is possible, I'll give you that, but I think we're an awfully long way from being able to prove it one way or the other.'

'I agree,' Bronson said. 'I'd love to think you were right, Angela, but it all sounds a bit too circumstantial and interpretive for my liking. You might simply be seeing what you want to see.'

'There's also the negative evidence, the evidence that isn't there,' Stephen said. 'A few abandoned Mandaean temples have been excavated in the past, and as far as I can recall none of them ever had anything like this strange inscription inside them. So either this isn't a Mandaean temple at all, which is in itself quite an exciting prospect, or if it is a temple, then perhaps this inscription is unique and something never seen before.'

'And I suppose the only other possibility,' Bronson suggested, as another thought struck him, 'is that the inscription was nothing whatever to do with the worshippers or the religion they followed.'

'What do you mean?'

'I mean maybe when the Marsh Arabs or the Mandaeans or whoever found this cave and opened it up, the inscription was already carved on the wall. Or it could have been put there by somebody else after the temple had finally been abandoned. The bottom line, really, is that until you've deciphered it, all we'll be doing is speculating, which is just a polite way of saying we'll be guessing.'

A few minutes later, Angela reduced speed as they approached a junction and then steered the Toyota off the main road and down a ramp. The new road was narrow, barely wide enough in some places for two vehicles to pass each other, and the surface was comparatively poor.

'It gets a lot worse than this once we're in the desert,' she said grimly, steering the Land Cruiser around a pothole.

The jarring ride wasn't conducive to conversation, and Bronson contented himself with staring out of the windows at the terrain around them, not that there was a great deal to see.

When most people think about a desert, their mental picture is of rolling sand dunes sculpted by the wind and the occasional palm tree or oasis. In reality, most deserts are not like this at all, and certainly that particular bit of Kuwait did not conform to this image. As far as he could see, the surface was rocky rather than sandy, and there seemed to be a complete absence of palm trees, though there were a few scrubby bushes dotted about the place.

'Here we go,' Angela said, about a quarter of an hour later, as she steered the Toyota off the road and on to the craggy surface of the desert. 'The satnav is almost useless to us now,' she added, turning it off. 'I'm just using the GPS.'

She pointed to the unit positioned in its sucker mount on the windscreen.

In a number of places there were tyre tracks showing that other vehicles had passed that way before, presumably other 4x4s and trucks belonging to the expedition. They saw no border guards or police, or indeed any signs of life at all, and a short time after they had left the road Angela announced that they were now in Iraq.

'We've only got about another fifteen clicks – kilometres – to go,' she said. 'Just under ten miles.'

They couldn't drive in a straight line because of the terrain. Angela had to keep weaving around hummocks and dips in the ground, and even then the Toyota pitched and rolled quite a bit. She also had to keep the speed right down, and it was almost half an hour later before she took one hand off the wheel for a brief second or two to point ahead of the vehicle.

'There we are,' she said. 'That's our home. Temporarily, of course.'

Bronson stared keenly through the windscreen at the tents – a dozen or so of them – that were just coming into view about a quarter of a mile in front. There were also a couple of smaller tents some distance away from the encampment – he assumed they were the toilets or wash rooms – and two longer lengths of material supported on poles over to one side, presumably shades erected over the excavation itself.

'It looks virtually deserted,' he said, a sudden sense of disquiet striking him. 'Where is everybody?'

Angela glanced at the dashboard clock.

'It's just after midday,' she said. 'They might be having lunch or taking an early siesta.'

'That makes sense,' Stephen remarked.

But Bronson stiffened, leaned forward in his seat and then turned to Angela.

'Stop the car,' he said, the tone of his voice making it perfectly clear that it was an order, not a subject for discussion.

Angela hit the brakes and the Toyota shuddered to an almost immediate halt.

'What is it? What's wrong?'

Bronson pointed through the windscreen.

'What's wrong is those birds,' he said, gesturing towards a large bird with dark plumage and lighter coloured feathers on its head and neck that had just flapped a few feet up into the air before settling back down again on the ground.

'I don't know much about birds,' he went on, 'but even I can recognize a vulture when I see one. There are an awful lot of them on the ground near those tents. I also don't know much about archaeology, but I do know that there shouldn't be a dozen vultures in the middle of a working archaeological camp. Something must be dead over there, something substantial, and I think it would be a really good idea to find out what it is before we go blundering in.'

6

South-eastern Iraq

For the first hour or so after they'd driven away from the encampment, Khaled had tried to study the pictures of the inscription on his laptop computer, and had transcribed the text, letter by letter, on to a sheet of paper. He knew that the next step would be a case of trial and error, until he worked out exactly what encryption system the originator had employed. To do that would take some time, and ideally he would need to be in a quiet room where he could concentrate, not bouncing around in the back of a jeep travelling across the Iraqi desert.

Nevertheless, he had spent a few unproductive minutes trying to crack the code using standard Atbash, having jotted down the sequence of letters at the bottom of the sheet of paper. But that had only converted the original gibberish into a different kind of gibberish, and eventually he'd given up. He tucked the paper away into the inside pocket of his jacket, and then leaned back in the seat to stare incuriously out of the window.

His mind ranged back over the events of the day, remembering the shocked expression on Mohammed's face as the senior archaeologist had recognized him and, probably at the same instant, had realized that his life was about to end. Khaled hadn't wanted to massacre the archaeologists, but he had known from the first – as soon as Mohammed had told him about the carving they had discovered – that he could not afford to let any of them stay alive. The quest on which he was embarking was far too important to leave behind any loose ends.

But as he sat there, something began to niggle away at his subconscious. He pictured the archaeologists standing, confused and frightened, in that small group surrounded by Farooq's men, as he'd been driven past them in his jeep. And then the confrontation, such as it had been, with Mohammed.

His face darkened as he realized, in that very instant, what he'd missed.

'*Tahouti*,' he muttered. It was an epithet more normally used by Iranians, and referred to a corrupt agent of Satan.

There was a walkie-talkie unit clipped to the dashboard of the jeep, and he told the driver to hand it to him. He lifted the unit to his face, pressed the transmit button and called Farooq.

'We have a problem,' Khaled said. 'Not everyone was there. We missed the woman.'

'I'd forgotten about her,' Farooq replied from the

passenger cab of the leading lorry, the bouncing of the vehicle slightly distorting his voice. 'Do you think she was hiding somewhere? My men checked all the tents, as you know.'

'I don't know,' Khaled admitted, his voice bitter. He checked his watch. He couldn't remember exactly what time they'd left the archaeologists' camp, but he knew it was at least two hours ago, and that meant a long diversion he could have done without. But there was no choice, and he knew it.

'We have to find her and silence her permanently,' he said. 'We need to go back to the camp, right now.'

'*Ma fi mushkila*,' Farooq responded: no problem.

Moments later, he ended the call, then used the walkie-talkie to issue new orders to his men.

Both the lorries slowed to a stop and then turned around to face the direction from which they had come, but for two or three minutes they didn't move, just remained stationary as they waited for the dust clouds to diminish so that the drivers could see where they were going. Then the small convoy, this time with the 4x4 jeep leading the other two vehicles, began to retrace the route it had taken earlier.

In the backs of the two lorries, Farooq's men checked their weapons and talked quietly amongst themselves. Perhaps Farooq would allow them to take their time over the woman. She was going to die anyway, so it really didn't matter if it was quick or slow.

7

Vicinity of Al Muthanna, Iraq

Angela tucked the car out of sight among the uneven dunes and dips that surrounded the camp, and turned it around to face away from the tents, as Bronson had suggested.

'Until we know what's going on here we should try to stay out of sight. We need to know we can get in that vehicle and then get out of here really fast if needs be,' he'd explained.

Only then had the three of them approached the silent encampment. Both Angela and Stephen had wanted to rush in there straight away, but Bronson had urged caution, suggesting that they should conceal themselves in a patch of sparse vegetation about a hundred yards from the tents and try to work out what, if any, danger lay ahead.

They had no idea what had happened in the camp, but the unmoving shapes they could now see on the ground – many of them surrounded by groups of squab-bling black birds – indicated that something catastrophic had taken place.

So for several minutes they just watched and waited.

'We have to get in there right now and find out what's happened,' Stephen said, his voice cracking with emo-tion. 'We can't just wait out here. We have to go and help them.'

He made as if to rise, but Bronson placed a firm hand on his shoulder and forced him to remain still.

'Not yet. Can you both take a look at the camp and tell me what, if anything, looks out of place there. Have any of the tents been moved? Are any missing?'

'It looks just the same to me,' Angela stammered.

'What about the vehicles?' Bronson asked. 'Is there an extra truck or anything parked next to your 4x4s? Or anywhere else.'

But neither Angela nor Stephen could see any vehicles they didn't recognize, and after another couple of minutes of seemingly interminable waiting, Bronson finally stood up and led the way towards the camp to investigate what had happened.

Even so, they still approached very cautiously, and from slightly different directions so that they wouldn't form such an obvious target as a group. But they saw nothing, and heard nothing, no indication at all of any movement in the camp. And then the reality became obvious, and the thing they had all dreaded revealed itself, as they stopped right beside one of the unmoving shapes.

'Dear God,' Angela gasped and clapped her hand to her face. She looked down at the body lying face down on the rocky ground, the man's back marked by at least four bullet wounds, the corpse surrounded by a pool of dried blood. 'Mohammed. I can't believe it. Oh my God.'

Bronson shook his head and took her arm, trying to turn her away from the corpse.

'You can't do anything for him now,' he said. 'Or for any of them, I'm afraid.'

She bent down and stretched out her shaking hand, but Bronson stopped her with a command.

'Don't touch him. He's dead, Angela. Don't touch anything. Either of you. I know it's hard to think like this right now, but this is a crime scene. What communication equipment do you have here?'

Angela just stared blankly ahead, clearly in shock as her mind struggled to process what her eyes were seeing.

Stephen's face was white and his breathing shallow. He, too, seemed unable to speak, but after a moment he turned to Bronson.

'There's a satellite phone,' he said, a tremor audible in his flat, expressionless voice.

'Right,' Bronson said. 'You two wait over there – stay away from this body. I have no idea how thoroughly or efficiently the Baghdad police will investigate this, but we must avoid doing anything to contaminate the scene. And we must let the authorities know what's happened out here. I'm going to check the rest of the camp to see if anyone has survived. Look after each other for a moment.'

It took him less than five minutes to confirm that every single member of the expedition was dead, and had been for at least a couple of hours, judging by the dried blood that surrounded the corpses. Each body displayed multiple bullet wounds, and some of them had clearly been shot by more than one weapon.

Bronson stopped by one body and looked down at it with a mixture of disgust and horror; even with his police background this was a sight that turned his stomach.

The wounds on this man, and the method of his death, were very different, as the sightless eyes in his severed head stared unblinkingly across the blood-soaked sands.

Bronson counted the bodies as he made his way around the encampment, trying to use his training as a police officer to think logically and work out what must have happened. Most of the corpses were lying close together in one particular area, while the body of the man Angela had identified as Mohammed and that of one of the younger Iraqi archaeologists were lying some distance away. After circling the camp, Bronson walked back over to where Angela and Stephen were waiting, the heaviness in his step making it clear that he had no good news for them. Stephen had his arm wrapped around Angela, trying to comfort her as they both struggled to deal with the shock of it. As Bronson approached, she looked up at him, an unspoken question in her eyes.

'I'm sorry,' he said. 'It was a massacre. The whole camp. And it wasn't random – this looks like a targeted terrorist attack.'

'Terrorists?' Stephen Taverner asked. 'You think terrorists did this? Why? This was an archaeological dig.'

Previously, his voice had been quiet and subdued, but the initial horror of their discovery had been replaced by a surge of anger. Anger tinged with the inescapable knowledge that he himself would certainly have been killed if he'd been in the camp when the attack took place – knowledge that would weigh heavily upon anyone's mind.

'I think Mohammed and one of the other men probably tried to make a run for it, and were shot down while they were trying to get away,' Bronson said sadly. 'Whoever did this really didn't care about leaving evidence behind them. Every fired cartridge case and every bullet that the authorities manage to recover from the bodies can be positively linked to a particular weapon. So that means that either these killers think they're above the law or, more likely, they're a bunch of terrorists and they know that they'll never be brought to justice because they expect to die fighting, so they don't care. The vast majority of the shots seem to have been fired from Kalashnikov AK-47s, judging by the spent cartridge cases I've seen. And that assault rifle is the weapon of choice for most terrorists around the world, because it's cheap, readily available and keeps on working pretty much no matter what you do to it.

'From what I've seen so far,' he continued, his voice laced with anger, 'I think that's the most likely scenario. There are four virtually brand-new Toyota Land Cruisers parked over there. If this had been a robbery of some sort, why wouldn't the thieves have taken them? I'm prepared to bet that when we check the tents we'll find that all the valuable stuff is still there. To come here, kill everybody and then just vanish back into the desert only really makes sense in two contexts. One possibility is that this was a straightforward terrorist atrocity, a group of Westerners and locals being identified and then targeted by a death squad to make a point to the world, just another unprovoked act of senseless violence and terror. The kind of action that's intended to make headlines around the world. But as this place is in the middle of nowhere it seems unlikely.'

'And what's the other option?' Stephen asked.

Bronson shrugged.

'The only other idea I've got is that the archaeologists were targeted by some group because of something specific at this dig. Something you've discovered.'

'But . . . we hadn't really found . . .' Angela trailed off.

'I know. That's what I mean. If that temple had been stuffed to the rafters with solid-gold relics studded with precious stones worth countless millions, then wiping out the people who discovered it and making off with the booty would make a certain amount of twisted sense. But I can't see anybody murdering every man in this group of archaeologists because they'd stumbled across an empty underground chamber. That's simply ridiculous. We're missing something here. Let's check the tents.'

Angela led the way to Mohammed's tent. All of the archaeologists had been accommodated two to a tent apart from Angela, as the only female, and Mohammed, the most senior.

In the space that in the other tents would have been occupied by a single campbed, Mohammed had a slim desk, the top covered in a layer of folders, paper and pens, held down by the chunky shape of a satellite phone, and with a stainless-steel Rolex watch sitting at one end of it. That, as much as anything else, was confirmation that robbery had not been the motive of the unknown attackers.

'Is anything missing?' Bronson asked.

'His computer and camera aren't here,' Angela said.

'Would he have worked on his laptop somewhere else?' Bronson asked.

'I doubt it. That's why he had this two-man tent all to himself, so that he could work in here. I never saw him take the computer anywhere else. Apart from anything else, it's virtually impossible to see anything on a laptop screen in sunlight. We did all the work on our laptops in our tents.'

'Okay. At least the phone is here, though.' Bronson turned to Stephen. 'While Angela makes the call, could you just check the other tents and see if all the other archaeologists have still got their laptops, cameras, watches and stuff?'

Stephen nodded agreement and walked away.

Angela glanced across at Bronson before she picked up the satellite phone, but he nodded for her to do so.

'Go ahead,' he said. 'This isn't a part of the crime scene, not really, and whatever else we do, we have to call this in. Do you know what the number is?'

Angela pointed at a printed list suspended by a length of string from part of the framework of the tent.

'Mohammed prepared this before we even set out to drive here. It's got every number that he thought we might need, including most of the British Embassy and consular officials based in this region.'

'It might be worth talking to them later, but for the moment just tell the police in Baghdad. I know Kuwait City is a lot closer, but jurisdictions will be important in this, and I'm quite sure that the Baghdad authorities will want to take the lead.'

Angela dialled the number from the list and, after speaking slowly and clearly to a succession of people who obviously understood little or no English, she was finally put through to somebody who could speak her language. She was good in a crisis, and explained succinctly what had happened, and then listened to the instructions given by the Iraqi officer. Then she ended the call.

'I presume he told us to wait here for them to arrive?' Bronson asked.

'Exactly, yes. And not to disturb the scene, just as you said. I suppose we really ought to tell the people at the Baghdad and Kuwait City Museums as soon as we can.'

'I don't think that's a good idea at the moment. Our only link to the outside world is that sat phone, and we really shouldn't use it in case the police want to contact us for any reason. Anyway, the Baghdad authorities will want to decide who needs to be told about this and when.'

'So what should we do now?'

'There's not a lot we can do, but if we can find some blankets or something I'll cover the corpses, if only to try to give these people a bit of dignity.'

Stephen reappeared while they were sorting out sheets and other coverings to use.

'There's not a single laptop, memory stick, tablet, mobile phone or camera anywhere here, as far as I can see,' he said. 'But they seem to be the only things missing. That doesn't really make sense.'

'You're right,' Bronson agreed. 'It doesn't.'

8

Iraq

When the convoy was about twenty miles from the camp, Khaled pressed the transmit button on his driver's walkie-talkie and ordered Farooq to stop the lorries. If the woman had been hiding somewhere in the camp, the last thing he wanted to do was make a direct approach, and then end up chasing her over the harsh desert terrain.

And it was also possible, he reasoned, that she hadn't been at the camp at all, but had been away obtaining supplies, in which case their best plan would be to lie in wait among the tents until she came back. He realized that neither he nor anybody else in the group had bothered counting the number of people in the camp or the vehicles parked there, which was a mistake. If they had, they would have known immediately whether or not anyone was missing.

Wherever the woman had been at the time of the

attack, Khaled knew that they would have to proceed cautiously to ensure that they managed to locate her and then kill her. They could not afford to allow her to escape with the knowledge of what was in the temple. And that meant a circuitous approach to the camp.

'Meet me at the jeep,' he ordered. 'And bring your map.'

Two minutes later, Farooq spread out his map on the bonnet of the 4x4, and for a few moments the two men just stared at the largely featureless terrain marked on it, the whole sheet a uniform sandy brown. Then Khaled glanced at the coordinates on his GPS unit, took a pencil from his pocket and drew a rough circle on the map. He changed the image on the navigation unit until it showed the location of the archaeological camp, and marked that spot on the map with a cross.

'We can't just drive there with the lorries,' he said, 'because if she's in a vehicle heading to the camp she could easily see us and just turn around and head the other way. And then we might never find her. If she's already at the camp, there are several 4x4 vehicles there she could use to get away.'

'The lorries will kick up a lot of dust and sand,' Farooq pointed out reasonably, 'even if I tell the drivers to go slowly, so we won't be able to approach without being seen.'

'Exactly.' Khaled pointed at the map. 'We will not drive to the camp at all. There's a track here that cuts down to the south between the camp and the border with Kuwait. Send one of the lorries down there and tell them to hold position near the route over the dunes that the archaeologists have been using when they drive to Kuwait City. They are just to watch, and to take no action until I give the order.'

Farooq estimated distances on the map by eye.

'If they stay on that track,' he said, 'then they'll be about ten miles to the east of the camp, and a lot further from where we are now. The walkie-talkies only have a reliable range of about five miles, so how will we remain in contact? We only have your satellite telephone.'

Khaled shook his head irritably. He hadn't foreseen that particular practical difficulty.

'But you told me that there is a satellite phone at the archaeological encampment,' Farooq added. 'I suppose that if the woman is there when we arrive, we can kill her immediately. If she runs for the border, we can use that phone to call the crew of the lorry and tell them to stop her before she gets there. That would work.'

'Yes,' Khaled replied slowly, 'it would. That's a good idea. Give my telephone to the crew and tell them what we want them to do.'

'What about the other lorry?'

'The men in the first lorry will cover the area to the east of the encampment, and if she does run, that will be the way I would expect her to go. But just in case she does something unexpected, I want you to send the second lorry along this other track to the west. I doubt if she would head that way, because there's almost nothing out there but desert, but we should still take precautions.'

'And where will you be?'

'I want you to ride with me in the jeep, and we'll go ahead of the second lorry on the westerly track. If she is in the camp, she will have found the mess we left and I've no doubt she'd be spooked by any vehicle approaching directly, but hopefully she would ignore a vehicle passing about a mile away. And that's how I plan to approach her.'

9

Vicinity of Al Muthanna, Iraq

Within about half an hour, Bronson had managed to cover all the bodies, and had weighed the material down with stones to stop it blowing off or being pulled away by the carrion birds.

By the time he'd finished, Angela and Stephen were visibly traumatized, but Angela's mood was now dominated by fury as much as by terror and sorrow.

'This is such a senseless waste of human life,' she said. 'I worked with all of these people, and I liked every one of them. Why the hell would anybody want to kill a bunch of archaeologists? It makes no sense, whether or not it was a terrorist action.'

Stephen had walked off to clear his head as soon as the last body had been covered, but about ten minutes later he came back, a puzzled expression on his face.

'I've just found something else that's rather peculiar,' he said. 'I went back and had a look at both the trenches,

76

and then I climbed the ladder down into the temple.' He paused for a moment, his gaze flicking between their faces. 'I don't know why it's happened, but the inscription has gone.'

'What do you mean it's gone?' Angela demanded. 'It's carved into the stone of the wall.'

'I mean it's not there any more. Somebody has chipped it away with a hammer and chisel, and all that's left is a clean smooth wall.'

The three of them immediately walked over to the second trench and climbed down the ladder and into the underground chamber, Bronson and Angela carrying torches that they'd picked up on the way.

'See what I mean?' Stephen said, shining his own torch at the wall in front of them, now entirely featureless.

Bronson shone his torch down at the floor of the temple, and moved the beam around, as if searching for something.

'What is it?' Angela asked.

'There's nothing here at all,' he said, puzzled. 'That means that after they chipped it off the wall, they collected all the debris and took it away, and the only reason they could have for doing that is to make absolutely sure nobody could reassemble the carved text after they'd destroyed it and all evidence of it was gone. It makes me wonder if this – this obscure inscription – is the reason these killers appeared here in the first place. Apparently whatever that encrypted carving means was clearly worth killing for.'

Although the air was stale and stuffy, and the temperature was if anything even higher than it had been on the surface, Bronson spent a couple of minutes looking around. He examined the carved human face above the altar as well as the altar itself, and also looked at the carved depression in the stone floor that Angela thought might have been something to do with a baptism ritual. Then he walked over to the ladder and climbed out of the temple to rejoin his two companions.

'This makes no sense,' Angela said again. 'Even if it was important, why was it necessary not only to obliterate it but also to kill everybody who had seen it?'

'Well, at least we know one thing now that we didn't before,' Bronson said, gesturing towards the shrouded bodies lying a few yards away. 'We now know that this wasn't just a random terrorist attack or a senseless massacre. This was a deliberate act and the crux of this matter was the inscription. That was their primary objective. That was why they obliterated it and took every camera and computer they could find from the camp that might have an image of the inscription on it.'

Angela opened her mouth to speak, but before she could reply Bronson's attention shifted and he fixed his eyes on the horizon over to the north.

'What is it?'

'I can see a dust cloud over there,' he replied. 'There's a vehicle approaching.'

Angela followed his gaze, but then shook her head.

'There's a track that runs out to the west of us. I think it links a couple of villages. It's probably just some local going about his business.'

'That's a pity,' Stephen said. 'I was hoping it might have been the police already, because then we could give them our statements and get back to Kuwait.'

'Not a chance,' Bronson retorted. 'We only made the call to the police in Baghdad about an hour ago and it'll take a lot longer than that for them to get here. Even if they're only coming here from Basra, which is the nearest big town, they'll still be at least another hour or two. There's no way they could have got out here so quickly.'

Stephen studied the dust cloud for a few seconds, then turned back to Bronson.

'You could be wrong,' he said. 'They could have used helicopters to get to Basra and then switched over to 4x4s for the last part of the journey.'

Bronson shook his head.

'If the police had access to helicopters, why wouldn't they land right here? No, I don't know who that is, but it isn't the Iraqi police.'

Bronson looked again towards the slowly moving cloud of dust and sand and shook his head. It was a shame it wasn't the police; he was about ready to get out of this place.

10

Vicinity of Al Muthanna, Iraq

Khaled was sitting in the passenger seat of the jeep staring through the windscreen at the collection of canvas tents that formed the archaeological camp, looking for any signs of movement.

But that wasn't all he was watching for. He was alternating his gaze between the camp and the road in front of the vehicle, waiting for a suitable location to initiate the next part of his plan.

And then he saw a steadily rising line of dunes on his left-hand side, and gestured for the driver to slow down. As soon the vehicle moved below the crest of the highest dune, he ordered the vehicle to stop, and the moment it did so Farooq and the other armed man in the rear seat opened their doors and climbed out on to the dusty track, pushing the doors closed as silently as possible behind them. The moment they were clear of the jeep, the driver accelerated away, so that if their progress had been observed, it would not be apparent that the vehicle had even stopped.

Farooq and his companion were still wearing sand-coloured camouflage clothing, which made them virtually invisible against the dunes, at least until they moved, so their approach to the encampment was slow and careful, taking advantage of every scrap of cover that they could find.

They stopped behind the sparse shelter afforded by a stunted bush growing near the base of a dune, and for a few minutes just stared at the rows of tents about half a mile in front of them. Even through the low-power binoculars Farooq was carrying, the camp looked almost exactly the same as it had when they'd left a few hours earlier.

But there was something different about the place that he couldn't immediately identify. Something had changed. Something that was niggling at his sub-conscious, either something that he'd noticed during the killings that morning or something that now seemed out of place.

He squinted into the brightness of the sky above as a faint motion attracted his attention.

And then he realized what that something was and a broad smile creased his swarthy face. He handed the binoculars to his companion and gestured towards the tents.

'Someone *is* there,' he said confidently. 'Or at least somebody *has* been there.'

'I don't see anybody,' the other man replied after a

few moments, as he stared through the binoculars. 'What did you spot that I didn't?'

'It's not in the camp,' Farooq said. 'It's above the camp. The vultures are circling and that could mean they've been driven away from the meals we kindly left them, but actually it doesn't. It's much simpler. They can't feed on any of the carrion for the moment because somebody has covered up the bodies. It must be the woman. Either she was hiding somewhere when we arrived this morning or she's arrived at the camp since we left. We're too far out for anyone to have just stumbled across this by chance.'

He took out his walkie-talkie, passed on what he had seen to Khaled, and then the two men continued their stealthy approach through the dunes, Kalashnikovs held ready in both hands, and their eyes scanning the camp in front of them, alert for the first sign of any movement.

11

Vicinity of Al Muthanna, Iraq

When Mikhail Timofeyevich Kalashnikov designed the
assault rifle that bears his name just after the end of
the Second World War, he was in part prompted to do
so by the poor quality of Russian military weapons at
that time, and in particular by their notorious unreliability. From the start, he was determined that his
assault rifle would work. At all times and under all
conditions.

And the reality is that the AK-47 will function even if
the mechanism is choked with mud or sand, or is full of
water, and it simply will not jam, overheat or break, and
that's why it's the weapon of choice for the armed forces
of over thirty countries worldwide, and the favoured
arm of virtually every existing terrorist group. Roughly
one hundred million of these rifles have been produced
both legally and illegally as counterfeit versions since
the design was finalized in 1948.

What Kalashnikov was much less concerned about was accuracy. The purpose of an assault rifle is to produce a high rate of fire – a theoretical 600 rounds a minute in the case of the AK-47, though the normal maximum is 100 rounds a minute – and to spray the enemy with bullets. A modern sniper rifle like the American Barrett M82 can reach out and consistently hit targets at well over a mile, but even an expert with the Kalashnikov would have to fire around five shots from a bench-rest or lying prone to hit a static man-sized target at less than half that distance. And if either the target or the shooter is moving, the effective range of the weapon drops dramatically.

And that, Bronson knew immediately as he heard the staccato clamour of an assault rifle being fired on full auto, was the only reason they were still alive. He grabbed Angela by the arm and pulled her down to the ground.

'What—' Stephen spluttered when Bronson reached up and pulled him down as well.

'They've come back,' Bronson muttered urgently, looking out to the north from the illusory shelter of the tent behind them.

He could see two figures perhaps four or five hundred yards back, both wearing camouflage clothing. What disturbed him in particular was that only one of them was moving, running towards the camp but keeping well out of the line of fire of the second man, who was pointing his Kalashnikov directly at the tents. These men clearly knew what they were doing: one getting close enough to guarantee killing shots, while the other covered the targets, keeping them pinned down.

'We've got to run for it, right now,' Bronson said, 'before they get any closer. Jink from side to side to throw off their aim, and run like hell. Back to the Toyota.'

Even before he'd finished speaking, Angela was on her feet, ducking and weaving as she sprinted away from the camp, still clutching the satellite phone. Bronson and Stephen jumped up and followed her, their feet pounding on the hard-packed sand and rock.

12

Vicinity of Al Muthanna, Iraq

As soon as the three figures appeared on the far side of the deserted encampment, the terrorist who had been running towards the tents – Farooq's companion – stopped. He braced himself, legs slightly apart, left hand holding the wooden fore-end of his Kalashnikov, his other hand wrapped around the pistol grip. He reached up and shifted the fire selector from full to semi-automatic, then took careful aim at the running figures.

The people he was trying to kill were over a quarter of a mile away and appeared to be little more than distant blobs over the iron sights of the AK-47. It would have been a difficult shot to hit a paper target at such a distance even in the relatively calm surroundings of a range. The shooter was panting from his exertions. Running even a short distance in the punishing heat of the desert was debilitating, and his targets were moving in such an erratic fashion that holding even one of them within his sight picture for more than a second or so was almost impossible.

But he tried.

He took two deep breaths to try to control his breathing, aimed the weapon more or less at the middle of the three distant figures and squeezed the trigger gently. The Kalashnikov kicked against his shoulder as the gas-operated mechanism ejected the spent cartridge case from the breech and loaded another round. He altered his aim slightly and fired again.

A few dozen yards behind him, Farooq mirrored his actions, firing single shots towards the fugitives.

But within seconds it became clear that the distance was simply too great and the targets far too elusive for there to be any realistic chance of cutting them down.

'Save your ammunition,' Farooq instructed, running up to his companion. 'Get after them and do not shoot again until you are certain of a kill.'

The other man nodded and ran off towards their quarry. As he did so, Farooq pressed the transmit button on his walkie-talkie.

He knew that the three fugitives had already made a bad mistake. He could see that they had just run past the vehicle park and had continued out into the open desert, presumably intending to escape that way or hide among the dunes, and Farooq knew that that was never going to work.

They were unarmed and on foot, and the easiest way to run them down was simply to summon the 4x4 and the lorry that was waiting out to the west of the encampment. Because however far and however fast the three fugitives ran, they could neither out-distance the vehicles nor hide from Khaled and the rest of his men.

'Yes?' Khaled responded.

'We see them, and Mahmoud is—'

'What do you mean "them"?'

'There are three of them. I think one is the woman.'

'It had better be her,' Khaled said. 'Where are they?'

'Mahmoud is following them, but they've headed off into the desert, out to the east. If you bring the 4x4 over here we'll be able to catch them in a few minutes.'

Over the open mike of the walkie-talkie, Farooq heard Khaled instruct the driver to start the jeep and head towards the encampment.

'You mean they ran out of the camp but didn't take one of the vehicles?' Khaled asked.

'Exactly. They ran straight past the vehicle park. I think they probably panicked when we started shooting at them.'

Khaled didn't respond for a moment, but when he spoke again Farooq could hear the urgency in his voice.

'How many jeeps are in the parking area?'

Farooq scanned the flat ground to the south of the encampment. 'I can see four.'

'That's why they're run into the desert,' Khaled snapped. 'They have five jeeps. They must have one of them parked outside the camp. You have to stop them. Right now.'

88

Farooq clicked the microphone button once in acknowledgement, but he had already started running in the same direction as Mahmoud and the three fugitives.

13

Vicinity of Al Muthanna, Iraq

Bronson would have been less worried if the men behind them had continued firing in their direction. The fact that they'd stopped meant that they were thinking. Instead of continuing to fire at them, the terrorists were clearly trying to close the distance as quickly as possible to get within range.

Their feet pounded on the hard surface as they headed down to the dip in the valley floor where they'd left the Land Cruiser. As the ground fell away, Bronson knew that they would no longer be visible to the two men who were chasing them.

'Just run straight,' he yelled, as the welcome bulk of the Land Cruiser came into view.

When they got about twenty yards away from the vehicle, Angela pressed the button on the remote to unlock the doors. The hazard warning lights flashed obediently. She reached out and grabbed Bronson's arm and then pushed the key into his hand.

'You drive,' she gasped, her chest heaving as she sucked in air through her open mouth.

Stephen wrenched open the rear door of the Toyota and clambered into the back seat, while Angela climbed into the front.

Bronson pulled open the driver's door, stuck the key in the ignition and turned it to start the engine even before he pulled the door closed. He engaged first gear, lifted his foot off the clutch pedal and simultaneously gave the engine full power, swinging the vehicle around to follow the faint tracks the Toyota had made when they'd arrived.

'Keep low,' he instructed as the vehicle surged forward.

He picked the obvious route, following the track and keeping the Toyota running in a straight line, to cover the maximum distance as quickly as possible, but he was watching the rear-view mirror at the same time, preternaturally alert for the first sign of danger. For the first indication that the pursuing men had reached a point from which they could see – and more importantly shoot at – the vehicle.

Suddenly, he saw the unmistakable figure of a gunman appear near the top of the dunes behind them.

'Hang on. Put the belts on.'

Bronson swerved to the right, straightened up briefly, then swung the steering wheel left, then right again, all the time doing his best to keep the big diesel engine running at high revolutions and the vehicle travelling as fast as possible.

He was acutely aware that the Toyota offered a much bigger target to the gunmen than the three of them had when they'd run from the camp, and he also knew that the metal bodywork of the Land Cruiser would offer about as much protection to a bullet from an assault rifle as a sheet of cardboard.

It wasn't like in the movies. In real life, bullets don't bounce off cars. They go straight through them.

But what he was really trying to do, apart from giving the gunmen a difficult, fast-moving and manoeuvring target, was to generate a big enough cloud of dust and sand to make the 4x4 virtually invisible. And judging by what he could see in the mirrors, he had certainly achieved that. The gunman he had seen on the dune had now completely vanished behind the yellowish-brown haze created by the speeding vehicle.

But even over the roaring sound of the big diesel engine, the repetitive crack of an assault rifle was still audible, some distance behind them. Bronson continued manoeuvring the heavy off-road vehicle as violently as he could, while still covering the ground as quickly as possible.

He glanced in the interior mirror at Stephen who was as white as a sheet. Angela, in contrast, looked remarkably calm, one hand holding the grab handle above the door, and the other braced against the dashboard as she stared out through the windscreen at the seemingly endless and largely uniform range of dunes that stretched out ahead of them.

'I don't know how to work the satnav, the GPS, I

mean,' Bronson said to her, changing up a gear, 'so can you input the next waypoint or whatever it is you would normally do to get back to Kuwait City?'

Angela nodded, used her right arm to brace herself against the dashboard of the car while she unclipped the unit from its windscreen mount with her other hand. She began altering the programming, a task with which she was obviously quite familiar. It took her less than a minute to change the route and destination, then she nodded and reattached the unit to the mount, and checked that the power cable was still connected.

'That's done,' she said. 'All you have to do is follow the arrow on the screen. That'll take us back to the border crossing point into Kuwait. Assuming these people don't catch and murder us first, of course.'

'But I can't even see them,' Stephen said from the back seat. 'They'll never catch us now.'

'Don't be too sure about that,' Bronson replied. 'Those two men didn't walk to the camp. They probably arrived in that vehicle we saw driving past on the road out to the west, and my guess is that by now they'll have gone back to it and they're already chasing us. I can't tell, because of all the dust we're kicking up at the moment, and I'm certainly not slowing down just to confirm that particular piece of bad news.'

14

Vicinity of Al Muthanna, Iraq

In fact, although Khaled had told the driver of the 4x4 to head straight to the encampment, Farooq and Mahmoud had still not climbed into the vehicle.

Mahmoud was following his latest orders, lying at the top of the sand dune aiming his Kalashnikov at the rapidly diminishing cloud of dust being thrown up by the speeding Toyota, and rhythmically firing rounds straight at it, guessing where the invisible target was most likely to be. There was always the chance that he might get lucky, but both he and Khaled knew that the vehicle was now so far away that there was almost no possibility of hitting it. And even if he did manage to do that, there was no guarantee the relatively small bullet from the assault rifle would do enough damage to actually stop the vehicle.

'I don't think that sat phone is here,' Farooq said, stepping out of a tent near the edge of the camp. Between them, he, Khaled and the driver had checked every single tent. 'We're wasting our time. We need to move out right now if we're going to catch them.'

The second lorry, Farooq knew, was already heading east on what they hoped would be an intercept course to catch the fleeing Toyota, but the chances of the truck being able to match – or even get close to – the speed of the Land Cruiser were extremely slim. Realistically, their best hope – in fact their only hope – was to contact the men in the lorry they'd sent off to wait near the track the archaeologists used in their journeys between the encampment and Kuwait City.

And without a satellite phone, that wasn't going to be easy.

Farooq jogged back towards the jeep, Khaled following close behind him. The camp looked almost exactly the same as it had when they'd left it a few hours earlier, apart from the sheets that had been placed over the bodies and weighed down with rocks. Neither man gave the sheeted corpses much more than a glance. Their concern was only with the living, with the female archaeologist whose knowledge of the discovery had to die with her – and as quickly as possible – and the two unidentified men who were with her and who would therefore suffer precisely the same fate.

Moments later, all four men climbed back into the jeep, the driver gunned the engine and with a sudden spray of dust and sand from all four wheels the vehicle accelerated away, across the open ground beside the encampment and then turned down the slope that led away from the tents. The driver was well used to driving in the potentially treacherous desert conditions – he'd been doing it since his early teens – and he had no doubt that he could catch the fleeing Toyota.

'Twenty minutes, maybe half an hour, and we'll be right behind them,' he said confidently.

Khaled nodded, but then shook his head.

'That might be too late because by then they'll be at the border,' he said. 'But if we can get within walkie-talkie range of the other lorry, then stopping them will be easy. There's nowhere they can run that the Browning won't be able to reach.'

15

Vicinity of Al Muthanna, Iraq

Bronson was trying to keep track of everything at once – the route ahead, the endless parade of dunes, the display on the GPS unit and the rear-view mirrors, though these were of little use right then because of the cloud of sand being thrown up behind the vehicle.

A thought occurred to him and he lifted his foot from the accelerator pedal.

'What?' Angela asked. 'Please don't tell me there's something wrong with the car.'

'Of course not. Toyotas don't break, not even out here.'

He slowed still further and as the dust cloud to the rear of the vehicle diminished noticeably he checked all three mirrors carefully. As far as he could see there was nothing in view behind, which was not too surprising given the speed at which they'd been travelling, but a vehicle following them was not what he was worrying about.

'So why have you slowed down?'

'Because we might be playing straight into their hands. I was just trying to make sense of what must have happened back at the camp this morning. We saw two men armed with assault rifles, but there must have been at least one other person in that jeep because it kept on driving past us on the track. These men aren't stupid.'

Bronson glanced at Angela beside him, and at Stephen's face in the interior mirror. Both of them looked apprehensive.

'Say there were two other people in the car as well, making five. I didn't count the bodies, but there were at least a dozen corpses back there—'

'Fifteen,' Angela and Stephen said simultaneously, and then Angela added: 'There were seventeen of us altogether in the team.'

'If only five people had turned up waving assault rifles and confronted three times that number of men, I would have expected far more people in the group to run away. Or to try to, anyway. It's the natural reaction. They would have known, once the first killing had taken place, that they were going to die, so why wouldn't they run and at least try to escape? So I think there must have been far more people involved in the attack on the camp than we've assumed so far. If there were more of them, say twenty, then running wouldn't have been an option because the archaeologists would have been completely outnumbered. That would explain why they died in that one small area. And if that is the case, I reckon there's a very real chance that the rest of these killers are some-where out here in the dunes, just waiting for a chance to take us down as well.'

Neither Angela nor Stephen responded to that remark and the bad news it implied.

'Is this the route you always follow when you go to Kuwait City?' Bronson went on.

'Yes.' Angela nodded. 'It's the straightest way of getting across the border, and most of the ground is reasonably hard, so there's not much chance of getting bogged down in soft sand or anything like that.'

Bronson indicated the arrow on the GPS unit, which was pointing precisely in the direction the vehicle was heading.

'So if anybody had been watching the camp, they would know what route you would follow on the journey.' It was more of a statement than a question, but both Stephen and Angela nodded.

'And that means,' Bronson added, 'that if there was a second group of terrorists out here in the dunes, all they would need to do is plant themselves somewhere near the route you always use and wait for us to drive into their ambush. And that's exactly where I think we're heading.'

He slowed down a little more and sat up straighter in the seat, scanning the surrounding area, trying to pick an alternative route to take. He nodded as if he'd made up his mind, swung the steering wheel to the right and began heading south, away from the direct route to the Kuwait border.

'If you keep going in this direction we won't get to Kuwait at all,' Stephen pointed out. 'The next border we cross will be into Saudi Arabia, and doing that would be a really bad idea for a whole number of different reasons.'

Bronson shook his head.

'We won't be going anything like that far,' he replied. 'I just want to move far enough away from your normal route to ensure that we don't get jumped by another bunch of guys hefting Kalashnikovs. I reckoned if we could head south for about five miles, then we could change direction back to the east and that would be enough of a safety margin to keep us out of trouble.'

About fifteen minutes later, Bronson pointed at the speedometer and began turning the vehicle to head east.

'We've covered just over seven kilometres since we turned south,' he said. 'That's not quite five miles, but it's probably enough of a buffer, and the terrain over to the left looks a bit easier to navigate than what's right in front of us.'

'You can navigate just with the compass,' Angela said, unclipping the GPS unit and doing something with the keypad to deselect the navigation feature. 'All it's displaying now is our geographical position as a lat and long, and the direction we're heading. And I suppose the good news is that if you're in this part of Iraq and you point the nose of your vehicle east, it's impossible to miss Kuwait. It's just too big,' she added with a faint smile, the first improvement in her mood that Bronson had noticed since they'd stumbled into the appalling carnage of the archaeological site.

He gave an answering smile, then switched his attention back to the terrain in front of them, picking the best route over and around the uneven dunes, now keeping the speed down to avoid creating a dust cloud that would be visible for a far greater distance than the vehicle itself.

Three minutes later, it became obvious that their problems were far from over.

16

Vicinity of Al Muthanna, Iraq

Khaled ordered the driver to stop the jeep near the crest of a range of dunes so that they could try to spot the vehicle they were chasing. Given the time they'd wasted searching for the sat phone at the archaeological camp, the only sign of the missing Toyota had been a distant cloud of dust and sand, and a few minutes later even that had disappeared from view.

At first, Khaled had assumed that the vehicle had just slowed down, to avoid being quite so visible, and would be continuing to follow the same track. But what now bothered both him and Farooq was what looked like a recent set of tyre tracks – or to be exact faint depressions in the sand that could have been tyre tracks – that led away from the established route and down to the south.

'If that is them,' Farooq said, scanning the horizon in a fruitless attempt to spot their quarry, 'they're heading straight for the Saudi Arabian border.'

'They won't go there,' Khaled said, with a confidence that Farooq suspected was not entirely justified. 'They'll still have to cross the border into Kuwait. All they've done is turn off route in case we were following them.'

'So do we follow these new tracks?'

'No.' Khaled shook his head firmly. 'We'd have to go too slowly if we were going to follow them. We'll stay on the original route and keep the speed up. The second lorry must be somewhere down to the south of us by now. Contact the driver on the walkie-talkie and tell him we think the 4x4 might be somewhere near him. And keep trying to raise the other lorry as well, because that's still in the best position to stop these people.'

A few seconds later, the driver steered the jeep off the dune and back on to the track towards the Kuwaiti border.

17

Vicinity of Al Muthanna, Iraq

'I think there's a truck behind us,' Bronson said. 'It's quite a long way back, but it looks as if it's travelling pretty quickly.'

Angela and Stephen both turned round in their seats to stare out of the side windows of the Toyota.

'Are you sure?' Stephen asked. 'I don't see anything.'

But even as he spoke those words, he saw a dark-coloured vehicle appear on the crest of a dune over to their right and then disappear from view as it drove down into the dip below.

'Now I see it. It could just be a supply vehicle of some sort,' he suggested. 'Or even a bunch of Bedouin on their way somewhere. We needn't assume the worst.'

'Of course it could,' Bronson agreed, 'but I really don't want to take the chance that it isn't, so I'm going to keep up the speed and maintain a decent distance in front of it.'

It wasn't a difficult decision to make. Trying to hide among the dunes was never going to work. The only thing that could save them, assuming that Bronson's concern about the possible identity of the people in the vehicle was correct, was speed. That it would make them visible to their pursuers was both inevitable and unavoidable.

He pressed his foot down on to the accelerator pedal and watched as the needles on the speedometer and rev counter rose in a synchronized movement.

'You're kicking up a big cloud of dust again,' Angela warned him.

'I know. But there's nowhere we can hide out here, so what we have to do is move as quickly as we can. We can't hide but we can run.'

Although there was no way of keeping out of sight, Bronson did his best, sticking to the dips between the dunes rather than driving up and over the crests.

But it was quickly obvious to all of them that the intentions of the people in the lorry behind them – and it was now closer and its size and shape could be seen – were probably hostile, because as soon as Bronson had increased speed, so did the other vehicle.

'Hang on,' Bronson said grimly, accelerating down the side of a dune and on to the level ground at its base. 'This is going to get rough.'

18

Vicinity of Al Muthanna, Iraq

In the cab of the lorry, the driver was following the very specific orders he had been given. As soon as they'd seen the Toyota, a couple of miles in front of them, he'd increased speed to try to get as close to the target as he could. The obvious problem was that although the lorry was, like all vehicles adapted for use in desert conditions, fitted with a permanent four-wheel-drive system and, in this case, a big turbo-charged diesel engine, its sheer weight and bulk meant that it was never going to be as fast as the vehicle they were pursuing. Although it had got closer to the target, the tail chase was a contest that the lorry was slowly losing.

But Farooq had passed one other piece of information to the driver, and as the front of the lorry crashed down over the top of a dune and he accelerated down the slope in front of him, he also snatched a glance at his GPS unit. Moments later he steered the truck over to the right, down a long narrow gully that ran fairly straight for about a hundred yards.

'Where are you going?' the man sitting beside him demanded, one hand clutching the fore-end of his Kalashnikov while he held on to the dashboard grab handle with the other.

'I'm following my orders. Wait and you will see.'

At the end of the gully, the ground sloped gently upwards on the left-hand side. The driver took another look at the display on his GPS then steered the truck up the slope. At the top, he hit the brakes briefly, then swung the steering wheel to the left and accelerated again. Immediately, the bone-crunching ride that everyone in the vehicle had been enduring eased noticeably, despite the fact that within a few seconds the lorry was travelling even faster than it had done before.

'Now I see what you mean,' the passenger said as he stared at the beaten track that stretched away in front of them. It was a long way from being a proper road, but it was relatively flat and level and mostly free of potholes and dips. 'How far does it go?'

'Only about three kilometres, according to Farooq, and then it turns away to the south. But that should be far enough for what he wants us to do.'

The driver knew that timing was everything. As the straight section of the track came to an end, he hit the brakes and shouted out, 'Get ready.'

As the lorry shuddered under braking, two of the men who'd been clinging on to the sides of the loading area clambered painfully to their feet and grasped the steel bar that ran across the truck directly behind the cab. The moment the vehicle came to a complete stop, one of them pulled a grey canvas cover off a long and somewhat bulky object located right in the centre, and directly above, the steel bar.

Underneath the cover – used only as a precaution to keep the worst of the sand out of the mechanism – the long black barrel of a Browning M2 half-inch machine gun gleamed in the sunlight.

The man designated as the gunner checked the weapon, ensured the belt carrying the ammunition was properly aligned with the breech and clear of obstructions, cocked it and then grasped the twin grip handles at the rear of the machine gun and swung it round to point the barrel towards the distant vehicle. Even for that powerful and heavy weapon, he knew that the 4x4 was at the very limit of its range, probably around a mile distant, but he had his orders.

The good thing was that although the 4x4 was travelling quite quickly, it was also following a reasonably straight course, making it an easier target.

He sighted the weapon, allowing a slight lead ahead of the vehicle, and raised the barrel a fraction to cater for the drop the bullets would experience in flight due to the effects of gravity.

'Quickly,' his companion urged. 'They'll be out of range in a few seconds.'

The gunner adjusted his aim, then pressed the trigger in a short and controlled burst.

19

Vicinity of Al Muthanna, Iraq

Bronson slammed his foot on to the brake pedal and simultaneously swung the steering wheel hard around to the left. The Land Cruiser rocked and lurched with the sudden change of direction, then surged forward as Bronson shifted his foot to the accelerator.

'What's happening?' Stephen demanded.

'That,' Bronson snapped, nodding his head at the ground over to the right of the vehicle, but not taking his hands off the steering wheel.

Stephen and Angela glanced in the direction he was indicating, but neither saw anything. Then, looking deceptively innocent in the harsh midday sun, a puff of sand seemed to erupt from the top of a nearby dune, followed immediately by two other flurries of dust and sand.

'What is it?' Stephen asked.

'They're shooting at us,' Bronson replied shortly. 'I

saw a kind of flicker from the back of that truck a few seconds ago.'

Stephen twisted round in his seat to stare over at the now stationary lorry. Then he shook his head.

'We must be at least a mile away by now. Surely they haven't got a hope of hitting us at that distance.'

'Not with a Kalashnikov,' Bronson replied grimly. 'But plenty of other things have the range.'

'Like what?'

'The Ma Deuce. That's what the American troops call the Browning M2 half-inch heavy machine gun. I don't know exactly what weapons those guys had mounted on the trucks, but quite often out here you'll find that anything much bigger than a jeep will carry a half-inch machine gun of some sort, and the Browning is pretty much the best of the bunch, so it's a really popular choice.'

'And that could hit us from over a mile away?' Stephen still sounded incredulous.

'Definitely. Its effective range is two thousand yards, but it's still dangerous at well over four miles. It fires between five hundred and six hundred rounds a minute, and that's about ten shells every second. Any single half-inch bullet hitting this Toyota could easily take out something vital – a tyre or the engine, say – and if that happens we're dead.'

'Jesus,' Stephen exhaled, and again turned to look towards the lorry.

The bigger the clouds of dust and sand Bronson managed to create the better, because that would obscure the 4x4 from view, and travelling in a straight line would be the height of stupidity, so he swung the Toyota left, away from the threat posed by the heavy weapon that was firing short bursts towards them. They couldn't hear the shots over the roar of the diesel in the Land Cruiser, but puffs of sand were erupting from the dunes near them, so it was clear they were still under attack.

Bronson dropped down a gear and pressed his foot hard on the accelerator pedal, sending the big Toyota barrelling down the side of a dune, the suspension bottoming as he reached the rocky level ground at its base.

On the firmer surface he could increase speed still more, which is precisely what he did, causing Stephen to seize the grab handle above his door with one hand and his seat belt with the other.

'If those bullets they're firing hit us, that'll be the end of us,' he yelled over the commotion. 'But the same applies if you crash this jeep.'

'I do know that,' Bronson replied, but didn't noticeably slow down.

He crested another dune, and for a split second all four wheels of the Toyota were turning in the air as it left the ground. It landed back on the slope on the far side of the dune with a crash that bounced all three of them around in their seats, but he continued to keep the power on, forcing the big vehicle to travel as fast down the slope as the conditions permitted.

'This isn't as dangerous as you might think,' Bronson

said, turning the steering wheel slightly to avoid a rocky outcrop that projected from the sand about fifty yards ahead of the Toyota. 'Sand dunes are formed by the action of the wind, and that usually means that the slopes on both sides are relatively gentle.'

Stephen didn't look convinced when Bronson glanced at his face in the rear-view mirror.

'And the chances of the bullets hitting us now are pretty much nil.'

'We haven't come that far,' Stephen said. 'We must still be in range of that machine gun.'

'We are, obviously,' Angela said, 'but what Chris means is that we're travelling away from them, and we were already close to the maximum accurate range of the weapon when they started firing. So they have to move, they have to follow us, if they're going to have any chance of hitting this vehicle. And one of the few things I do know about weapons is that trying to hit a moving target from another moving target is virtually impossible.'

She gasped for breath as the Land Cruiser again lifted off the ground and then crashed down once more.

'That is what you meant, isn't it?' she asked.

Bronson nodded. 'Got it in one.'

A couple of minutes later, Bronson began to back off the speed. He hadn't seen any signs of further firing from the lorry, and the vehicle itself was now at least two miles behind them, maybe three or more. They were safe, at least for the moment.

And then, off to the left, Bronson saw an almost

identical dark shape, and in that instant he realized he was facing a clever ambush. The reason the pursuing lorry had fired at them – apart from trying to stop the Toyota and kill them, obviously, which would have been a bonus – was to force them over to the north, and within range of the other heavy machine gun he had no doubt was mounted on the second truck.

The vehicle appeared to be stationary, or at least it did when he first saw it, but within a few seconds it was clear that either it had been moving very slowly or the driver had just started off. Which deduction was correct was irrelevant, because almost immediately the vehicle came to a stop on the crest of a dune, and seconds later Bronson saw a sudden flicker from above the cab.

Somebody on the lorry was firing a weapon at them, and this time there was no doubt at all: at 600 yards, the Toyota was well within range of the Browning.

20

Vicinity of Al Muthanna, Iraq

The first bullets from the half-inch machine gun mounted behind the cab of the second lorry chewed up the sand less than thirty feet in front of the Toyota.

Their only defence – apart from simply driving out of range, which wasn't going to happen any time soon – was to get out of sight. To drop down into the gullies that lay between the dunes.

Bronson hit the brakes and swung the wheel hard over to the right. The Land Cruiser lurched and swayed, and then headed straight down the slope.

He'd reacted as quickly as he could, but he still thought it might have been too little, too late, as he saw the explosions in the sand marching steadily towards them.

A second later the back of the vehicle seemed to lift up bodily into the air from some immense impact. The rear window shattered, greenish-blue jewels of safety glass flying in all directions.

Angela wasn't a screamer, but she instinctively ducked down in her seat and squealed in terror. Stephen dived for the floor, shouting expletives.

When Bronson took his eyes from the terrain in front of him for the briefest of instants he could see the exit hole punched through the roof of the Toyota.

'We're okay,' he said. 'One bullet hit the car, but no serious damage.'

'Jesus Christ,' Stephen said, the terror in his voice obvious.

'Stay low, both of you,' Bronson instructed in the chaos. 'I'm going to try to keep in the valleys, where the dunes will hide us. Or at least hide most of the vehicle.'

But already he was running out of options. The valley down which he was driving was rapidly coming to an end, and in front of them was the side of a gently sloping dune.

Stopping wasn't an option. Instead, Bronson dropped the Toyota down a gear, and pressed his foot hard on the accelerator pedal. The big turbo-charged diesel engine roared its defiance and the 4x4 powered up the slope, clouds of sand being blasted away from the low-pressure tyres.

'Hang on!'

Angela and Taverner gripped whatever they could find as the Toyota again powered into the air over the crest and crashed down on the opposite side of the dune, the impact driving the breath from their bodies.

Bronson lifted his right foot from the accelerator as

the vehicle lifted off the ground, but immediately pressed it down again the instant the tyres were back in contact with the sand. He was concentrating on getting the hell out of the killing ground as quickly as possible, but still found a second to take a look out of the side window to check the lorry whose inhabitants were determined to murder them.

The faint flicker from above the cab told him that the weapon was still firing, but the lorry was on the move now, the driver obviously trying to close the distance between them.

As long as the lorry was moving, Bronson knew that there was less chance of the machine gunner – no matter how good or competent he was – being able to hit them. Angela was quite right: trying to hit a moving target from a moving vehicle was as near impossible as made no difference unless they were really close together, and Bronson estimated that they were already almost half a mile apart.

But even as that thought crossed his mind, another salvo of bullets from the heavy machine gun tore up the sand just feet behind the Toyota. It seemed that the gunner was more competent – or simply a lot luckier – than Bronson had anticipated.

Then the Land Cruiser dropped down the slope, the dunes on its left-hand side providing a natural barrier impervious to even the heavy-calibre bullets being fired from the truck, and for a few precious seconds they were safe.

It was a cat-and-mouse game they were playing and

Bronson guessed that there was only one possible outcome. The gunner on the lorry now knew the direction they were heading, and every time the Toyota drove out of one of the dips between the dunes, as it inevitably had to do, there was a greater and greater chance of him hitting the vehicle with his next salvo. And when that happened, they were as good as dead.

Even if they weren't killed by the bullets that would perforate the thin steel of the Toyota, Bronson had no doubt that the men in the back of the truck would arrive within a few minutes to finish the job with their assault rifles or pistols.

What he needed, apart from a miracle, was some way of keeping out of sight, of keeping the vehicle below the top levels of the dunes until he could drive out of range of the weapon. The problem was that the dunes simply marched like a giant frozen sea, each crest followed by a dip and then by another crest, and in order to get away Bronson was being forced to continually climb over crests before descending into the relative safety of the shallow valleys beyond.

Again he powered the Toyota up the side of the dune in front of him, and again he felt the unmistakable sensation as it left the ground, and then the crash as the tyres hit and the suspension compressed all the way to the stops.

Even over that noise, the hammering of the machine gun was still audible, and again the Toyota shuddered as another one of the heavy bullets smashed into it.

Glass from one of the side windows at the back of the

vehicle sprayed all around the interior. And at the same instant the opposite window blew out as the bullet continued its journey through the Toyota before burying itself in the sand a few feet away.

This time Angela screamed.

'Jesus Christ,' Stephen shouted again, the panic evident in his voice. 'I felt that go right over my head.'

But again they'd been lucky. Any lower and, as Taverner had just pointed out, the bullet would very probably have killed him. And a couple of feet lower than that and it could have taken out the drivetrain or gearbox, which would have signed a death warrant for all three of them.

They were out of sight of the lorry again, Bronson steering the 4x4 along the bottom of a dip. This time he decided to stay down for longer, even though that would mean they weren't putting much distance between them and their pursuers, because as far as he could tell that shallow valley ran like a section of an arc around the location of the lorry. But at least the gunner couldn't possibly know where his target would appear next, and that just might give them an edge.

Bronson eased the vehicle further over to the left, picking his spot on the opposite side of the valley carefully, choosing the lowest dune that he could see, and then he steered the Toyota up the slope and over the crest and down into the next valley of sand.

This time, no shots followed as the 4x4 appeared from the dip. Bronson drove the Toyota down the opposite slope and at the bottom reversed direction to head back the way they'd come, hoping that the gunner would be expecting him to do the opposite.

Again he picked an area where the crests were the lowest, and accelerated the vehicle as hard as he could. As he steered it over the crest and down into the next dip, he saw the long barrel of the machine gun swing towards him, but too late for the gunner to open fire before the Toyota disappeared again. And they were about another couple of hundred yards away, and distance was vital. Distance would keep them alive.

Then, right in front of him, Bronson saw another valley in the sand that intersected with the one he was driving along, but this one tracked away from the position where the gunmen's lorry was parked. He didn't hesitate, just swung the Land Cruiser into it and accelerated hard.

It wasn't all that long, and at the end another wall of dunes rose up, but that didn't matter. They were now another couple of hundred yards further away from the lorry, and would – or so Bronson hoped – be coming back into view somewhere that the gunman wouldn't expect.

And when he crested the dune, he was proved right. No shots came their way, and when he checked the rear-view mirrors he estimated that they were now about a mile, maybe even a little further, away from the armed lorry.

'I think we're clear now,' he said cautiously, picking the straightest route he could and winding up the speed, while still weaving slightly from side to side, just to continue offering as difficult a target as he could. Though in reality he knew that the plume of sand the tyres were already chucking into the sky was probably their best defence.

Then through the blown-open window on the right-hand side of the vehicle Bronson heard another volley of shots, though he had no idea where the bullets struck. All three of them looked in that direction, to see the first lorry they'd avoided bouncing over the dunes straight towards them, but still about a mile away from the Toyota.

'They're wasting their time firing at us,' Bronson said. 'We're right at the limit of his range and the truck's all over the place.'

They continued to hear sporadic firing from both vehicles for another few minutes, but no other rounds hit the Toyota, and the sounds drifted further and further into the distance as they accelerated away.

Twenty minutes later, without further incident, they crossed the border into Kuwait and could all relax for the first time since they'd left the camp.

'We should tell the Kuwaiti border guards what's happened,' Taverner said.

'Probably not a good idea,' Bronson replied. 'I had a few dealings with Arabs when I was in the Army, and their mindset is very different to ours. If we tell them we've been shot at, the most likely outcome would be for them to arrest us, on the grounds that clearly some kind of crime has been committed and we were on the spot at the time. And if we were there, then we must obviously have been involved. Once news of the massacre at the archaeological camp breaks, we'd probably be the prime suspects for that as well. We'd be lucky to ever get out of jail.'

'So what do we do?' Angela asked.

'We head for the hills,' Bronson replied. 'We've all got our passports with us – I hope – so we park this 4x4 at the airport in Kuwait City and buy tickets on the first flight out of Kuwait that isn't going to another Arab country.'

'Why?' Angela asked.

'Because if the Kuwait authorities are alerted and discover that we are on an aircraft operated by an airline based out here, they could always instruct the crew to turn it round and bring us back, or land somewhere else en route where we could be arrested. That technique is much less likely to work if we're being flown out using a Western European airline. Even a fairly short-haul flight would do. Then, once we're in Greece or Italy or wherever, we buy another ticket and keep moving until we get back to Britain. Then we go to the police and tell them what's happened and let the authorities sort it out.'

'Suppose they don't believe us?' Stephen asked. He had perked up considerably the moment they'd turned on to the road inside Kuwait that paralleled the border.

'I'd rather take my chances with British justice than sit in an Arab court hoping for the best. I took a bunch of pictures of the dead bodies on my phone before we left the camp, and that will help establish our innocence.

My arrival time at Kuwait Airport should be enough to prove that the killings must have taken place well before our arrival. I'll take some shots of the damage to this jeep as well before we fly out, and that should substantiate what we tell them.'

21

Vicinity of Al Muthanna, Iraq

'My men did their best, Khaled,' Farooq said, 'but the woman was lucky. And whoever was driving that car knew what they were doing. We didn't anticipate that. My gunner is certain he hit the vehicle at least twice, but obviously the bullets missed the engine and anything else that would have stopped them.'

Khaled nodded. There was no point in recriminations, and he was very aware that the main reason the woman was still alive was because of his original mistake.

He and Farooq had done a quick headcount of the bodies of the archaeological team while they were looking for the satellite phone, and he was now aware that one of the men was also missing. He guessed that archaeologist was one of the two men accompanying the woman, though he still didn't know who the second man could be.

'So what will you do now?' Farooq asked.

'I will decipher the inscription and follow the trail that it reveals,' Khaled said. 'That is the most important task, and the reason for everything we have done.'

'So you'll have to forget about the woman?'

Khaled shook his head.

'No. That trail is still fresh. I have a good idea what she's likely to do and where she'll go. These people are very predictable. I have contacts I can task to find and follow her, and when they track her down I will see that she is silenced for ever. Bring me the sat phone. I have calls to make.'

22

Kuwait City

Their first look at the departure board at the airport was not encouraging. There were plenty of planes leaving, but almost every flight was not only operated by an Arab-owned airline, but was also flying to an airport in another Arabic country, precisely the combination Bronson most wanted to avoid.

'We'll take that one,' Bronson said, coming to an immediate decision. 'The Nile Air flight to Alexandria.'

'Pardon me for asking,' Stephen said, 'but isn't Egypt an Arab country?'

'It is,' Bronson agreed, 'but it's not a Gulf Arab state, and right now that looks to me like our best option. If you've got any better ideas, now's the time to share them.'

There was only a short queue at the Nile Air ticket counter, and apart from the clerk nobody so much as glanced at them as Bronson bought the tickets. None of them had even heard of the airline, but the aircraft was a modern Airbus A320. Boarding was on time, the three-and-a-half-hour flight passed entirely without incident, and after the aircraft touched down in Alexandria they walked straight through customs and immigration.

The next problem was the complete lack of any useful onward destination from Alexandria, and after a few frantic minutes checking schedules and departure times, they knew they had only one option: get to Cairo. They left the airport after hitting a couple of the ATMs hard and piled into the first taxi they saw outside. There was a train service between Alexandria and Cairo, but even if it left spot on time it would get them to the airport precisely five minutes before the next possible flight took off. And that was never going to work. Their only hope was to put their trust in the ability and competence of an Egyptian taxi driver.

'I hope you know what we're doing,' Angela said from the back seat, pulling her seat belt as tight as it would go.

Bronson glanced over his shoulder, gave her an encouraging nod and then waved a fistful of Egyptian pounds in front of the driver's face.

'Cairo International,' he said, 'as fast as you can.'

Getting from place to place quickly on Egyptian roads is never easy. The traffic, especially near the major cities, is invariably horrendous. The road surfaces frequently alternate between new smooth tarmac and stretches where the metal layer has almost completely disappeared to reveal the rutted and potholed base below the road. And, of course, there are frequent police checkpoints, toll booths, wrecked vehicles and other obstructions to impede progress.

But Bronson remained hopeful. The distance between the two cities was a little over 100 miles and there was even an almost direct road – the Cairo–Alexandria desert road – that was virtually all dual carriageway. Once they'd cleared the traffic around Alexandria, providing they didn't run into the tailback after a major accident, and the driving conditions permitted the taxi driver to really wind it up, Bronson reckoned they ought to cover it in just under two hours. And that would be just enough time.

The biggest problem, really, was getting out of Alexandria.

'Is this the evening rush hour?' he asked the driver in English, as he looked through the window at gridlocked lanes in both directions.

The man shook his head, so Bronson tried again, this time in French.

That produced an immediate response, and the two of them had a brief but animated conversation, the driver gesticulating in both directions, but finishing up by pointing ahead of them.

'What did he say?' Angela asked.

Bronson half turned in his seat to face her.

'He knows what the problem is,' he replied, 'because he can see it, and there's been some stuff on his radio as well. A lorry has broken down, just stopped dead, in the middle of the road at the next intersection. He's going to try to work his way around it, as soon as a gap opens up.'

In fact, a gap didn't so much open up as be created by the driver. He sounded his horn in a long continuous blare as he swung the steering wheel to the right, sticking the nose of the Mercedes directly in front of a Toyota pickup. The moment the car in front of the pickup moved, he slid further over, angling the taxi towards a side street that appeared mercifully clear of traffic, the entire manoeuvre accompanied by a cacophony of noisy blasts from horns and hooters but, perhaps surprisingly, no angry gestures from the drivers he was inconveniencing. If he'd tried the same manoeuvre in a London street, Bronson guessed it would have ended in blows.

At the end of that street was a set of traffic lights showing red. The driver slowed, but didn't stop – and neither did the three cars in front of him and the two behind – simply pulling out of the junction, sounding the horn and joining the traffic flow on the cross street. That manoeuvre caused Bronson to press his foot hard down on the imaginary brake in front of him, and take a firm grip of the grab handle on the door. But they didn't hit anything, and the other cars parted to allow them in.

'Jesus Christ,' Stephen muttered from the back seat, invoking the deity yet again.

Bronson waited until they were travelling in a straight line once more, in harmony with the surrounding traffic, before he spoke again to the driver in French.

He listened to the man's reply, and then laughed.

'What?' Angela demanded.

'He's just told me he's heard that in England the drivers always obey the traffic lights. And that in Italy the drivers ignore the traffic lights. But here in Egypt, the traffic lights are only for decoration.'

'That explains a hell of a lot,' Angela said darkly.

But that was the last major hold-up they encountered, and within a few minutes the Mercedes was heading away from Alexandria on the desert road. The driver did well, holding the Mercedes saloon at well over an indicated 100 kilometres an hour when he could and travelling as fast as the conditions permitted when he couldn't. They didn't meet a significant amount of traffic and they didn't see a single accident, and they stepped out of the taxi at the departure building at just after nine forty-five. Bronson didn't count the money, just handed the wad to the driver as he stepped away from the vehicle.

'Where are we going now?' Stephen asked.

'Well, we've got the same problem at Cairo as we had at Alexandria,' Bronson replied. 'No flights to anywhere where we actually want to go. That's why we're heading for Sharm el-Sheikh. But look on the bright side.'

'There's a bright side?' Angela asked.

'Oh yes. Nobody would realistically expect us to be following the route that we're taking, so if anyone is after us, they probably have no idea where we are right now, or where we're heading.'

They caught the flight with minutes to spare, and exactly an hour later the EgyptAir Boeing 737 touched down precisely on schedule in Sharm at half past eleven.

Then Bronson felt they could breathe again, and for the first time since they'd left Kuwait they had time in hand, because the next flight he'd picked – to Milan – wasn't scheduled to depart until two thirty in the morning.

He insisted that they delayed buying their tickets until about an hour before the flight was due to leave, to minimize the amount of time the opposition would have to work out where they were and to do anything about it. When he decided that the time was right, they again bought return tickets as they'd done on the previous two flights to arouse less suspicion.

They passed through the security check without incident and sat down in the departure lounge. It looked as if the flight would be at least half full, judging by the number of people already waiting at the gate, but they were able to find three seats off to one side where they sat and waited for boarding.

There was, clearly, only one topic of conversation that interested them. None of them could understand the reason for the apparently senseless massacre of their colleagues out at the dig site. They kept their voices low, just in case any of the other passengers, most of whom appeared to be Arabs, could understand English.

'It just doesn't make sense,' Stephen said for about the third time.

'The inscription in the temple . . .' Angela said. 'Whatever it said has to be really important.'

'Pity we'll never know what that was,' Bronson pointed out, glancing at Angela. 'Or is there something you should be telling me?'

'You know me too well, Chris,' Angela said with a slight smile. 'You know the way I work. The very first time I went down into the temple I took my camera with me. I have plenty of pictures of the inscription. We can look at them right now if you want. If it is worth killing for, we need to work out why as soon as we can.'

Bronson smiled back.

'Actually, I thought you might have done something like that, because I know you do enjoy a puzzle.'

'So do you.'

'That's why I'm a copper, I suppose,' Bronson replied. 'And this could well be the biggest puzzle we've ever got ourselves caught up in. Just as much as you do, I want to find out why the hell that inscription was so important it had to be destroyed, and why everybody who'd seen it was murdered. There's nobody near us, so can we take a look at the pictures now?'

Angela nodded, glanced around them, then pulled her camera out of her carry-on bag and switched it on. She navigated through the gallery until she found the image she was looking for, and handed the camera to Bronson.

He stared at the small image for a few seconds, then shook his head.

'It's not what I was expecting,' he said. 'It looks quite

rough, like it was done in a hurry, or by somebody copying something unfamiliar.'

'You can see it better on a big screen, obviously,' Angela said, taking back the camera, 'but you're right: it was quite roughly carved.'

Stephen had barely even glanced at the screen of the camera; he just kept nervously looking around the departure lounge.

'Do you think we're still in danger?' he asked.

'After the efforts they made to kill us today,' Bronson said, 'I think you can safely assume that if those people can possibly do so, they'll kill us immediately. But it's a bit different assassinating someone on the streets of London than machine-gunning a jeep in the Iraqi desert. Once we get back to Britain, my guess is that we'll be safe enough, especially if we do the obvious and post pictures of the inscription on the Internet, which will release the images into the public domain. They'd probably still like to tie up the loose ends, but they wouldn't actually achieve anything if they did murder you.'

'Cold comfort,' Angela said, 'but comfort all the same.'

The talk ranged back and forth, but without them reaching any conclusion that made sense of what had happened. Although they were talking together, all three of them were supremely conscious of their surroundings, and in particular the possibility of police officers or airline officials approaching them. Not that they could have done anything much if that had happened. But eventually they boarded the Meridiana Boeing 767 to Milan without incident. As they buckled up their seat belts, Angela breathed a sigh of relief.

'Are we really safe now?' she asked.

'We're safer, but I wouldn't say we're actually safe yet,' Bronson replied. 'Just work out the timing. The police from Baghdad will have reached the camp this afternoon, and when they found that we weren't waiting for them as they instructed they would immediately have started looking for us, because that's how the corporate police mind functions. They would know, and if they didn't know they would definitely have guessed, that about the only place we could go would be Kuwait, and if I was running the investigation absolutely the first thing I'd have done would be to block the two of you from getting on any aircraft, going anywhere.'

Stephen looked around anxiously, as if already checking for a policeman brandishing handcuffs to be approaching him down the aisle of the aircraft.

But Bronson shook his head.

'I think we're okay for the moment,' he said reassuringly. 'I reckon it would have taken at least two or three hours for the wheels to start turning, and even if they began by running checks on credit card usage, it will still take them a significant amount of time to find out where we went once we left Kuwait. The electronic trail will basically stop in Alexandria, and they might well assume that we went to ground somewhere there. Obviously they'll eventually discover that we flew down to Sharm el-Sheikh, and from there up to Italy, but I doubt if there'll be any kind of a reception committee waiting for us in the arrivals hall at Milan airport. I just don't believe that they could get the information in time to move that fast.'

Ten minutes after they'd boarded, and three minutes after its scheduled departure time, the Boeing lifted smoothly into the air and climbed swiftly up to its cruising altitude.

23

Milan

It was early morning, a few minutes after six, when the aircraft touched down in a damp and muggy Milano Malpensa airport. They passed through customs and immigration without any problems, and immediately made their way to the departure side to check on outbound flights to London.

'We're in luck,' Bronson said, pointing at the board, which showed two scheduled flights to London, both leaving at around eight.

But when they presented themselves at the ticket counters, they discovered that not only were both flights fully booked, but there were around a dozen people on the waiting list for each one.

That really only left them with two other options. They could find a hotel or get out of Milan using a different form of transport than an aircraft, and in Bronson's opinion, keeping moving was far more important than getting some sleep.

Stephen had a different point of view.

'Do we really need to do this?' he complained. 'I'm completely knackered.'

'We all are,' Angela snapped, 'but Chris is just trying to keep us alive, and I'm going with him. If you want to stay here, that's entirely up to you.'

Stephen looked from one to the other, and shook his head.

'I can't see how they could possibly trace us this far in such a short time. This is Milan anyway, it's not like we're still in the Middle East. I'm going to find a hotel near the airport, get some sleep and then fly back to London this afternoon or sometime tomorrow.'

'I really don't think that's a good idea, but it's your choice,' Bronson said. 'One word of advice, though. When you check in, make sure you use a different name and pay in cash. Definitely don't show the clerk your passport or anything that can identify you. Tell them that you've been robbed and that all your personal documents have been stolen. That way, if anybody does manage to trace us here, they'll have no way of telling where you went after we disembarked from that aircraft.'

Stephen nodded absent-mindedly. 'Thank you for everything you did back there,' he said.

He hugged Angela, shook Bronson's hand, and walked away towards the exit from the arrivals hall.

Angela watched him go, a thoughtful expression on her face.

'I'm tempted to say he's right, you know,' she said. 'This could be a bit of overkill on your part.'

Bronson shrugged. 'Maybe it is. Maybe not. I just really don't want to take the chance, especially not if you're likely to be in the firing line. Doing this should hopefully break the chain completely. Nobody – not the men following us or the Iraqi police or anybody else – should know that I'm involved at all yet, so the paper trail that you've left from Kuwait City will end right here in Milan, and there'll be nothing to show where you went or what you did after you walked out of the airport.'

Angela nodded. 'You've talked me into it,' she said. 'Do you want me to go with you to the desk?'

'Definitely not. I don't want anybody here to remember us being together. There's a café opening up just over there. Grab yourself a coffee and buy some soft drinks and a couple of sandwiches or something for the journey, and then walk out of the building. I'll pick you up outside.'

Bronson's Italian was fluent, and hiring the mid-sized Peugeot was a reasonably simple process. Quicker than he had expected, he was handed the keys and directions to the car rental parking area. A few minutes after that, he pulled up outside the door of the arrivals hall to allow Angela to place her bags in the boot and climb into the passenger seat of the car.

'How far do you want to go? Today, I mean?' Angela asked as she did up her seat belt.

'All the way, if possible,' Bronson replied.

'It is a hell of a long drive, though,' said Angela.

'I know, but I won't be happy until we're back in the

UK and this is behind us. Anyway, while I'm driving you can get started on working out what that inscription is all about.'

The built-in satnav steered them through the outskirts of Milan until they picked up the ring road, the *Tangenziale Ovest di Milano*, to the south-west of the city. Near the district of Pero, Bronson turned on to the *Autostrada Serenissima*, which ran almost due west towards the French border. Driving through Switzerland would have been a shorter route, but he didn't want any possible problems at the border, and thanks to Schengen there were no border controls of any sort between Italy and France.

While they drove, Angela talked, partly to rehash what they knew about the putative temple, the obliterated inscription and the killings, but mainly, Bronson knew, to keep him awake as the seemingly unending tarmac of the autostrada unrolled in front of them in the early morning. Simply staring at it was hypnotic, and there was surprisingly little traffic at that time of the day so any kind of an external stimulus was a bonus.

They made it into France and as far as an autoroute service station beyond Lyon before Bronson finally admitted defeat.

'I'm sorry,' he said, 'but that's it. If I try to drive any further I'm going to fall asleep at the wheel.'

'There's no hotel here,' Angela pointed out, 'so shall we just stay in the car?'

'Unless you've a real problem with that, yes. I just

need to close my eyes for a few hours, and then we can get on the road again.'

They ate the last of the sandwiches Angela had bought at the airport in Milan, then reclined their seats as far back as they would go and closed their eyes.

Bronson was snoring in minutes.

24

Milan

Stephen Taverner had enjoyed a much more comfortable time. The bedroom in the hotel was a decent size with a surprisingly luxurious en suite bathroom. The facilities passed him by, though, as all he could think about was getting some sleep.

In fact, he didn't get anything like as long a sleep as he had been hoping: just after nine thirty that morning he was awakened by a knock at the door, and he stumbled over somewhat groggily to find out who it was. When he peered through the security spy hole he saw a man standing there in a white coat with a laden trolley beside him.

'I didn't order room service,' Stephen said.

The waiter replied to him through the closed door in passable English.

'I know that, sir,' he said, 'but we have a problem in the dining room and so all our guests are receiving a complimentary breakfast in their suites.'

For a second or two Stephen hesitated, the lure of the still-warm sheets in the bed competing with the appetizing prospect of fresh coffee and warm pastries. Then he released the safety chain on the door and turned the handle.

The instant he did so, the door was pushed open violently from the corridor, the side of it catching him a glancing blow on his head, which sent him staggering and tumbling to the floor. By the time he had recovered his senses, the waiter had pushed his way into the room along with the trolley, and was standing looking down at him, the white coat discarded behind him. Another man, heavily built, wearing a dark suit and exuding an air of menace, stood beside him, and both of them were holding automatic pistols of some kind, each equipped with a bulky suppressor. Behind the duo stood another figure, much smaller and slight. He, too, was dressed in a black suit that even to Stephen's untutored, and at that moment also largely unfocused, eyes, looked extremely expensive.

Stephen glanced to one side, wondering if he could possibly escape, but the room door was already closed and the security chain in place. The lethal inevitability of the situation dawned on him and filled him with panic.

For several long seconds, none of the three men spoke, just stared down at the frightened archaeologist, their expressions impassive. Then the small man stepped out from behind his two companions and took a pace forward.

'My name is Mario, and I have been asked to obtain some information from you, Mr Taverner.' His voice was soft and refined, his English perfectly fluent. 'If you wish to avoid a considerable amount of pain it will be in your own interests to tell me what I need to know. Matters like this can always be handled in at least two ways, and I'm extending to you the courtesy of letting you choose which.'

Taverner suddenly felt a warm dampness at his groin and realized that he had wet himself, the unmistakable menace implicit in what the man had just said simply terrifying him. He also realized in that moment of crystal clarity that he really should have taken Bronson's advice and registered at the hotel under a false name and paid for the room in cash. But he had been mentally and physically exhausted when he'd arrived and hadn't really taken Chris's words very seriously – handing over his credit card and signing in with his real name had just seemed easier all round.

The man who'd been wearing the waiter's jacket noticed the change in colour of the pyjama bottoms Stephen was wearing, and a smirk appeared on his face.

'What do you want to know?' The archaeologist's voice quivered with emotion. 'I'll tell you anything I can. Anything I know,' he added.

'I know you will,' Mario replied. 'That has never been in any doubt. Let me start very simply by asking if you know where I can find' – he broke off for a moment to look at a piece of paper he took from his pocket – 'a woman called Angela Lewis?'

Stephen shook his head and the small man's face changed instantly, the indifferent, slightly benign, expression replaced by one of unmistakable hostility.

'Do you mean you don't know or you won't tell me?' he asked. 'There is an important difference.'

'No, no,' Stephen stammered. 'I really don't know. I mean, I know what she intended to do, but I've no idea where she is at the moment.'

'Don't try to be clever with me, Taverner. Just answer the question. I'm asking you politely at the moment, but that can always change. In an instant.'

'Look,' Stephen said, 'all I know is that Angela and her ex-husband decided not to fly back to Britain but to drive there. I couldn't face doing that – I was just too tired – so I came to this hotel to get some sleep and then fly back this afternoon. I don't know if they hired a car and are still driving or if they've stopped to sleep in a hotel. Or they might have changed their minds and stayed somewhere here, or even taken a train out of Italy. I really don't know.'

He was babbling in his eagerness to convince his unwelcome visitors that he was telling the truth.

'We flew together from Kuwait City to Alexandria, then from Cairo to Sharm el-Sheikh and finally to Milan, but we separated in the arrivals hall at the airport. The last time I saw them they were standing together and talking. But I swear I have no idea where they are now.'

The three black-suited men stared down at Stephen, and for a moment or two none of them responded. Then Mario nodded.

'This woman's husband, or ex-husband, I think you said. Does he have a name?' he asked, taking a pen from his pocket and preparing to write on the paper he was still holding.

'Yes, yes. His name is Chris Bronson.' Stephen didn't even hesitate in implicating Bronson.

'Spell that for me.'

Stephen did so, and the small man put away both the paper and the pen.

'That's better than nothing,' he said, almost to himself. 'If he hired a car, he must have used a credit card and produced his driving licence. We can work on that.'

He reached back into his pocket, took out the piece of paper again, wrote something else on it, then tore off a strip and handed it to one of the men standing behind him. He switched to rapid-fire Italian, clearly issuing instructions, and when he'd finished the man nodded once, holstered his pistol after removing the suppressor, and left the room.

After the door had closed behind him, Mario glanced around the room before looking back at Stephen's cowering figure.

'Do you have a camera, Mr Taverner?' he asked.

'What?'

'It's a simple enough question. Just answer it. Do you have a camera?'

'Yes, I do. It's in my case, over there.'

'And I see your laptop is already out and on the desk. Good.'

Mario looked back at Stephen.

'There's just one other answer I need from you,' he said. Then he asked another question that made no sense at all to the frightened archaeologist.

'Yes, of course,' Stephen replied when he realized that the Italian was expecting an answer. 'We all did,' he added.

Mario nodded, took the paper from his pocket again, presumably to check that he had covered everything he needed to do, then replaced it and nodded again.

'Now I don't think we need to detain you any longer, Mr Taverner.'

A wave of relief washed over the terrified archaeologist.

'I would hate you to be late for your next appointment,' Mario added, with a wintry smile.

'Appointment? I don't have any appointments.'

'Oh, I think you do, Mr Taverner. In this case, you have a very important and final meeting. With your maker.'

Stephen's eyes widened in horror as he realized what the man was saying, but before he could move, or even say anything, Mario made a single gesture and his companion took a half step forward, aimed his pistol at Stephen's chest and pulled the trigger. A simple execution.

The weapon coughed once, the noise sounding like a heavy, wet slap, and the archaeologist slumped backwards as the bullet tore through his heart. For good measure, the gunman fired twice more, once into his chest and the third bullet through his forehead.

Then he calmly unscrewed the suppressor from the end of the barrel and slipped it into his jacket pocket and replaced the pistol in his underarm holster.

'An easy morning's work,' Mario said in Italian. 'Pack up his laptop and charger, then find his camera and check for anything else that could contain images.'

Before the two men left the room they took half a dozen photographs of the dead man, including close-ups of the bullet wounds. The contract that had been accepted by them had been quite specific in a number of details, but the two most important conditions were that any piece of electronic equipment capable of storing images was to be recovered and then sent by courier to an address in Baghdad, and unambiguous photographic evidence of the termination of the principals was to be supplied before the agreed payment would be released.

The problem was that because the targets had split up, he had only been able to fulfil a part of the contract, and the probability was that the Lewis woman and her ex-husband were now beyond the reach of his criminal organization. But at least he hoped he would be able to start following the trail and establish how the two people had left Milan.

It would be fairly easy to find out if they had hired a car, if Taverner had been right in his belief, and his contacts in the *carabinieri* would be able to provide both a description of the vehicle and the registration number. In that case it could possibly be traced as it made its way through France. Of course, tracing it and stopping it were two entirely different matters, but that would not be his problem.

He had already instructed his man to begin checking with the car hire companies, and it shouldn't take too long for the results to come in. With his influence, things tended to happen immediately. He'd told his man to initiate checks on all rentals for the two hours after the Sharm flight had touched down, to allow time for them to have passed through customs and immigration. Only if that produced no results would he start asking questions at the railway stations in the city.

Less than ten minutes after Stephen had been shot, the two dark-suited men walked out of the hotel and across the street to where two other men waited in a black Alfa Romeo saloon, the smoked-glass windows making it impossible to see who was inside it.

'Give me a phone,' Mario said, as the Alfa nosed its way out into the traffic, another Alfa following a few yards behind it.

The man sitting in the front seat beside the driver opened the glove box and took out a pair of latex gloves, which he pulled on, and a mobile phone. He unclipped the back, checked that a SIM card was already inserted, slid a battery into position and replaced the back panel. Then he switched on the mobile and passed it back.

The small man consulted the piece of paper again and pressed the buttons on the keypad to dial a mobile number in Iraq. All the phones used in this kind of third-party operation were burners – cheap mobiles purchased in bulk from a wholesaler – and the SIM card inserted in each of them would be used to make exactly one call before being disposed of, and no numbers were ever programmed into their memories. Each mobile would only be used half a dozen times before being dumped as well. Members of the Mafia who needed to make telephone calls memorized the appropriate numbers, and if additional numbers had to be used, as in this case when the organization was carrying out a contract on behalf of another group, then those numbers would be written down on small slips of paper. Paper could be burned or swallowed in an emergency, but data stored electronically on almost anything could always be retrieved, and that was a potential problem.

'We have had partial success,' Mario said when his call was answered. 'We have located and spoken to the man in question and obtained what we needed from him.'

Calls from one mobile to another were essentially encrypted, but like all people involved in criminal activities, the small man was always circumspect in what he said. You never knew when information might get into the wrong hands.

'But the lady and her husband had already left. We believe they decided to continue their journey by car, and I should be able to confirm that this morning. Do you still wish to speak to her?'

The man in Baghdad paused for a moment while he digested this unpleasant piece of news.

'Did you get an answer to my other question?' he asked.

'I did,' Mario replied, 'and he said the answer was yes. In fact, he said everybody had done so.'

Khaled cursed briefly and fluently in Arabic, then switched back to English, their only common language.

'Very well,' he said. 'In that case I will certainly need to reach her. Do you know anybody who could talk to them on my behalf?'

'Possibly, but finding them will not be easy, and it might be better to wait until they get home. I definitely have friends there who could contact them.'

That was about as clear a statement of intent as Mario was prepared to say on an open line: he knew that trying to find the targets in France would be difficult, perhaps impossible, but once the Lewis woman reached Britain, she would probably think she was safe and certainly wouldn't feel the need to hide. So eliminating her there would be comparatively easy, a simple matter of locating her house or apartment and then subcontracting the killing to an organized crime group based in Britain.

'I'll have to think about it,' Khaled said, after another pause. 'If I decide that that is the best option would you be able to organize it?'

'Of course. There will be some additional expenses for my friends, but I presume that would not be a problem.'

'No.'

Moments later Mario passed the phone back to the man in the passenger seat. He snapped the back off the mobile, removed the battery and took out the SIM card. He produced a small pair of scissors, snipped the card into four pieces and dropped them out of the side window one at a time as the vehicle sped through the streets. Then he took a small plastic packet containing a new and unused SIM card, opened it, slid it into the slot in the phone, and replaced the plastic back before putting the phone back into the glove box, along with the battery. Simply having the battery in place offered at least the possibility that the mobile could be tracked, even if it wasn't switched on, which was why the phone was only powered up for the time it took for the call to be made. Finally, he peeled off the latex gloves and put them and the remains of the SIM card packet into a small plastic bag that he would dump later.

Before long the small convoy reached its destination, a large and palatial villa set in extensive grounds surrounded by a high wall topped with razor wire a few miles to the north of Milan.

In an air-conditioned room built into the basement of the property and protected by solid concrete walls and a steel door that would resist anything short of a rocket-propelled grenade, a trusted and experienced computer specialist oversaw the IT facilities of the Milan family of the Cosa Nostra.

Mario walked down to the computer room and handed the operator a piece of paper on which he had written two names: 'Angela Lewis' and 'Chris Bronson'.

'I need their addresses, where they work, and a couple of decent photographs of each of them.'

The operator glanced at the sheet and shook his head.

'Lewis is a pretty common name,' he said. 'Is there anything else you can tell me about her?'

'She probably works in London,' Mario said, 'and she's an archaeologist.'

The operator nodded.

'Then it shouldn't be too difficult,' he agreed. 'How soon do you want this?'

'Today, if possible. It may be necessary to place a contract on her and, if so, our client will want it done within twenty-four hours.'

25

France

When Bronson woke with a grunt and a snort it was early afternoon, the sunshine bright on his face. For an instant, he had no idea where he was, though he did know that he was extremely uncomfortable, with a crick in his neck that felt like it would be with him for most of the day.

Then realization dawned, and he looked over to his right to see Angela lying flat out on the reclined passenger seat, looking at him with a single blue eye through a tangle of blonde hair.

'You're awake,' Bronson said, stating the obvious.

'Yes, I am,' his former wife said somewhat testily. 'In fact, I've been awake for most of the morning, thanks to your snoring. It was a somewhat unpleasant reminder of our brief married life.'

'I do recall you complaining about my snoring then. What's the time?'

'Just after one thirty. I know we should get back on the road quickly, but before we do I absolutely insist on a coffee at least. And ideally a croissant or something to nibble. I'm not that nice to be around when I'm hungry, and I'm hungry right now.'

Bronson nodded and reached for the door handle.

'So what's the plan?' Angela asked, as they sat at a corner table in the autoroute restaurant, two coffees and a plate of pastries in front of them.

Bronson glanced at her and shrugged.

'I don't really have one,' he replied. 'I'm sort of making it up as I go along. Random decisions are going to make our movements as unpredictable as possible, and hope-fully keep us one step ahead. What I wanted to do was get you out of danger, which meant getting you out of Iraq and away from Kuwait as quickly as possible. Even if those terrorists have access to the most sophisticated surveillance and tracking facilities, they can't possibly know where you are right now. The trail would have stopped at Milan. They probably don't even know which country you're in.'

'I know all that,' Angela said. 'But if they want to track me down in Britain – and there was plenty of information about all of the team at the camp – they certainly could.'

Bronson nodded.

'I hadn't expected the trail to stop in London,' he said, 'because the fact that they were prepared to slaughter an entire archaeological team just to stop anyone seeing that inscription shows they're completely ruthless and dedicated to the cause. It's the inscription that's the core of this whole mess. That's why I suggested publishing your photographs of it online, because once it's out there and anyone can see it, their attempt to keep it quiet will obviously have failed and there would be no point in targeting you any more.'

'Unless those bastards have long memories and decide I should die just because I was involved. Simple revenge. What little we know about them suggests that their philosophy is the exact opposite of the forgiving kind. Let's face it, we were really lucky to get out of Iraq. A few seconds more or less, the guy behind the machine gun aiming with a bit more care and those vultures would be feasting on us by now.'

'And there was me thinking it was all down to my skill behind the wheel,' Bronson said with a slight smile. 'But they didn't just turn up at the encampment on the off-chance that you'd found that temple and there was an inscription inside it, did they? It was targeted and premeditated.'

'God, I never thought of it like that. How could they have known? It had to have come from an insider.'

'Yes. As far as I can see there are only two possibilities,' Bronson said. 'Most probably somebody told them, though it's just about possible that they hacked into an email account belonging to one of the archaeologists. I mean, presumably finding the inscription wasn't a secret, so it's likely that one of the team might have told his wife or a work colleague or somebody what they'd found.'

'But that means—' Angela began, but Bronson interrupted her.

'Unless we're way off beam, it means somebody definitely expected the inscription to be found. Not necessarily by your team, and not necessarily at that location, but somebody knew it was out there in the desert somewhere. Whoever it was must have been waiting for some sign that it had been found, and then he sent in the men with the guns. This wasn't some off-the-cuff operation, this was a deliberate attempt to obliterate the inscription and murder everyone unfortunate enough to know anything about it. It was carefully planned. And if you and Stephen had been there when they arrived, it would have been entirely successful.'

'Yes,' Angela said, 'it would. Even if one of us had mentioned the inscription in an email, Mohammed had told us not to send out any pictures of it, or of the temple. That information would have been released as a part of our report on the expedition, the official document detailing everything we'd found.'

She shook her head angrily.

'What gets me is that it's so bloody unfair. Archaeology isn't supposed to be dangerous – unless a trench collapses on top of you or something – and this expedition was meant to be a bit of gentle digging in a site that looked mildly interesting. The only reason I was there was to help out with the conservation of any ceramics we found and to give my opinion on the dating of the relics. And now I'm on the run from a gang of murdering thugs who want to kill me not because of what I know, but because of something that I've seen.'

'We've been here before, Angela my love, and we've proved on several occasions that archaeology can be extremely hazardous to your health. This is just another situation where we're on the side of the righteous and facing a bunch of people who have our worst interests at heart. Don't worry. We'll get through this. We make a good team. Now, let's get back on the road.'

26

Baghdad, Iraq

To say Khaled was unhappy barely even hinted at the degree of his irritation.

What should have been a simple operation had gone disastrously wrong. The woman and a man he now knew to be her former husband had escaped the best efforts of Farooq and his men, along with another archaeologist who Khaled hadn't even known wasn't at the camp.

The only piece of good news was that the contract he had placed with the Italian had been completed, and Taverner had been taken care of in Milan. But where Lewis and her husband were at that precise moment, he had only the vaguest idea. If Taverner had been telling the truth, they were probably somewhere in the middle of France driving towards the channel ports in a hire car, and trying to locate them in that vast country would be a complete waste of time. A hit at the channel ports would also be too problematic because of the security measures in place at border control. About the only option he had left, Khaled realized, was for a contractor in Britain to find out where the Lewis woman lived and then eliminate her. But that couldn't be done for at least a couple of days. A wait, even that short, seemed interminable.

There was one piece of good news, though. At least the inscription that had been carved on the stone wall of the underground temple appeared to be precisely what he had expected and hoped for. He still hadn't managed to decipher the encrypted text, but he was certain that he would soon work out the very basic cipher that had been used the better part of one millennium earlier by an unknown scribe.

And then, he would have all the clues that he needed to commence his search.

Khaled walked across his spacious office to the wall opposite his desk, where a large safe stood. He pulled a set of keys out of his pocket, selected a butterfly key which he used to undo the main lock, then inserted another key into a different lock and gave it a half turn to the right. The door remained firmly closed, and he then entered a six-digit code on the keypad beside the locks. As he entered the final number, the internal bolts slid back and the door swung open.

Inside were four shelves, three of them containing boxes and packets holding particularly precious relics, while the top shelf held a number of ancient books and much more modern folders. It was one of those, the cardboard a dull greenish colour, that he selected and carried back to his desk.

He released the elasticated bands that held the cover closed. Inside were several colour photographs showing dead bodies, men, women and children, the corpses twisted in the agony of their dying, the limbs and abdomens bloated and distended. But Khaled barely gave the pictures a second glance. What Saddam Hussein had done to the Marsh Arabs was old news, his bombing raids and the use of various lethal concoctions from his chemical warfare armoury just another fading memory in the consciousness of the world.

He put the photographs to one side and then slid out from the folder a sheet of parchment that was almost entirely covered in Arabic script. The ancient document was encased in a specially designed plastic folder that was fitted with a hermetic seal, allowing air to be sucked out of the interior and effectively store the parchment in a vacuum. He picked up the plastic folder and for a few moments just stared at the old leather and the faded script, then placed it reverently to one side. He picked up a high-resolution photocopy of the parchment text and studied that for a second or two.

But it was the next sheet in the green folder that he spent the longest time looking at, although he knew most of what was written there by heart. This was a page of modern writing paper on which he had carefully transcribed the writing from the parchment, allowing double spacing so that any ambiguities could be addressed in the blanks between the lines. There had been a few places where the meaning of the Arabic text was less than completely clear, and he had written alternative possible explanations for some of the words and phrases.

But no matter which interpretation of details of the text he considered, the meaning and thrust of the basic information was perfectly clear. The fact that the temple and the inscription had been found was sufficient proof of that. In fact, once he had read and understood the Arabic text on the parchment, which had come into his possession almost twenty years earlier, he had known beyond doubt that the structure existed, buried somewhere under the sands in the trackless wastes of the southern Iraqi desert. He'd also known it was inevitable that sooner or later somebody would find it.

It had turned out to be later, and obviously it would have been better if a smaller group of people had been involved in its discovery, but ultimately the death of a handful of archaeologists, several of them not even Iraqis, was insignificant compared to the importance of the find. The downside was going to be the very obvious publicity generated by the massacre when news about it finally broke internationally. That would make any activity in the southern part of Iraq difficult to achieve without coming under the unwelcome scrutiny of the media, but Khaled both hoped and expected that the trail he would be following would start a considerable distance away from the underground temple. Very probably, in fact, it would actually begin in a different country.

He spent a few more minutes looking at the contents of the folder, refreshing his memory, then replaced all the papers and photographs within the cover and put the document back in the safe.

He had barely sat down again at his desk when his private mobile phone, the number known to only a handful of people, rang. He glanced at the screen but saw only that the originator was a withheld number.

'Hello,' he said cautiously in English.

'This is Filippo,' the heavily accented voice at the other end said, and Khaled immediately recognized the codename the Italian contractor had selected. 'The electronic equipment you asked us to source for you is already on its way by courier. It should arrive tomorrow.'

That, Khaled knew, was simply a reference to the laptop computer, camera and any other electronic gizmos that might have been in Taverner's possession. Another loose end had been tied.

'Good,' he said. 'Any news on the other matter?'

The Italian sounded quite pleased with himself when he replied.

'I have been in contact with a colleague in Britain and he has already discovered the home address of the woman. As soon as you decide the action you want to take I can issue him with appropriate instructions. Her companion's address is proving more difficult to determine, but he is still investigating that and should have a result by the end of the day. Do you wish to issue any instructions at this stage?'

Khaled thought for a second or two before replying.

'No, not yet,' he said. 'It is important that both are dealt with simultaneously, if possible at the same location and ideally in what appears to be an accident. The electronic equipment must be recovered at the same time. Call me when your contact has not only identified both addresses, but also knows where these two people are.'

'As you wish. Our contract is now complete. Can you ensure the agreed funds will be sent as soon as you receive the goods?'

'I've already prepared the transfer,' Khaled replied.

'Excellent. I will call you with news as soon as I have it.'

27

Milan

Stephen Taverner's body was discovered a little after midday. The Englishman had failed to check out – he had only booked the room until noon – or to answer the telephone on three separate occasions, and this had concerned the reception staff because he had told them he was intending to catch an afternoon flight to London.

What's more, one of the room service waiters had failed to return to the kitchen after delivering two room service breakfasts, and the manager was far more concerned about that minor mystery. After repeated knocking on Taverner's door, he used his override key card to open the door and found himself looking at the breakfast trolley standing in the room close to the dead body of the Englishman.

It wasn't the first time the manager had discovered a body in a hotel room, though it was the first time he'd encountered somebody who'd very clearly been murdered, and he knew the drill. There was not the slightest point in checking the corpse for a pulse – even to a layman and at a distance it was obvious that the man had been dead for some time – so, shocked as he was, he did what the training manual told him to do.

He had already touched the outside door handle with his bare hands, so he knew his own fingerprints would be on it, and if he touched the inside handle he would probably smudge any prints the departing killer might have left. So he didn't do that. What he did do was use his internal communicator to contact the reception desk and tell them to call the police and an ambulance, and to explain that a man had been murdered, giving the room number.

The response from the *carabinieri*, relayed to the manager from reception desk, was exactly what he had expected. The room was to be sealed, nobody allowed in or out, and the police were on their way.

The manager had already used his handkerchief to close the door, and he then summoned a porter from the lobby to stand outside it until the police arrived. His mission to find the missing waiter then took on a new urgency. Unless the waiter himself had murdered the Englishman for some reason and then fled – which seemed extremely unlikely – then something else must have happened to that man.

The search didn't take long. In a linen closet at one end of a corridor, the manager discovered the silent and unmoving body of the missing man, crouched down on the floor on his hands and knees, almost as if he was praying. The manager's cursory examination showed a complete absence of blood, but a very obvious red mark around the dead man's neck indicated that he had been either strangled or garrotted.

When the *carabinieri* arrived outside the hotel, to the inevitable accompaniment of a self-generated fanfare of sirens and squealing tyres, the manager was waiting for them in the lobby to explain that the body count had doubled since his staff had made the initial call.

'Before we go up to the room,' he said to the two senior detectives, 'you need to know that I've just found a second body, a member of my staff, hidden in a linen closet, and it seems fairly clear to me that the two cases are related.'

'We'll be the judge of that, thank you,' the senior *carabinieri* officer snapped. 'There could be any number of explanations for two bodies being found in the same hotel on the same day. There's no need to look for a connection that isn't necessarily there.'

'Of course,' the manager replied equably. 'I'm just not entirely certain how many unconnected explanations there can be that will explain a dead waiter stuffed in a linen closet and missing his jacket, nametag and badge, and a man shot to death in a room down the corridor, a room in which I also found the waiter's jacket and the breakfast trolley. But,' he added with a smile, 'you men are the experts, not me. Shall we go up, gentlemen?'

Two hours later, both bodies had been certified as dead, by far the easiest and shortest part of the entire proceedings, and had then been removed after dozens of photographs had been taken of the corpses in situ. The specialist investigators had then moved in to examine the two established crime scenes while another group searched for the third one. There was no doubt that the Englishman – his passport identified him as Stephen Taverner – had been murdered exactly where he was found, but the situation with the waiter was different. He could have been marched at gunpoint down the corridor and into the linen closet and strangled there, or he could have been attacked somewhere along the corridor itself. But the carpet and beige walls had so far revealed no signs of a struggle at any point.

A team of detectives was already looking at the hotel CCTV recordings, but without any particular expectation of finding anything, because the coverage was very limited, basically just a couple of cameras on each floor beside the lifts which provided a few shots of the corridors towards the bedrooms. Numerous people had been seen entering and leaving the building throughout the night – an entirely predictable characteristic of an airport hotel – and the vast majority looked like tourists or businessmen.

Inevitably, the unexpected arrival not only of several police vehicles but also of the vans and cars belonging to the crime scene investigators attracted the attention of the press, and the barter system immediately began to bear fruit for the reporters. They quickly found that chambermaids and cleaners, working for the minimum wage, were only too happy to share what they knew – or what they thought they might possibly have heard, in many cases – in exchange for folded high-denomination euro notes. News of the murder was broadcast on the local radio stations around lunchtime, and went out on the wires to other media outlets during the afternoon.

By that time, the only piece of information that was not publicly available was the name of the dead Englishman, simply because the Italian police were making arrangements to inform his family in the UK before the news broke.

28

France

When Bronson and Angela reached the vicinity of
Orleans Angela managed to tune into British Radio 4.
After a few minutes, the programme ended and then a
man with a very deep BBC voice began reading the news.
Bronson turned up the volume – both he and Angela were
desperate to hear whether or not news of the events in
Iraq had broken internationally. If they had, they both
guessed the massacre would be headline news.

It soon became clear that nothing had been released
about it by the Iraqi authorities, but just before the end
of the broadcast they both registered the importance of
one other breaking news story: the body of an
Englishman, believed to be an archaeologist, had been
found murdered that morning in a hotel in Milan.

When the broadcast ended, Angela reached up and
switched off the radio. Her hand covering her mouth in
horror, she turned to Bronson.

'That was Stephen,' she said quietly, 'wasn't it?'

Bronson sighed heavily. 'I'd like to say that it wasn't, that it was just a bizarre coincidence, but I don't think it was. I'm sorry,' he said, and squeezed Angela's shoulder.

Angela was staring straight ahead through the windscreen, taking in deep breaths to steady herself.

'They got to him so quickly. I mean, how did they manage that?' Her voice was quiet with shock.

'Realistically, he wouldn't be that difficult to find. If they had access to the airline schedules of Kuwait City our three names would have popped up as probably travelling together, because we bought tickets at exactly the same time.'

'But they were in Iraq! They couldn't have got to Milan any quicker than we did. It doesn't make sense.'

Bronson shook his head.

'Unfortunately, crime is a business these days – an international business, in fact – and it's quite common for one criminal organization to contact another one in a different country to arrange a particular job. In fact, and especially with assassinations, this is a really good technique – from their point of view – because it provides a complete separation between the person who actually orders the killing and the victim. The murder is committed by someone who has never met the victim and has no possible links with him, and that type of crime is virtually impossible to solve.'

'I didn't know that,' Angela said. 'So you think someone in Iraq just picked up a telephone, rang a contact in Italy and told him to find us and kill us?'

'That's about the size of it, yes. Obviously you can't just open up a telephone directory, look under "M" and expect to find the Mafia listed, but there's a lot of international cooperation between criminal organizations in those areas where they're not directly competing with each other. In fact,' Bronson added, 'what probably saved us was the time it took the men in Iraq to establish their bona fides.'

'Sorry, you've lost me.'

'Even in the criminal world, committing murder is still pretty serious, and it would take a lot more than one phone call to convince some Mafia *capo* to send out a group of his soldiers to track down and kill three people. There would have been checks and double checks and then they'd have to agree the fee and the payment method. All that would have taken time. My guess is that our aircraft had probably already landed in Milan several hours before the Italians were ready to move, and they were playing catch-up all the way.'

Angela shivered. 'So if we'd taken a later flight somewhere, or the men in Iraq had moved quicker, the Italian killers might have been waiting for us at the airport?'

'Yes. That was why I was so keen to get out of Kuwait as quickly as possible.'

For a few minutes, they were both silent, the gravity of the situation weighing heavily on them. Then Bronson glanced across at his former wife who was still staring straight ahead through the windscreen at the unwinding road in front of them.

'I'm starting to have second thoughts,' he said.
'What about?'
'What we do next. I think it's time for Plan B.'

29

Baghdad, Iraq

Khaled took off his reading glasses and rubbed his eyes. He had been studying both the photographs of the inscription found in the underground temple and the written copy he had made of the text. He felt as if he had been looking at the enigmatic characters for the entire day, though in fact he'd only been sitting there for about three hours. But the text – such as it was – still made absolutely no sense to him. It was clearly encrypted, because no combination of letters in the text formed a recognizable Latin word, and he was reasonably certain that it was Latin.

He tried character shifting, a refinement of basic Atbash, which meant starting the first letter of the reversed alphabet at some random point, which gave a further twenty-six possible ciphertexts to try, none of which had worked. He'd then again tried character shifting but using the ciphertext alphabet written forwards rather than backwards. That produced another twenty-six possible combinations, and once more none of them had worked.

All he'd so far managed to establish was that something rather more complex than Atbash had been used to encrypt the message. And, realistically, about the only two possibilities were that a code word of some sort had been included within the ciphertext, or perhaps the cipher itself was entirely reliant upon a number of code words instead of a reversed alphabet.

Both techniques were known to have been used as early as the mediaeval period, and because of one single piece of information – the date of an event that took place in Western Europe – which had been included within the text on the parchment in his possession, Khaled knew that the inscription could not possibly have been written prior to the early part of the fourteenth century. So a cipher that utilized code words was entirely feasible.

The problem, obviously, was working out which word, or combination of words, had been used.

Khaled was by no means an expert cryptographer. Because of his job he had become familiar with the basic techniques, and rather than trying to peer into the mind of a mediaeval scribe to guess what names or words he might have chosen almost half a millennium earlier, he decided to approach the problem from a different direction, by using frequency analysis.

In English the six commonest letters in order are E T A I O N, the list including four of the five vowels. So if a piece of English-language text, encrypted using a simple letter-substitution code, is analysed, whatever letter occurs most frequently in that piece of text is most likely to represent the letter 'E', and the second commonest the letter 'T', and so on.

Latin was obviously going to be different, but Khaled had very quickly located an analysis that had been performed on a number of pieces of mixed-genre Latin texts amounting to nearly 300,000 words. The results, posted on the Internet, were in fact not that dissimilar to English, the commonest letters being I E A U T S, these six letters together amounting to over 55 per cent of the text, and the first three accounting for almost 32 per cent of the total. Obviously different types of text would have produced different results, but he felt this information was a good guide.

He took a fresh sheet of paper, printed a photograph of the entire inscription and worked his way methodically through the first half-dozen lines, crossing out each letter on the photograph as he noted it down on the paper, and putting an additional line beside each letter as a simple counting mechanism each time it reoccurred. That produced a kind of table of popularity for the letters used on the inscription, which he cross-referred to the list on the Internet and pencilled in substitutes accordingly.

That, infuriatingly, didn't make any better sense, and for a couple of minutes after he had completed the letter substitution Khaled just stared blankly at the paper in front of him.

And then it was as if a light began to dawn, and he suddenly realized that as well as encrypting the original text, the man who carved the inscription had added one other simple layer of complication. A complication that in fact Khaled should have guessed a lot earlier, purely because it *was* an inscription.

Once he saw how the original text – and he now knew that it definitely was Latin – had been encrypted, deciphering it was simply a matter of time, and within a little over half an hour Khaled was looking at the original plaintext. Or at least, he was looking at the original plaintext of roughly half the inscription.

But the lower half of the encrypted text stubbornly refused to yield to anything he tried, even frequency analysis, and he guessed that some entirely different encryption method must have been used. This was interesting in its own right, and attracted his professional attention, but on a personal note it was just extremely frustrating. There had to be, he assumed, some clue or indication in the section he had managed to crack that would indicate how to decipher the rest of it.

And then he saw something that he hadn't noticed before. There was a piece of the inscription that he had ignored because he'd assumed it was simply decoration, placed there by the sculptor in an attempt to make a rather uninteresting-looking inscription slightly more attractive. And he'd been wrong.

Between the section of the inscription that he had managed to decrypt and translate and the part that had so far resisted his efforts was an incised line made up of a series of small square crosses, all apparently identical. But now he could see how important the line was because it separated the two parts of the text. It was another indication – if any was needed – to show that a different decryption technique would be required to display the plaintext of the characters that had been chiselled into the rock to form the lower part of the inscription.

As a final check, he then effectively reverse-engineered the part of the cipher he'd successfully cracked and confirmed that it was Atbash, but with the addition of two proper names, one at the beginning of the reversed alphabet and the other at the end, giving multiple options for the encryption. And the names the author had chosen, with hindsight, were entirely predictable, given what he already knew – or at least guessed – about the origin of the inscription and the men who had ordered it to be carved.

He spent another hour trying every combination of names and variants he could think of, attempting to crack the lower section of the encrypted text, but got absolutely nowhere. And there appeared to be no clue within the plaintext he had written out to suggest what word or words might have been used to form the cipher. It looked very much as if the second section needed something else to allow it to be decrypted, and that did make sense of a phrase that appeared towards the end of the plaintext.

But he wondered if he even needed to decrypt the remainder of the text, because the information contained within the inscription seemed enough in its own right, within certain limitations. Although the statement he had decoded was clear enough, it was also in one sense frustratingly obscure.

Khaled checked his decryption a couple of times and looked at the few possibilities for alternative meanings, and then for a minute or so he just sat and stared at his best guess of the translation of the original Latin script, the only bit of the inscription that actually mattered to him. It was far from specific, but interpreting what it meant – or more accurately the location to which it referred – wouldn't be that difficult.

He smiled to himself. With any luck, his quest would be over within a matter of days.

But there was no time to waste, because of the woman who had got away. She had escaped from the camp and then vanished from Milan before she could be silenced. She was probably somewhere in France at that very moment, running for her life. But what concerned Khaled more than anything was not the fact of her continued existence, but the unpleasant knowledge that – according to the dead archaeologist in Milan – she, like all the other members of the team, had taken copious photographs of the inscription.

And, sooner or later, she would go to ground somewhere and when she did Khaled had no doubt that she too would manage to decrypt the enciphered text and make exactly the same connection that he had. And if she had the slightest inkling of the importance of the object the inscription referred to as the 'hoard', then almost certainly she and her former husband would join the race.

Time really was of the essence, and Khaled knew he would need to move as quickly as he could once he'd worked out the meaning of the clue he'd uncovered. And he would also need some help. Or, to be completely accurate, some muscle. He opened his briefcase, took out his personal mobile phone and dialled Farooq's number.

'I need you and six of your men,' he said without preamble when his call was answered. 'And make sure you have your passports, because we will almost certainly need to fly somewhere at short notice, probably somewhere in Europe.'

'You mean you don't know where?' Farooq asked. He sounded surprised.

'Not yet,' Khaled replied. 'I've deciphered the inscription, but I still need to work out exactly what the text means.'

'What about weapons?'

'Hopefully we won't need them, but if we do we'll have to find them at our destination. Anyway, warn your men and hold yourself ready.'

Khaled ended the call, opened up a web browser and began searching for a location that matched the description he'd managed to decipher.

30

France

'And Plan B is what, exactly?' Angela asked.

'Basically,' Bronson replied, 'it's not so much a plan, more like an anti-plan. Instead of doing what they might expect, we do the opposite, and stay unpredictable. I've no doubt that Stephen was forced to tell his killers that we planned to drive to England, and if we do that there's a good chance there'll be a man with a long rifle waiting for us somewhere near the Channel port or outside your apartment building.'

Angela stared at his profile for a few moments before she spoke.

'You're serious? You really think they won't give up until they've killed me?'

Her voice was calm and level, but there was no mistaking the fear that lay behind her simple questions.

'They massacred a whole camp of people and then had Stephen murdered,' Bronson said in reply. 'Italy's a long way from Iraq, but they had no trouble reaching out and killing him in Milan within just a few hours. So, yes, I'm serious. Mind you,' he added, 'we've been here before, facing the same kind of threat.'

'I know,' Angela said, 'but when it happened before, at least we had a good idea what the motive was. This time, it just doesn't make sense. How can the knowledge contained in an inscription carved over half a millennium earlier be so important – or so dangerous – that everybody who sees it ends up dead?'

'The only way to find out is for you to decipher it,' Bronson said simply. 'Do you think your photographs are good enough to let you transcribe the letters and work out what the plaintext says?'

Angela nodded.

'That wasn't why I took the pictures,' she said. 'At the time, the inscription was just a curiosity, and the photographs were intended to show the entire layout of the underground temple, but they're certainly clear enough to let me transcribe every character.'

'I think we should go to ground, lose ourselves completely for a while. Once you've worked out the meaning of the inscription, we can decide what to do next.'

'That won't get them off our backs, though.'

Bronson nodded. 'I know. The trouble is that at the moment we have no idea why they want us dead, so what we need more than anything else is information. And pretty much the only source is that inscription. Once we know what it says, we'll have a better idea why it's worth killing for and hopefully what we should do about it.'

'So we just drop off the radar?'

'Exactly. For the time being, I think that's our safest course of action. And the first thing we need to do is get rid of this car. If they traced Stephen to his hotel room, there's no doubt at all that they'll know about this vehicle.'

A few minutes later they reached the Auxerre-Sud junction of the Autoroute du Soleil, and Bronson steered the car down the off ramp. Auxerre wasn't a huge town, but it was big enough to have a number of vehicle hire agencies and, luckily, one of them was the same company that they had approached in Milan. He handed over the vehicle, explaining to the counter clerk that they had changed their plans and were now going to take a train to Paris and then fly to London from there. That, he hoped, would help muddy the waters if their anonymous pursuers managed to track them to that agency.

About a quarter of an hour later they sat down at an outside table at a pavement café, their bags tucked against the wall behind them, and ordered the menu of the day, plus a coffee for Bronson because he was going to be driving, and a large gin and tonic for Angela because she looked like she needed it.

'So we've got rid of the car,' Angela said, taking a long swallow. 'What next?'

'We max out our credit cards, draw as much cash as we can. With the resources these people seem to have,

I've no doubt they'll be able to pinpoint our location if we pay hotel bills with cards, so we need the cash if we're going to stay out of sight. Out of electronic sight, I mean. Then we find ourselves another car, hopefully from a small agency.'

'We'll have to use a card for that,' Angela pointed out, 'unless the rules have changed.'

'I know, but there's nothing we can do about it. But it will take them time to find out what we did after we handed back the first car, and even if they get the details of our new vehicle, France is a really big country and finding us won't be easy. We'll make sure of that. And then we disappear. Just take a look at the map and pick somewhere at random. Find a hotel and get started deciphering the inscription as soon as we can.'

'Okay. A hotel would be helpful because I'm going to need the Internet. My Latin isn't too bad, but I'll need some pointers about deciphering the text. I'm not an expert in cryptography.'

They left Auxerre in a small and anonymous three-year-old Citroën a little over two hours later, having raided the ATMs and drawn out a couple of thousand euros between them. Their natural inclination was to head towards Paris and the Channel ports, but that was probably what anybody trying to follow them would assume they'd do, so instead Bronson steered the dark blue C3 south-east, following a road that more or less paralleled the autoroute, and taking turnings as and when he felt like it.

'Do you know where we're going?' Angela asked.

Bronson shook his head.

'No, and that's the point. If I don't know where we're going, nor will anybody else. What I want to do is put about thirty miles between us and Auxerre, because that will create a huge search area for someone trying to find us.'

Around three-quarters of an hour later, he steered the Citroën into the car park of a hotel lying just off the Route de Paris on the outskirts of Avallon and not too far from the local airport. The parking was behind the building, which meant that the car would be out of sight of the road, and a large sign beside the main entrance extolled the virtues and facilities of the premises. These included the obvious essentials like en suite bathrooms and central heating, but also advertised coffee-making facilities in each room and, in quite large letters, free Wi-Fi.

The proprietors only spoke basic English, but Bronson's French was more than up to the task, and they chose a double room on the first floor overlooking the road.

'Are you sure about the double?' Bronson had asked, somewhat surprised at Angela's insistence. Their relationship was still somewhat fragile and sharing a room was unusual rather than normal.

'Just book it before I change my mind,' Angela had replied. 'It's going to attract a lot less attention. And after what we've been through in the last day or so, I don't think I want to be on my own.'

In the hotel room, Angela immediately opened up her

computer and navigated to the folder containing the photographs of the inscription.

Bronson sat beside her as she studied the pictures she'd taken.

'It really isn't what I expected,' Bronson said, staring at the image on the screen. It was many times larger than the small image he'd previously looked at on her camera, and he could see the inscription clearly for the first time. 'I'd envisaged a neat carving, maybe inside a shield or escutcheon, something like that. But that just looks so crude.'

The image showed a flat area of rock, brilliantly illuminated by the flash from the camera and on which every detail stood out clearly. There was a roughly carved border around the outside of the text, and the incised letters were carved in a simple and basic fashion with no attempt at ornamentation of any sort. It looked as if the carving had been done in a hurry by somebody whose only aim had been to ensure that the individual letters were perfectly readable.

'That's one of the things that struck us about it as well,' Angela said. 'We came to the conclusion, maybe wrongly, that the inscription was a copy of something else. Maybe a piece of text written on a parchment or something of that sort, and the inscription was just intended to be a permanent record.'

'In other words, it's not the inscription that's important, it's the message. It's the information, rather than the form in which that information is conveyed.'

Angela nodded. 'Exactly. Now, I think the easiest way

to tackle this is for you to take a pencil and paper and copy down the inscription as I read it out, letter by letter. Once we've done that, I can try to work out how the encryption was done.'

Bronson opened his own computer bag and took out what he needed, then sat at the other end of the small desk in the room and wrote down each letter as Angela read it out from the image on the screen. It wasn't a large piece of text, and it didn't take long for Angela to finish. There were a few instances where extra clarity was needed, and on these she looked at different pictures of the inscription until she was satisfied that she had correctly read every single letter.

'And I suppose that,' Bronson said, putting down the pencil he'd been using, 'was the easy bit.'

'Correct.'

An hour or so later, Angela had followed the same logical process as Khaled had done hours before and had in front of her a new version of the inscription, produced not by any form of Atbash but simply by frequency analysis.

She was staring at it, her head in her hands.

'I must be missing something,' she said. 'This looks almost right, but it just doesn't make sense.' She pointed at one section of the text. 'It still looks like gobbledegook, but less obscure, somehow.'

Bronson walked over to the side of the room and made a couple of cups of coffee, then returned to the desk and put one of the cups in front of her.

'It'll come to you,' he said confidently. 'I know you.

You'll keep going backwards and forwards over this until you finally crack it.'

Angela suddenly stiffened.

'Out of the mouths of babes and sucklings,' she murmured, grabbing another piece of paper.

31

Iraq

The biggest problem Khaled had encountered in his search for a possible location was the sheer number of places that could be described in a way that matched the crucial words in the deciphered inscription, that could be below a 'lost temple'. There were far more destroyed temples, buildings lost to the world through neglect, natural catastrophe and, inevitably, war, than there were places of worship still standing.

There were obvious filters that he could apply – it had to have been in existence at least as early as the thirteenth century, for example – but that still left dozens of possibilities. The other problem he faced was that although he knew that many Christian churches – and in his opinion these could be generically described as 'temples' – had crypts lying underneath the building, this fact was rarely a matter of public record. The number of places he found that were described as having such a structure was vanishingly small, and he was quite certain that subterranean chambers existed below many buildings that he had initially dismissed.

Khaled pushed back his chair, stood up and paced back and forth across the carpet in front of his desk. It was a habit he had acquired years earlier, as the worn track in the carpet mutely testified, but it did seem to help him think more clearly. And after only a couple of minutes, a thought popped into his mind, an idea that might focus his search significantly. But first, he needed to check his translation of the inscription again.

He sat down in front of the computer and pulled up the transcription he had prepared. He scanned down to the appropriate section, and then nodded. It was something of a jump, but it seemed to him to make sense. It all hinged on the interpretation of a single word, a word chosen by a man over five hundred years earlier.

He looked again at the decrypted Latin, and then navigated to an online Latin dictionary and entered the word *hypogeum* into the search field. He'd done it before, and the result was exactly what he had expected. It wasn't even an unusual word, and had been in use during the entire period when Latin had been the predominant European language – but just to make absolutely certain he brought up three other different Latin dictionaries, one after the other, and checked the results in those as well.

They all agreed. The translation was simple: the word meant a crypt or a vault, or some other kind of underground chamber, and that was what had prompted his re-examination of the text. The question really was whether or not the mediaeval author of the inscription had thought the same way that he was now doing.

Because there was another word, a word much more commonly used than *hypogeum*, and which indicated almost exactly the same kind of thing, but with one subtle difference. In Latin, the word *crupta* – the root of the English word 'crypt' – also meant an underground chamber, but one that was additionally used for rites, for religious services of one sort or another. If Khaled was right in his interpretation, the mediaeval author was specifically stating that the 'hall' was not used by the temple above it for any kind of religious function, and – making another leap of deduction that might well not be justified by the evidence – might not even be in any way a part of that temple. The writer could simply have been referring to two entirely separate buildings: a temple, or to be exact a place where a temple had once stood, and some kind of hall cut into the ground some distance underneath it.

And if that were the case, then there was one very obvious location that sprang into his mind.

There was also, he supposed, trying to rationalize and justify his deduction, a piece of what might be described as negative evidence as well. By simply using the word *templum*, meaning the temple, rather than one of the other fifty or so words in Latin that could be employed to refer to a place of worship, and by not specifying where that temple might be located, the author could have been alluding to the best-known such structure of his time. Khaled had spent some years in Britain and, to take a modern example, if most citizens there heard a reference to 'the abbey', he guessed that most of them would immediately assume that the speaker was referring to Westminster Abbey because that was the most famous such structure in the United Kingdom.

And although the mediaeval world was geographically diverse and well separated, culturally and religiously it was a very small place and he was reasonably confident that most people in Europe and the Middle East in those days would know exactly which temple the author of the inscription would have meant.

Khaled turned back to his browser, thought for a few seconds, then entered an entirely different search string and scanned the list of pages that had been generated. At the top of the third screen was a hit that he thought seemed promising, and this time the page of inform-ation that was shown after he'd clicked the link was precisely what he was hoping to see. He now knew – or at least he hoped he knew – what the author of the inscription must have been referring to.

He read it all twice, then picked up his mobile phone and called Farooq.

They needed to move quickly, but the good news was that they didn't have quite as far to go as he had expected.

32

France

'What?' Bronson asked.

'I think that could be it,' Angela said, quickly jotting down a series of letters. She turned back to her laptop, accessed a website and typed rapidly. Then she nodded in apparent satisfaction.

'What?' Bronson asked again.

Angela pointed to one of the words in the latest version of the inscription that they had produced.

'See this word here?' she asked, and Bronson nodded. 'Frequency analysis suggests that the word is "siruf", and that's not a word in Latin that I know. In fact, it's not a word that any of the online Latin dictionaries recognize. But if you reverse the letters it turns into "furis".'

'I'm none the wiser,' Bronson said.

'No, but you are better informed, my dear. "Furis" might not be a Latin word that you've ever encountered, but I know what it means. It's the Latin for "thief". And look at this' – she pointed at another sequence of letters – 'that is "sirotpecretni", which again is not a Latin word, and it doesn't even look like Latin. But write it backwards and you get "interceptoris". "Interceptor" is now an English word with an entirely different meaning. But originally it was a Latin word, and it meant a usurper. I think the person who prepared this inscription used Atbash with a code word or words added to the alphabet to make decryption more difficult and then as a final refinement he reversed the ciphertext in its entirety, writing every word backwards. In fact,' she added, 'I probably should have guessed that that was a possibility, just because we're talking about an inscription.'

'Why?'

'Because most people are right-handed, and if you're carving something on a piece of stone you'll naturally hold the chisel in your left hand and the hammer in your right. If you do that, your left hand obscures what you've just carved if you work from left to right, but not if you work from right to left. This is why we believe that some languages, like Hebrew, run from right to left because most of the early examples were inscriptions of various sorts. The language got established by being carved in that way, and nobody ever bothered changing it to run in the opposite direction.'

Their coffee grew cold as they reversed the inscription, transcribing it letter by letter, Angela reading out each one in reverse sequence while Bronson wrote out the text.

'There don't seem to be any breaks between these words,' he said. 'Or if there are, you're not telling me where one word ends and another one starts.'

'That's because as far as I can see there are no breaks in the inscription and I've seen nothing like an interpunct anywhere in the text, which is more or less what I expected.'

This time it was Bronson's turn to look puzzled.

'An interpunct was a small dot or occasionally a tiny triangle that was used in ancient and classical Latin script to separate words,' Angela explained. 'But it fell out of use round about AD 200, and after that Latin was written in what was known as *scripta continua* – basically, continuous script without any spaces – for about the next half a millennium. After that, the custom of inserting spaces between words was used.'

'But if you think this inscription is mediaeval, wouldn't you expect to find spaces?'

'If this were a regular inscription or piece of Latin text written on parchment, then I would absolutely agree with you. But this inscription looks to me as if it was a copy of a piece of earlier text and, more importantly, we know it was encrypted. If the scribe or mason who produced it had included spaces to separate the words, that would have made deciphering it easier, which would have defeated the object of the exercise.'

Deciphering the Latin was the first step. Once they'd completed that, or at least the first part of the text, because the section written below a faint but a distinct line that ran across the middle of the inscription defied all her efforts, Angela spent another fifteen minutes or so using an online Latin–English dictionary to translate the text. Then she sat back in her seat, read through what she'd written, and glanced at Bronson.

'And?'

'And what?'

'And what does it say, obviously?' Bronson asked.

'Oh. Well, not as much as I was hoping, frankly, and certainly not what I was expecting. And that lower part of the inscription still appears to be complete gobble-degook, so I guess that will need some other code words or something, maybe even a different decryption method, before we can read what it says. The section I have translated seems to be a condemnation of some unnamed man. It refers to him as "the thief" and "the usurper" – the two words, oddly enough, that I first recognized in the text when we realized how it had been encrypted – but his identity is never confirmed. It's almost as if the author would have expected anybody reading it to know precisely who he was talking about. A bit like Christianity today, I suppose, where a church could be referred to as the "house of the lord", and nobody would be in any doubt which particular lord was meant.'

'That would be a reference in a positive sense,' Bronson pointed out, 'but from what you've said this is definitely a negative reference, maybe something to do with the forces of evil, with the Devil, perhaps. After all, in most religions if you accept the existence of God, logically you must also accept the existence of God's counterpart, the Devil. Without the threat of going to Hell, how

194

could the priests persuade their flock to do what the Church wanted them to do? Could that be it?'

Angela shook her head.

'That's a good suggestion,' she replied, 'but it doesn't really work with this text. This doesn't read like a threat of eternal damnation or anything of that sort, it's more a sort of lament, really. It's as if it refers to a member of the Church – or of a particular religion, in this case – who has taken something and used it for his own purposes, though it doesn't say what was taken or how it was used. But there is a reference right here' – she pointed to a sentence towards the end of the translated inscription – 'to an object, or rather objects, of some sort that the writer refers to as the "hoard" or "cluster".

'The problem is that almost every Latin word has a number of different but related meanings, and although it's generally considered to be a precise language, there are obviously different ways of interpreting any piece of text, and especially one that's at least half a millennium old. There may well have been different meanings ascribed to particular words at the time when it was written, meanings that may never have been recognized by scholars and researchers. We know, for example, that this word – *acervus* – had multiple meanings. It usually referred to a large quantity of something, hence the translation as a "cluster" or a "hoard", but it could also mean a funeral pile or even a treasure of some sort.'

'That sounds more interesting,' Bronson said. 'The idea of treasure always raises my interest level. So the short version is that the text might be referring to a cluster of something, or even a hidden treasure, but you have no idea what, although it is whatever this usurper stole.'

Angela shook her head. 'Not exactly, no. The first part of the inscription refers to this thief or usurper, but unless I'm reading it wrongly the cluster or treasure is something different, something that justified the claims being made. A kind of positive proof that the unnamed man was a thief. Some object that would prove the case against him, if you see what I mean.'

'But it doesn't say what it was? Or who he was?'

'No. Though it does give a hint that this cluster of objects had been secreted somewhere. As I said, each word has more than one possible meaning and interpretation but the relevant section reads something like "within the chamber under the lost temple where the objects were deeply hidden there the key will endure for eternity". The phrase that's least subject to different interpretations is "deeply hidden", but the basic meaning seems clear enough. Something – something of considerable importance to the author of this text – was buried in some kind of underground chamber.'

'But what about this key that's being referred to? What do you think that is? A key for a chest or something like that?'

Again, Angela shook her head.

'I think it's simpler than that,' she said. 'An iron or bronze key intended to open a lock couldn't really be described as something that would endure for eternity, because eventually it would rust or corrode. I think this piece of text is telling us that we need to find this chamber and that when we do there'll be some kind of a carving or inscription that will act as a key to decipher the rest of the inscription, the bit that we haven't cracked so far. That could easily be described as a key that would last for ever.'

'So what you're saying is that this somewhat bizarre inscription that was hidden in a temple buried under the sands of Iraq is actually trying to send us off on some kind of a treasure hunt? I'm assuming, obviously, that these objects, this anonymous cluster of things, will have some kind of a value even today, that it is treasure of a sort.'

'You might be right,' Angela said, 'but equally these hidden objects could simply have been valuable documents of some sort, priceless half a millennium ago but essentially worthless now. On the other hand, I suppose it is just about possible that when – or rather if – we manage to follow this trail to the end we might find ourselves looking at something with very real value. The question, really, is whether or not the trail is worth following. Are we going to find ourselves in more danger if we do embark on this hunt than if we just walk away and try to hide?'

Bronson didn't respond for a couple seconds, then he nodded.

'Two things,' he said. 'First, I don't think any document or something of that sort would be sufficiently valuable for the clues to its location to be carved on to the wall of an underground temple. To me, that just doesn't make sense. I think whatever the inscription refers to has to be something of real tangible value.'

'And the second thing?'

'It's pretty obvious that those men are on the hunt as well, and after what happened in Iraq and Milan I have no doubt at all that they will never give up. For whatever reason, the knowledge contained in that inscription is so important to them that they've decided that anyone who finds out about it has to die, and what they know has to die with them. I think that even if we walk away from all this, we'll be in exactly the same danger as we would be if we carried on looking. In fact, it might even be more dangerous, because we'll be more static targets if we go back to Britain. My vote is that we carry on, keep following the trail and try to stay one step ahead.'

'Very inspiring,' Angela said with a slight smile. 'But the obvious problem is that right now I have no idea at all where we should start our search. Have you?'

'No,' Bronson admitted, and looked down again at the sheet of paper on which Angela had written the deciphered and translated text. 'This chamber,' he said after a few moments. 'You're sure it must be somewhere underground?'

Angela pointed at another part of the translated text.

'As certain as I can be, yes. The Latin word used is *hypogeum*, and the Latin adjective *hypogeus* specifically means "underground", so I think we're looking for some sort of room that lies underneath a temple.'

When she said those last few words, a distant memory

stirred somewhere in Bronson's brain, and he leaned across to the keyboard of Angela's laptop.

'What are you doing?' she asked.

'I just had an idea.'

He input a four-word search string into the browser and pressed the enter key as they both stared at the screen. He clicked on the top entry.

'There you are,' he said when the page had loaded. 'I think that's probably somewhere near the place that the line in the inscription is talking about, the *Minheret Hakotel*, if that's how you pronounce the Hebrew: the Western Wall Tunnel in Jerusalem that leads to the Hall of the Hasmoneans. That's probably the most obvious location that could be referred to as the hall under the lost temple. It's arguably the most famous temple that doesn't actually exist any more anywhere in the world, and has been since about the start of the second millennium. If we're going to keep following this trail, our next stop has to be Israel. And there's something else,' he added, scrolling down to look at the rest of the information.

'What?' Angela asked.

'The other thing that might be relevant is that the most famous – or notorious – residents of that vanished temple weren't the Jews who built it or the Muslims who've occupied the site for the last fifteen hundred years, but the Knights Templar. They took their name from the alleged location of the Temple of Solomon on the Temple Mount, and according to legend they spent the first few years they were in Jerusalem excavating the chambers and passageways that lay within the Mount. And of course the Templars were more or less contemporary with the inscription, if your dating of it is anything like accurate. So maybe what we're looking for has got less to do with the Marsh Arabs of Iraq than with the best-known of all the Western Christian mediaeval military orders.

'And that,' he added, 'brings an entirely new possibility into the mix.'

33

Jerusalem

Pretty much the first thing that Farooq did after he and his companions had landed and made their way into the city from the airport was assemble his men in a café a couple of blocks outside the Old City, and make a telephone call to a local number. It was answered almost immediately, and the conversation that followed was short and largely monosyllabic, at least at Farooq's end. Less than a minute later, he ended the call and gestured to two of the men to accompany him.

'We should be about half an hour, maybe a little longer,' he told the four others still sitting in the café. 'The meeting place is on the outskirts of the city. Wait here until we get back.'

Then Farooq turned away and raised his arm to hail a cab that had just turned into the street.

In fact, it was just over an hour before the three men returned to the café. Farooq glanced around, but as far as he could tell they were unobserved. People were passing in the street, talking together, looking at maps, wielding cameras and all the other tourist-oriented activities that are an enduring and inevitable part of daily life in a city like Jerusalem. More to the point, nobody appeared to be paying them the slightest attention.

He nodded to his two companions, each of whom took two obviously heavy packets from their pockets and passed them over, one to each of the other four men.

'Don't open them now,' Farooq instructed. 'Wait until you're alone. They're a mix of different makes, a couple of Brownings, a Sig and a Walther, but all nine milli-metre and each with twenty rounds of ammunition.'

'Only twenty rounds?' one of the men asked.

'That's nearly one hundred and fifty between the seven of us,' Farooq replied. 'And you all know that we're not here to get involved in a firefight. The weapons are for your personal protection and for use against the infidels if the need arises, though in this environment a quieter assassination method would obviously be more appropriate. That is why you also each have a knife and a garrotte.'

He looked around the group.

'When you open the packets, you'll see that the magazines aren't loaded and the shells are loose, so you may wish to do something about that sooner rather than later. The three of us have already prepared and loaded our weapons.'

'What use is a pistol wrapped up in a bit of paper with an empty magazine?' another of the men said. 'I'm going to the restroom to load mine right now.'

Without waiting for a response, he pushed back his chair and strode into the café, heading towards the lavatories at the back of the building.

Over the next twenty minutes the other three men followed their colleague's example, visiting the stall in the male lavatory, to unwrap, check and then load the pistols Farooq had purchased. Finally they reassembled at the café table.

'So what do we do now?' one of the men asked.

'We do nothing,' Farooq said. 'Khaled has not told me yet when he will be arriving, but it will probably be sometime today, or tomorrow at the latest. Once he gets here we can do whatever it is that he wants and then return to Iraq. Or that's what I hope, anyway.'

'You still haven't told us why we're here.'

'I haven't told you because I don't know,' Farooq replied. 'But he's paying us, and paying well, so we'll just have to wait and see what he intends to do.'

'How long do we wait, then?'

Farooq shrugged. 'As long as it takes.'

34

France

'No matter what you may have heard or read about the Knights Templar,' Bronson began, 'and there's a hell of a lot of stuff out there that is complete fantasy, there is one indisputable fact about the end of the order, when the Templars were purged. At the time the order was arguably the richest single entity in the whole of Europe, possessing and controlling more wealth than many nations. Most history books will tell you that the operation to seize the assets of the order was kept entirely secret, and was a total surprise to the Templars. But in fact it seems much more likely that they knew about it well in advance and hid the treasure somewhere.

'Nobody's ever been able to prove it, but if you look at the circumstantial evidence there doesn't seem to be much doubt about what happened. In 1307, the order was a vast multinational corporation. I can't remember the numbers involved because it was some time ago that

I read about it, but in all there were tens of thousands of Templars, knights, sergeants and all the other people involved, but only a few hundred were actually arrested throughout the whole of France when the French troops arrived to carry out the king's orders. Either his troops were incredibly stupid and incapable of finding all of the Templars, which seems extremely unlikely, or they simply weren't there to be arrested.

'And it is a documented fact that Philip the Fair – Philip IV of France – was virtually bankrupt before he ordered the arrest of the Templars, and he was still virtually bankrupt after the order had been purged. The cupboard was bare. And it's been established that he knew the kind of assets the order possessed because a few months before he came up with his devious master plan, he'd had to take refuge in the Paris preceptory of the Templars to avoid an angry mob. So the assets that formed the backbone of the Templar order had almost certainly somehow been spirited away.'

'You seem to know a lot about it,' Angela said.

'I've always been interested in the subject,' Bronson said. 'I'm a detective, I'm supposed to solve crimes, and what happened to the Knights Templar was undeniably a criminal act. Philip claimed that he suspected the order of indulging in heretical practices, but that simply doesn't hold water. In those days, in the mediaeval period, heaven and hell were real and virtually tangible, and the word of God – or more accurately the word of the incumbent sitting on the throne of St Peter in the Vatican – was the ultimate truth on almost any subject.

Heresy, meaning anything the Church of Rome dis-agreed with, was a mortal sin, and anyone who engaged in heretical practices was likely to end up being excommunicated, which – according to the belief system of the time – meant that they would be denied a place in heaven for all eternity.

'In extreme cases, once the various inquisitions got involved, being excommunicated meant they got off lightly, because all the inquisitions basically functioned in exactly the same way. They started from the assumption that the individual being investigated was guilty and all his or her protestations of innocence were simply attempts to mislead and hoodwink the church. There was no possibility, in their eyes, of any innocent person being accused, so really all they were doing was establishing the degree of guilt. And in order to obtain the confession that they needed – the confession that would save the soul of the heretic – they indulged in the most horrendous and inventive tortures that the mind of man could devise. They were forbidden to spill blood, so they dislocated joints using things like the *strappado*, broke bones, burned off the feet by roasting them in a fire, pulled teeth and probed the sockets with red-hot spikes and, ultimately, tied people to stakes and set fire to the wood that surrounded them, burning them alive. All this, of course, in the name of a gentle and merciful God, who was extremely conspicuous by his absence from the torture chambers of the Inquisition.'

'You feel really strongly about this, don't you?'

Bronson shook his head and smiled somewhat ruefully at her.

'Sorry,' he said. 'I'll climb off my high horse right now. I suppose it all comes down to my personal dislike and distrust of religion. Of all religions, in fact.'

'Enough of that,' Angela said, squeezing his arm. 'I think you rather lost the thread of where you were going. You were telling me why you believed that the purging of the Templars was a crime.'

'Oh yes. That's right. All I was going to say was that if Philip the Fair genuinely believed that the Templars were guilty of heresy and engaged in heretical practices, then for the sake of the souls of the Templars themselves he should have acted immediately, and sent in the inquisitors. No, he was a deceitful and duplicitous, not to mention treacherous, man. He'd actually allowed Jacques de Molay, the Grand Master of the Order, to act as a pallbearer at the funeral of one of Philip's own relatives just a week or so before the arrests took place. In those days such a job was an honour and would only be performed by a member of the immediate family of the deceased or somebody who was an important and valued family friend. If Philip had genuinely believed that the Templars were guilty of heresy, there is no way that he would have allowed the leader of the order, by implication the biggest heretic of the lot, to take part in such a ceremony.'

'And by that time Philip must already have made his plans to swoop on the Templars?'

'Weeks earlier at least,' Bronson agreed. 'Getting his

sealed orders to his various military commanders and assembling troops in the right positions throughout France would have been a long process in those days. Messages could be sent as fast as a man on a horse could gallop, but the soldiers would have had to march to their destination, and that would have been the slowest part of the entire process. No, the whole thing – the arrests, the trials and everything else – was a set-up, an operation set in action simply to allow Philip the Fair to get his hands on the assets of the order. Only, as I said before, he didn't, because they'd disappeared.'

Angela was silent for a few moments, then she glanced at the computer screen, at the pages scattered across the desk, and finally at Bronson.

'Are you saying what I think you're saying?' she asked. 'Do you really think that the inscription we found has got something to do with the lost treasure of the Knights Templar?'

Bronson shrugged and spread his hands wide.

'I genuinely have no idea,' he said. 'If it has, I think it's the first tangible clue ever found that might give some indication of what happened to the Templar assets, which would explain the lengths these terrorists have gone to in order to cover it up. What I do find interesting is that the text you've deciphered seems to point us towards the Temple Mount in Jerusalem, which is where the history of the order really began, and it is definitely telling us about a hoard, a collection of objects or possibly even a treasure, depending on how you translate the Latin word, that's been hidden. That just seems to be too intriguing a possibility to ignore.'

Angela nodded briskly.

'You're right,' she said. 'I agree with you. The Temple Mount could well be the location referred to in the inscription, though adding the Templars into the mix is a bit unexpected. I also think the idea that we could be on the trail of the Templar treasure is something of a stretch, but I'll keep an open mind on that. So, yes, we are going to keep following this trail, and the sooner we can get ourselves out to Jerusalem the better.'

35

Jerusalem

The two biggest problems Bronson had encountered in booking a flight were that the majority seemed to arrive in Israel in the very early hours of the morning, and most also involved an intermediate stop at Brussels, Amsterdam or Rome. He was keenly aware from what they knew had happened to Stephen that it would be fairly easy for someone to track down their whereabouts once there was a record of them booking a flight.

It cost more – a lot more, in fact, almost double – but eventually he'd found a direct Air France Airbus out of Charles de Gaulle to Tel Aviv, and they'd bought the tickets when they'd arrived at the airport the following morning, at the very last minute.

As they had expected, security on arrival at Ben Gurion Airport was both obvious and comprehensive, and it took some time to get through the system and into the arrivals hall.

'Shall we hire a car?' Angela asked.

'That's probably not a good idea,' Bronson replied, scanning the crowded building as he spoke. 'We've already left an electronic trail by using a credit card to pay for the flight, and if they are as organized as they seem to be, they'll already know that we're here in Israel. It'll take longer, but I'm sure we'll be a whole lot safer if we just become two more anonymous passengers on a bus. And according to my map it's not that far to Jerusalem.'

They headed to the bridge on the second floor of the airport and crossed over it to the bus stop for the short ride to the Egged bus station at Airport City. There, they disembarked and took the next available number 947 to the Central Bus Station in Jerusalem, a journey that was completed in just under an hour and a quarter.

'Shall we look for a hotel first?' Angela said as they stepped into the bright sunshine of late afternoon.

'Definitely. We'll take a taxi to somewhere near the Temple Mount and see what we can find. On the map it looks like about two miles from here to the Old City, which would take us a while to walk. Not to mention that we'd probably get lost if we tried.'

Modern Jerusalem surrounds and entirely encloses the Old City, but planning laws have mandated against high-rise buildings and most development has been restricted to the higher ground, leaving the valleys as open spaces, so it provides a sensation of space and openness. And it was a British regulation, imposed when

Great Britain governed the area, that specified local limestone – Jerusalem Stone – was to be used for all the façades. Pinkish-white in colour, the shade changes throughout the day as the light alters, meaning that the colours and appearance of the buildings, of the whole city, in fact, changes as well.

A quarter of an hour later, Bronson paid off the cab driver at the Jaffa Gate, the gate to the west of the Old City near the Tower of David and one of the busiest entrances penetrating the sixteenth-century wall – built on the orders of the Ottoman ruler Süleyman I – that surrounded the ancient heart of Jerusalem. In his hand were three business cards for local hotels, given to him by the taxi driver.

The Old City lay before them, within the mediaeval wall. It was not particularly big – very roughly square shaped, with the Temple Mount occupying about half of the eastern side, directly opposite the Jaffa Gate, and a little over half a mile from north to south and roughly the same from east to west. Within the boundary wall the Old City was divided into four quadrants representing the dominant religions that had occupied Jerusalem over the centuries. Running clockwise from the north, there was the Muslim district – which included the Temple Mount – then the Jewish, Armenian and Christian districts.

All three of the hotels the driver had suggested were in the Christian and Muslim quarters and were, the man had assured them, both very high quality and very reasonably priced. They passed along a section of the main axis of the ancient city, skirting the permanent Arab market or *suq*. One of the most dominant features of Jerusalem life, it was crowded with shoppers talking and haggling over the prices asked for goods.

They walked east along David Street, heading directly towards the Western Wall, but then turned north up Shuk ha-Basamim Street and continued past the Alexander Nevski Church. One of the hotels recommended by the taxi driver was only about a hundred yards in front of them.

Jerusalem has been a melting pot of cultures and religions for centuries, and the streets teemed with people. Orthodox Jews, black hats perched seemingly precariously on the tops of their heads and black curls dangling down both sides of their faces, bustled around, some alone, others in small groups talking earnestly together. None of them ever seemed to smile. Arabs moved steadily through the crowds, their pace relaxed and sedate. Tourists from almost every nation on the planet stood and walked and talked and took photographs of the almost indescribably ancient buildings.

And as a constant reminder of the state of religious and political flux that characterized Jerusalem, and of the troubles that sporadically flared up between the nations, armed Jewish soldiers stood on corners, their eyes flicking from one face to another, looking for the first sign of trouble, their hands resting on the pistol grips of their Galil assault rifles.

But perhaps even more than the diversity of the people, it was the buildings that entranced them. The sense of age, of centuries, millennia even, was almost palpable. It was as if the countless years of occupation by disparate civilizations had weighed down the buildings and the streets, investing the very structure of the city with an unmistakable sense of timeless occupation. Above all, Bronson detected a sense of sadness, as though the fabric of Jerusalem, the very stones themselves, had somehow absorbed some of the emotions experienced by the inhabitants when the peace of the city had been brutally shattered by one or another of the invading armies that had breached the defences over the millennia and, all too often, massacred everyone they found inside the walls.

'This is quite a place,' he said, painfully aware of the complete inadequacy of his words to convey more than a fraction of what he was feeling.

'Yes,' Angela replied thoughtfully, and Bronson could see that she was feeling exactly the same way.

The hotel stood on the corner at the crossroads they were approaching and, as far as Bronson could see, it didn't look too bad.

'This should do us,' he said as he led the way to the main entrance.

Twenty minutes later, they were standing side by side in their compact double room on the first floor of the building, and looking out of the window across the rooftops of the Old City towards the Temple Mount.

'It looks bigger than I remember it,' Angela said. 'The Mount, I mean.'

'Last time we were here, if I remember correctly, we

were a bit too busy to do any sightseeing, and I doubt we'll get much opportunity now either. The chances are that our pursuers are here already, either because they've tracked us or because they've also managed to decipher the first part of that inscription. They can't know about this hotel, of course, but they'll know that the only reason we would have for flying to Israel is because we think the clue referred to in the inscription is here, some-where under the Temple Mount. So we'll need to keep our eyes open and stay alert. They'll have photographs of us by now, or at least of you, culled from some pro-fessional journal, so they're already one step ahead of us.'

Angela looked worried at his last remark.

'In a country like this,' she said, 'my fair skin and blonde hair are going to really stand out. When we leave the hotel I'll put my hair up and wear a hat or scarf or something. I guess I'll need to do that anyway, especially if we're going to any of the religious sites, like the Kotel tunnels behind the Western Wall.'

'That should be our first stop,' Bronson agreed. 'And with a bit of luck it might be our last stop as well, assuming that whatever we're looking for is still there.'

'But what are we looking for?'

'Now that is a bloody good question. And our biggest problem. Logically I'd assume it must be a carving or another inscription or something of that sort – some-thing that will provide the code word that we need to complete the decryption. What I'm hoping is that it will be recognizable, that it will have some characteristic or feature that will link it to the inscription you found in Iraq. But, frankly, I think we'll just have to look at everything and photograph as much as we can and hope that we'll somehow spot what we're looking for.'

'I feel like the odds are against us. And one more thing: I thought that the Kotel tunnels only ran along the very edge of the Temple Mount, and that most of the chambers were deep under the Mount and completely inaccessible from all entrances. If we take the translation literally, we should be looking for a cavity under either the Dome of the Rock or the Al Aqsa Mosque, depending upon what we believe is meant by the word "temple", and one thing I do know is that there is no possibility at all of getting into those subterranean rooms.'

'You may well be right,' Bronson said. 'It's entirely possible that the key, whatever it turns out to be, will be hidden way beyond our reach, and if that's the case we'll have to rethink. But it's worth trying, and maybe we'll get lucky. If there's nothing in the tunnel system that we can access, the only other possibility, I suppose, is that we try a little bit of discreet unauthorized surveying, and see if we can find anything that way.'

Angela looked at him for a few seconds before she replied.

'I hope you're not suggesting what I have a horrible feeling that you *are* suggesting,' she said.

36

Jerusalem

Farooq sat opposite Khaled in the hotel room the Iraqi had booked, and for a few seconds just stared at him. Then he shook his head slowly, trying to choose his words carefully.

'I understand what you want us to do,' he said, 'but I'm not sure that we're the right people for this kind of work. My men are freedom fighters, fighters for Islam. That's what we know, and what we've trained for. When you first requested our services, you told me that we would be facing infidels, legitimate targets that we could engage in the name of the prophet, peace be upon him. And what you asked us to do we did, to the best of our ability. But this is not our fight.'

Farooq paused for a moment, his dark brown eyes fixed on the face of the older man.

'I have no complaints about your work,' Khaled said, 'but I would like to remind you that you and your men

217

have been extremely well paid for what you have done so far. You may be fighters for Islam, but you're also mercenary soldiers.'

'I don't dispute that, but the point is that this has nothing to do with money. We came to Jerusalem on the understanding that you needed us to perform the same kind of services, to locate and kill more of that group of infidels who had opposed us in Iraq. We have obtained weapons as you instructed, but what you are now asking us to do is completely different.'

Khaled nodded. 'I would agree with you if this were just a simple matter of exploring a cave or cellar, but what I want doing is far more dangerous than that. It is possible that we might encounter the couple who escaped us in Iraq, in which case we can cut off that particular loose end, but we will also probably have to contend with armed Israeli police and soldiers. This will not be a simple matter of exploration, and I really do need the protection and help that only you and your men can offer. And, let me remind you, I am offering you a substantial fee for your services.'

Khaled paused for a moment, sensing that he would have to do far more to convince the younger man to provide the assistance that he needed. It would mean taking him even further into his confidence – something he was reluctant to do for several reasons. But he saw no real alternative.

Marshalling what he hoped would be the final and most decisive argument, he leaned forward in his seat and unconsciously lowered his voice, despite the fact that they were quite alone in the room.

In the other armchair on the opposite side of the small glass-topped coffee table, Farooq mirrored his actions.

'I have never explained to you what this quest is for,' Khaled began, 'or not in any detail, anyway.'

Farooq nodded. 'I have had all the information necessary to complete the tasks you set us.'

'Exactly,' Khaled replied. 'But for you to fully appreciate the importance of what I'm trying to do, I would like to explain precisely why I was so excited when I learned about the inscription in the underground chamber, and why I was so determined that none of the archaeologists would be permitted to live after they had seen it.'

'I assumed you had a good reason for issuing that order.'

Khaled didn't reply directly, but simply nodded and then slightly changed the subject.

'About twenty years ago,' he began, 'a piece of ancient parchment came into my possession. That in itself was by no means unusual. In my profession I am frequently required to examine and authenticate such documents. In this case, the provenance of the relic was indisputable. It had been held in a storeroom at the museum for the better part of half a century, and had been rediscovered, so to speak, when that room was being cleared prior to redecoration. The parchment was included within a bundle of other written materials, and the whole lot had been passed to me for assessment, in case any of the documents had historical importance or significant value. I scanned every piece of parchment I'd been given, but none, apart from that one obviously, was of any particular interest.'

'What was so important about the parchment?'

'I still don't know its precise origin, but the material was covered in carefully written Arabic script, and my best estimation was that it had originated in the middle of the fourteenth century, or perhaps a little later.'

Farooq made a waving gesture with his hand, encouraging Khaled to get to the point of the matter.

'The text on the parchment referred to a particular relic that has been lost to history for over two millennia. In fact, most people doubt that it survived beyond the middle of the first century. But what that document said was quite unequivocal. It not only stated that the relic had survived – at least until the time that the document had been written – but it also claimed that information relating to the relic's present location was included on an encrypted inscription on the wall of a Mandaean temple – an underground temple – somewhere in southern Iraq. It even gave directions to that temple, but time and the shifting sands of the Iraqi desert meant that none of the locations it referred to were still identifiable. That was why I was so excited when I learned what the archaeological team had stumbled across.'

'And what relic did the text refer to?' Farooq asked. 'Presumably it was something of considerable value.'

To his surprise, Khaled shook his head decisively.

'No. In fact, the object neither had nor has any

commercial value whatsoever, though you could argue that its symbolic value was priceless. Or, just to be completely accurate and clear about this, it had a huge symbolic value in the mediaeval period, but today I suspect that it would simply be regarded as a curio, nothing more.'

Khaled looked at the puzzled expression on the face of the younger man.

'I'm sorry, Farooq, but you're the first person I've ever talked to about this. I fully appreciate that none of it really makes much sense at the moment. Why would I order the deaths of fifteen or twenty archaeologists when all they've discovered is information about the location of an ancient relic that has no monetary value?

'In fact, it's not the relic itself that is important. It's the belief system that surrounded the relic and which drove the actions of a particular group of men. These people venerated that object above all others, and that is why it's so important. Because when the organization to which these men belonged ceased to exist, not only was the relic hidden in a place of safety, but the considerable assets that they possessed – assets that today would be worth a literal fortune – were almost certainly hidden in precisely the same location. You see the implication, of course. So there is money involved – riches beyond anything you could possibly imagine.'

Farooq nodded.

'That is why I began this quest. That is why the archaeologists had to die. I couldn't risk any of them making the same connection that I did and finding the relic before me. And if I succeed in this quest – with your help – I'm fully prepared to share whatever we find with you. I know your group is often short of funds. Well, trust me, Farooq, because if we find this relic and what I believe to be hidden with it, then you will have more money at your disposal than you could ever possibly spend. You could start a *jihad* against the infidel West that would last for a hundred years, that would drive them from our homeland and into the sea, never to return.'

Khaled paused for a moment, wondering if he had overstated the case, if the hard sell had perhaps been too hard for Farooq to believe. But the gleam in the young man's eyes gave the lie to his fears.

'We will do this,' Farooq said, his voice soft but determined. 'We will do what you want in return for a share of whatever you find. What division do you suggest?'

'Half for you and your group, and half for me,' Khaled replied. 'I have the information needed to follow the trail, but I need you and your men to ensure that we aren't stopped or beaten to it. We're complementary to each other.'

Farooq nodded.

'Agreed,' he said. 'That is generous.'

'I need you with me, fully committed. If you felt I was being greedy, then perhaps I wouldn't be able to count upon your wholehearted support.'

'Now,' Farooq said, 'are you prepared to tell me what this mysterious relic is that we're searching for?'

Khaled shook his head.

'No,' he replied. 'Instead, I'll let you tell me. You're an educated man, and I think you should be able to work it out. Let me list the clues for you. We have a relic that was venerated and arguably priceless until the Middle Ages, but which today because of changes in belief systems around the world would only be considered a curio. It was not only of crucial importance to that one group of men that I alluded to, but also to the Mandaeans of southern Iraq. The men who had custody of the relic fell from grace but left behind them an enduring mystery in the form of the almost complete disappearance of all the assets they were known to possess. Now,' Khaled added with a smile, 'with all that information to hand, what relic do you think we're looking for?'

Farooq sat in thought for perhaps half a minute, then a broad smile crossed his face and he nodded. Then he spoke just six words.

At his response Khaled also nodded, stood up and extended his hand.

'That,' he replied, 'is precisely what we are seeking.'

37

'You can't just kick down a door and wander about under the Temple Mount,' Angela said.

Bronson's face was a picture of injured innocence.

'I don't recall suggesting we should deliberately try to break into the closed spaces down there,' he replied. 'On the other hand,' he went on, with a slight smile, 'if we did decide to take a quick look in the areas that are off-limits to tourists, I don't think we'd find it too difficult.'

'You do know that the Israeli police and soldiers are armed, don't you? And that they very probably have orders to shoot first and find out what the hell's going on sometime later?'

'I do know that,' Bronson agreed, 'but the point about doing a kind of unauthorized expedition is that the only danger will be accessing the tunnel system. Once we've got the door open and we're inside, we'll be completely invisible.'

Angela shook her head.

'You're mad,' she said. 'Quite, quite mad.'

'Very possibly,' Bronson said agreeably, 'but sometimes a touch of insanity – or at least the willingness to take a chance – is exactly what's needed.'

'In my opinion, breaking into the chambers underneath the Temple Mount would amount to quite a bit more than taking a chance,' Angela replied. 'On the other hand, I don't have any problem whatsoever in taking one of the Kotel tunnel tours so we can at least see what we're up against.'

Bronson nodded. He knew Angela as well as any man knows the woman with whom he has spent the better part of his life, and he had been quite certain that, once she had decided they were on the trail of something of major historic importance, she wouldn't be prepared to let a minor inconvenience like a locked and barred gate, or even wandering platoons of armed soldiers, deflect her from her course. They had spent time in Jerusalem before, on an equally perilous quest, and had come through that unscathed, and Bronson was confident that they could do the same this time. Or at least, they would have a damned good try.

'That also sounds like a plan,' he said enthusiastically. 'Let's go right now. We don't really have any time to lose.'

'But we can't just turn up,' Angela reminded him. 'We'll have to pre-book a tunnel tour.'

At the back of the desk in the hotel room was a small wooden box containing a number of printed leaflets advertising various attractions, including Hezekiah's Tunnel, the Church of the Holy Sepulchre and the Western Wall Tunnels. She picked up one of the tunnel tour leaflets and dialled the number.

'Good,' she said, replacing the phone in the cradle. 'There's an English-language tour in just over an hour, and there's enough space on it for the two of us to join in. Let's go.'

It wasn't that far from the hotel to the Kotel Plaza, and they made it with over half an hour to spare.

'The Wailing Wall,' Angela said, as they stopped as if by common accord and stared in awe across the open space to the vertical wall that dominated the area.

They looked at the mass of people gathered at the foot of the wall, some obviously praying, their heads moving back and forth somewhat in the manner of chickens feeding, while others busily forced scraps of what looked like cloth or paper into the spaces between the massive old stones.

'Remind me why it's called that?' Bronson asked.

'The root cause of the name goes back nearly two millennia,' Angela explained. 'In AD 70 the Romans destroyed what was known as the Second Temple and virtually the entire Jewish population was forced to leave the city.'

'Hang on. I know quite a lot about the mediaeval history of this area, but not too much about the earlier stuff. Why was it called the Second Temple?'

Angela shook her head. 'It was a lot more than a name,' she replied, and glanced at her watch. She pointed

226

at a nearby café with three or four vacant tables outside. 'We've got a few minutes before the tour starts. Buy me a coffee to sustain me, and I'll give you the potted history.'

They sat down at one of the tables. Bronson ordered two coffees and then looked expectantly at Angela.

'Right,' she said, 'according to the history of early Judaism, the Ark of the Covenant was moved from one sanctuary to another over the years, until King David captured Jerusalem, and moved the Ark permanently to the city. The idea was to fuse three separate things – the Judaic monarchy, the Ark and the holy city itself – into a single entity that the various tribes of Israel could regard as the centre, something that would be a unifying force. King David chose what was then known as Mount Moriah, now the Temple Mount – the place where legend stated that Abraham had erected the altar on which he intended to sacrifice his son Isaac – as the location for the temple that would house it. David never lived to see the temple finished, but it was completed during the reign of his son Solomon, and finished – if my memory serves me correctly – in 957 BC.'

'So that was the First Temple,' Bronson said.

'Exactly. It acted as a sanctuary, the final resting place for the Ark of the Covenant, and as a place of worship for the entire people. Oddly enough, the building wasn't that big, but it had a huge courtyard in which thousands of people could stand. The temple contained five altars and three rooms, and the most important of those was the Holy of Holies where the Ark was kept, a room that only the high priest could enter and only on Yom Kippur, the Day of Atonement.

'The First Temple stood for a little under half a millennium, but in about 600 BC the Babylonian king Nebuchadnezzar sacked the place and removed all of the temple treasures, very possibly including the Ark of the Covenant, though of course the ultimate fate of that relic has never been established. According to the Bible, it was supposed to be made of acacia wood that was then covered in gold leaf, so there's a possibility that it may simply have rotted away over the centuries. There have been all sorts of claims about where it ended up, but the truth is that nobody knows for sure. Anyway, Nebuchadnezzar came back about fifteen years later and completely destroyed the building. He also captured much of the Jewish population and hauled them off to Babylonia as slaves. Less than a hundred years later, the Persians defeated the Babylonians and the descendants of those Jews were allowed to return to Jerusalem, where they rebuilt the temple. This was the Second Temple, erected on the spot where the First Temple had stood, but a significantly smaller structure than the original.'

She paused for a moment as the unsmiling waiter delivered two small cups of coffee and a surprisingly large bill.

'Interestingly,' she went on, taking a cautious sip, 'the Second Temple also lasted for about half a millennium. It had been desecrated but it was still standing when Herod the Great, the King of Judaea, came to power in 37 BC, and he ordered the temple to be rebuilt, a process that began in 20 BC and took almost half a century.'

'So Herod wasn't entirely bad news,' Bronson suggested.

'Nobody is entirely bad news,' Angela commented drily. 'It was claimed that even Mussolini made the trains run on time, though of course he didn't. But you're right: Herod wasn't all bad. It was a major rebuilding programme. They started off by doubling the size of the Temple Mount, then raised and enlarged the Temple, facing it with stone, and built a number of additional chambers and facilities, and the new building again became the centre of Jewish religious life in the city. What happened next, really, was the fault of the Jews, because in AD 66 they rebelled against Roman rule, which was at least understandable as it was a rebellion against an occupying power. The Jewish Revolt was put down by the Romans with massive bloodshed and ended in AD 73 when the fortress of Masada finally fell, the defenders committing mass suicide rather than submit to Roman rule. As a part of the campaign, in AD 70, the Romans completely destroyed the temple, which is where I started the story.

'And then the Romans deported most of the surviving Jews. They were forbidden to return to Jerusalem until the early Byzantine period, about three hundred years later, and even then they were only allowed to visit the city on the anniversary of the destruction of the temple. The only bit of the building that was left – and in fact it wasn't actually a part of the temple at all, merely one of the supporting walls – is what we're looking at now, the

Western Wall. The Jews who visited realized that the temple had gone for ever, and so they began praying at the closest point to the original structure, and they howled and lamented their loss, hence the Wailing Wall.'

'And those bits of paper that some of them are forcing between the stones are prayers?'

'Yes,' Angela said. 'In fact, all this is really to do with *Shechinah*. That more or less translates from the Hebrew as the "divine presence", but actually it's rather more complicated than that. The word *Shechinah* is not so much God but more the place where God would be expected to reside. And in Orthodox Judaism, that location would have been the Holy of Holies in the innermost chamber of the First Temple, where the Ark of the Covenant would have been kept. Even after the First Temple was destroyed, the assumption was that the divine presence would have remained in the same place within the Second Temple, and when that was reduced to rubble the spirit would have stayed in the same location, and the closest point to that spot on the top of the Temple Mount that is still accessible to the Jews is the Wailing Wall. So that's the place where they leave their prayers.'

'I thought there was some theory that the Ark had ended up in Ethiopia, assuming it ever existed and had managed to last the centuries,' Bronson said.

'Yes, it has been suggested, though I don't believe it,' Angela replied. 'According to legend, a place called Aksum in Ethiopia was where the Queen of Sheba lived, and she was believed to have married Solomon, the man who built the First Temple. They had a son, Menelik, who became the first Emperor of Ethiopia, and he's supposed to have travelled to Jerusalem and, presumably with Solomon's permission, removed the Ark and carried it back to his own country. There's a small chapel there, lived in by a single priest, whose only job is to guard the Ark, which is never displayed or seen by anyone else. That's the first problem, because he could be guarding something completely different, or even looking at an empty room.

'But, there's another very obvious problem with this story. The Ark of the Covenant was the single most important treasure that the Jewish people possessed, and I can think of no cogent reason why Solomon would have given it away. During his reign there was no threat to Jerusalem or to the Temple, so there would have been no reason to take it elsewhere for safe keeping. But even if it had been, once the perceived danger had passed presumably it would have been returned, and that's not what the legend says happened. If Solomon had given away the Ark, and the people had found out about it, he would probably have been lynched, because it really was that important to them. The whole point about Solomon's Temple was that it was intended to be the final resting place for the relic, the sanctuary where it would remain for ever, so for me this theory really doesn't hold water.'

Angela took a last sip of coffee then glanced across the Kotel Plaza to where a group of people had begun to assemble near the Western Wall Heritage, the entrance to the tunnel system.

'That must be our tour,' she said, gesturing towards them. 'We should probably get over there.'

Bronson left some money on the table and they strode across the plaza to wait for the tour to begin.

The walk through the tunnel system took a little over one and a quarter hours, but neither Bronson nor Angela were concentrating entirely upon what the guide was telling them. Instead, they kept to the back of the group, looking about them in all directions and taking pictures of anything and everything they saw – any kind of carving or inscription that could possibly be construed as a key.

Not that anything they photographed looked particularly hopeful. There were occasional marks on the stones, some of them possibly left by the masons who had fabricated them, others clearly carved graffiti of one sort or another, most probably dating from countless centuries earlier, and other occasional marks for which they had no obvious explanation.

But at the end of it, neither of them seriously believed that they'd seen anything that could possibly be what they were looking for, and both were feeling somewhat despondent when they emerged from the tunnel system.

'We'll need to look at these images on the computer just to make sure,' Angela said, 'but I didn't see anything that appeared to be even slightly hopeful. Did you?'

'Nothing,' Bronson replied flatly. 'I still think it was

worth taking the tour, but I'm afraid you're probably right. This key that the inscription talked about is most likely to be in one of the chambers right under the Temple Mount, and the only way we're going to be able to find it is to pay a nocturnal visit and hope we can get deep inside the structure.'

Angela nodded but didn't respond.

'I checked the door locks when we went in,' Bronson continued, 'and they're better than I had expected, but they're certainly not top quality. I'm not an expert, but I'm pretty certain that I could pick them, as long as I had about five minutes without interruption. And I didn't see any cameras inside the tunnels or any infrared detectors, so if we could get in there we'd be safe enough unless they've got some guard prowling around during the night who might come along and check the doors. And even then, I might be able to lock the door from the inside.'

Angela glanced at him as they walked along, heading back towards the hotel. 'You're determined to go through with this, aren't you?'

'I'd rather we didn't have to,' Bronson replied, 'but right now I don't see any alternative. If we walk away I think there's a good chance that both of us will be targets of that terrorist group. Our best option is to try to beat them to whatever it is they're looking for. But I don't want you to get involved,' he added. 'I can go back in there myself. There's no need for you to take the risk as well.'

'Not a chance,' Angela said. 'You'll need somebody to

hold the torch and keep a lookout while you're working on the locks. Plus, two pairs of eyes are better than one if we do manage to get into the locked chambers. What I'm trying to say is that where you go, I'm going to go as well, so you'd better start getting used to it.'

Bronson gripped her hand and squeezed it.

'Thanks,' he said simply.

38

Jerusalem

'It all looks quiet enough,' Angela murmured.

She and Bronson were standing on the Kotel Plaza opposite the Wailing Wall, about twenty yards or so down a side street, a position from which they could see almost all of the open space in front of them. They'd been waiting for about ten minutes and in all that time they'd seen only two people – a couple walking arm in arm – cross the square. At a little after two in the morning, the lack of activity was hardly surprising, and exactly what they were hoping for.

'Right, then,' Bronson said quietly. 'There's no time like the present, I suppose. Let's go.'

They stepped forward, arm in arm, looking as much as possible like a couple returning from a night out. The last thing they wanted was to be stopped, since in the pockets of Bronson's lightweight jacket he was carrying three pairs of pliers and two screwdrivers, half a dozen crudely made skeleton keys that he had fabricated during the afternoon, as well as his version of a torsion wrench, a device to apply turning pressure to the barrel of a lock. It was, by any standards, a comprehensive, if home-made, DIY burglary kit, and he was in no doubt that if he was stopped and searched, he would be spending the rest of that night in a police cell.

They wandered casually across to the Wailing Wall, and for a few seconds just stood beside it, again checking that they were unobserved. Then they moved into the shadows cast by the Western Wall Heritage building and stood motionless for a moment.

'So far, so good,' Angela murmured.

'That was very definitely the easy bit,' Bronson said. 'From now on, if anybody sees us or stops us, we're in big trouble.'

He bent down to examine the lock on the outer gate, while Angela shone a light so that he could see what he was doing.

That afternoon, as well as buying the tools that were now in his pocket, Bronson had also purchased four torches, two small and two larger and more powerful, and half a dozen spare batteries for each. He'd then taken one of the small torches and placed electrical tape over the glass so that the beam of light it emitted was reduced to little more than the diameter of a pencil. That, he knew, would give him more than enough light to work by, but hopefully would not be bright enough to attract the attention of any passers-by.

He gripped the handle of the gate firmly, but even as

he did so, something totally unexpected happened: the gate swung open silently at his touch.

'What?' he muttered.

'It's already open,' Angela whispered, stating what was surprisingly obvious to them both.

'They definitely wouldn't have forgotten to lock it,' Bronson said, equally quietly. 'I don't think we're the first intruders to get inside here tonight.'

Angela gripped his arm.

'You mean they're already here? Somewhere inside the tunnel? We should go back, just forget this.'

'I really don't want to do that.' Bronson's tone was firm. 'Whatever they're doing in the tunnels, they're bound to leave traces. That means the Israeli authorities will know that someone was in here, and they'll immediately step up their security. The only chance we have of getting in there is tonight. Right now, in fact. Whoever's inside won't know that we're behind them, so hopefully we can just follow them while they do the searching for us.' He paused. 'Look, are you still up for this?' he asked. 'You know, right now you can still walk away. I can do this by myself.'

Angela didn't respond for a moment, her face a pale oval in the dim moonlight. Then she shook her head.

'If those are the same people that massacred my colleagues in Iraq,' she whispered, 'then I definitely don't want to go in there tonight. Walking into a black tunnel where there are men carrying guns isn't my idea of good thinking, and you shouldn't go in there either, not without a weapon.'

He touched her arm in reassurance.

'If it is those men, then if they're armed at all they'll be carrying pistols, and pistols aren't going to be too much use in a confined space like the tunnel and spaces under the Temple Mount.'

He reached down and picked up a length of rebar – the steel reinforcing bar used in concrete – that was lying on the ground just outside the doorway.

'Down there in the dark, this will probably be more use than a pistol. I'll be okay.'

Angela's face was barely visible in the moonlight, but Bronson could still see from her expression that she was terrified for him.

'There could be a dozen of them in there,' she said, 'just waiting for you to walk in. We should go, just forget all about this,' she added, repeating herself.

For a few seconds, Bronson contemplated doing just that, taking the easy option. But he knew that if they didn't get to the bottom of the mystery neither he nor, more importantly, Angela, would ever be safe. There was no option. He had to get in there, no matter what the risks. And having come this far he was desperate to solve this mystery too. He shook his head.

'I doubt very much if there are that many inside. And they'll be looking in front of them, searching for this key thing, not behind, where I'll be.'

For a long moment, Angela just stared at him, her eyes unblinking as if she was committing his face to her memory. Then she bowed her head and nodded.

'I really don't want you to do this, Chris. But I know

I won't be able to stop you. I can't go with you, I just can't, but I'll stay out here and listen. And if I hear anything, then I'm going to call the police.'

'Good.' He put a hand on her shoulder. 'Stay close and keep your ears open. I'll be fine.'

And a second later Bronson, a black-suited figure barely visible against the night sky, was gone, stepping inside the gate and out of sight.

In the square, Angela took out her mobile and checked the signal strength and the amount of charge remaining in the battery – both indicated nearly the maximum – then made herself as small as she could, squatting down beside the entrance to the Western Wall Heritage, where hopefully she would not be seen, but would still be close enough to the entrance to hear anything happening inside.

39

Jerusalem

The Western Wall Tunnel runs under the outmost portion of the Temple Mount, part of it behind the Wailing Wall, though this section of the tunnel is only about ninety yards long, while the structure as a whole extends to about five hundred yards.

Over the years, various excavations, authorized and unauthorized, have been made in and around the area, with the result that within the tunnel there are a number of closed-off spaces to which visitors have no access.

Of course, that presupposes that the visitors have not entered the tunnel complex equipped with bolt croppers, pry bars and other tools that would facilitate the opening of a locked gate or door.

Farooq was keenly aware of the problems he would face in the dark and confined spaces beneath the Temple Mount, and he had chosen only two of his men to come with him on his nocturnal expedition. All were carrying their pistols, as well as the tools that they had thought they would need.

They had done their best to prepare themselves as well. The previous evening he and Khaled had spent a considerable length of time online researching everything that was known about the subterranean structures within the Temple Mount, including the detailed maps produced by Charles Warren, the British army officer who had entered the spaces during his three-year dig in Jerusalem in the latter half of the nineteenth century.

They didn't know exactly what they were going to find when – or rather if – they managed to get into the chambers under the Temple Mount itself, but thanks to Charles Warren at least they had a good idea of where they needed to go.

If Khaled's assumption was correct, and the inscription's 'lost temple' was one or both of the vanished Jewish temples that had originally stood on the Temple Mount, then what they needed to do was to get into one of the chambers below the Dome of the Rock. As Muslims, both men already knew that one famous chamber existed underneath the present mosque.

Accessible by a stairway was a carpeted prayer chamber known as the *Br al Arwah*, the Well of Souls, from which could be seen the crack in the Foundation Stone supposed to have been caused by Muhammad ascending from it to heaven and the rock splitting as it tried to follow him. In early Jewish times, the chamber was reputed to have been where the Ark of the Covenant was placed for safety while Jerusalem was under attack, and according to legend the relic might still be hidden somewhere in that cave. Islamic teaching states that the Well of Souls is where all the spirits of the dead will assemble at the end of the world, awaiting the final judgment of God.

But that cave was accessible only from within the Dome of the Rock, and was in any case so well used and documented that the presence of any mysterious inscriptions or carvings would have become common knowledge long ago. No, Khaled was quite certain that the chamber – the *hypogeum* – that they sought lay below, perhaps some distance below, the Well of Souls, and would only be accessible from underneath.

If they were to take the translated text of the inscription literally, then they should be searching the area that lay directly below the Dome of the Rock. And that meant surveying the wall that had been constructed around the buried portion of the Foundation Stone to form a large chamber, and checking the areas that Charles Warren had named on his map the Great Sea and Cohain's Mikva, their original purposes and reasons for their names forgotten in the grey mists of ancient history. They might even have to go as far over as the Eastern Wall and the Shushan Gate.

Farooq had waited until just after one in the morning before he and his men had approached the Western Wall Heritage building. He knew that was taking a chance, because they were more likely to be seen at that time of night by residents returning home. But they were only going to get one chance, one night during which they could explore the underground labyrinth, because as soon as their intrusion had been detected, security would be put in place and after that the only way back in would be to use considerable violence. So the earlier they could get inside, the better.

Part-way along the tunnel, the light from the torch Farooq was holding glinted on a series of vertical black bars, and he widened the focus of the torch to show the entire structure. It was a heavy metal gate secured not with a lock into the frame but with two substantial heavy-duty padlocks, one at each end of a thick horizontal steel bar.

He bent forward and inspected the padlock at one end of the bar. It was a high-quality unit, but like every lock ever made it had a weakness, and his visual inspection quickly revealed what that was. The hasp was thick stainless steel, which would have been difficult to either cut through with a hacksaw or sever using a set of bolt-croppers. But the metal plate to which it was attached was much less substantial.

'Mahmoud, use the croppers and cut here and here,' he instructed, pointing to the metal above and below the hasp of the padlock.

The man he'd addressed extracted a set of heavy-duty bolt-croppers from the canvas bag he was carrying and closed the jaws of the tool around the metal, then steadily squeezed the ends of the handles together, his face tensing with effort.

After a few seconds there was a sharp crack as the croppers did their work. Immediately, Mahmoud opened the jaws of the tool and closed them over the top of the steel plate. He pressed the handles together, and again there was another cracking noise as the jaws snapped together, having severed the metal. The section of the plate that he'd cut out tumbled to the floor.

'Do the same again at the other end of the bar,' Farooq instructed, then pulled the padlock towards him.

It didn't come free, and when he shone his torch at the end of the metal bar he realized that there was just enough left of the circle of steel to hold the hasp of the padlock in position.

'Hand me a pry bar,' he ordered, and the other man standing beside him reached down and removed the tool from Mahmoud's bag.

Farooq inserted the tip of the steel bar behind the hasp of the padlock and pressed sharply down on the other end of the tool. The padlock was immediately freed from the steel embrace of the door frame and tumbled down to land with a thud by Farooq's feet.

Moments later, Mahmoud completed the second cut on the frame at the other end of the bar, pulled the padlock out of position and then lifted away the steel bar from in front of the metal gate.

Farooq reached out, grasped the steel bar on one side of the gate and pulled it open, the hinges protesting with loud squeals. It sounded as though that particular entrance hadn't been used in a very long time. Behind it was what looked like a normal wooden door, and for a moment Farooq wondered if they would have to pick the lock or break it down, a noisy option that he really wanted to avoid. But when he reached out and turned the handle, the door opened, though not without a certain amount of shoving to get the aperture wide enough to step through.

Beyond, another void beckoned – even blacker, if that were possible, than the unlit tunnel. Farooq aimed the beam of his torch through the doorway, then led the way inside.

When Farooq switched off the torch for a moment, the darkness was impenetrable, though as their eyes adjusted a faint bluish glow became evident, a glow that moved very slightly as he turned to look at it. After a second, he realized that it was the barely luminous numbers on the face of the analogue watch Mahmoud was wearing on his wrist.

Farooq slid the small torch into his pocket and took out a much larger one with a long aluminium barrel and pressed the button to turn it on. He swung the beam around them in a semicircular arc so that they could see what lay to their front, and then turned round to check the wall behind them.

The massive stones of the inner wall extended in a more or less straight line behind them in both directions, while in front the ground was lumpy and uneven, a mixture of dark earth and protruding rock, presumably the bedrock upon which the Temple Mount had been built. A short distance in front of them, another wall, formed from equally substantial blocks of cut and dressed stone, paralleled the structure to their rear, though this was nothing like as long.

Farooq took a printed copy of the Warren map from his pocket, unfolded it and studied the shapes and dimensions of the structures the English army officer had identified well over a century earlier.

'I think we're somewhere near Warren's Gate,' he said, his voice seeming unnaturally loud in the silence of the subterranean chamber. 'If so,' he went on, 'that wall right in front of us' – he moved the beam of the torch left and right over the ancient greyish stones – 'must be the perimeter wall around the Foundation Stone. And that means the *Qubbat as-Sakhra*, what the infidels refer to as the Dome of the Rock, is almost directly above us. It seems that we have entered the underworld of the *Haram Ash-Sharif* almost exactly where we had planned.'

Farooq lowered the beam of his torch slightly, illuminating the rocky and broken ground directly in front of them, and led the way over to the wall.

'You two go around it to the right,' he instructed, 'and I'll go left. Remember what I told you: if you see any kind of carving or inscription, especially if it's enclosed in a border like the one in the photographs from the underground temple in Iraq, take several photographs of it and remember its position, because I will want to see it as well. We are not interested in anything painted on the wall, only carvings, and not just initials or individual letters. The key we are seeking will almost certainly be two or more words.'

The three men separated, the other two switching on their own torches as they walked away, and began working their way along the wall.

Farooq knew the history of the Noble Sanctuary as well as any Muslim – it was, after all, the third most holy Muslim shrine after Mecca and Medina – and he was supremely conscious, not just of his close proximity to the *Qubbat as-Sakhra*, but also to the Foundation Stone itself, the last place on earth that the prophet Muhammad trod after his Night Journey and immediately before he ascended to heaven.

He was also aware – and this produced an entirely different emotion – of the tens of thousands of tons of stone and bricks and masonry and wood and other materials that lay above them, a colossal weight that was supported, at least in part, by the wall that he was now inspecting, a wall that looked substantially less impressive in the light of that knowledge. Farooq put the thought out of his mind and concentrated on the search at hand.

He reached the corner without having seen anything of interest, the ancient stones appearing largely featureless apart from the marks made by the nameless masons who had dressed them two millennia earlier. He shone his torch ahead of him and immediately saw a potential problem. Close to the wall were two oblong stone structures that he guessed had been referred to by Warren as Cohain's Mikva. Those were not the problem, and he would examine them as part of his search, but directly behind them was another wall, a structure that abutted the wall around the Foundation Stone, and which extended up to the north.

He checked the map again, just to confirm his

suspicions: he was walking into a dead end and would have to retrace his steps in order to inspect the entire boundary wall. Even then, there was one section that, according to the map, would be forever out of reach, a short section that lay on the other side of the wall he had just seen, and which was enclosed in a kind of triangular shape by a second wall extending to the north. On the other hand, if it was inaccessible to him he would have to assume it had also been inaccessible to the author of the inscription.

Farooq shrugged and continued forward, playing the beam of his torch over the entire surface of the wall from the base to the very top. He reached the wall junction, scanned along the north wall as well, and checked all around the two oblong stone structures.

Disappointed, he turned and retraced his steps. There was no sign of Mahmoud or Salim, but he knew they would have had a much larger section of wall to inspect than the area he had studied. He could hear them talking somewhere in the darkness, and strode along the wall, playing his torch over the stones as he headed towards where they had to be.

Again, the stones in the wall presented an entirely featureless aspect.

Not for the first time, Farooq began to doubt Khaled's assumptions and beliefs. By any standards, they were exploring the chamber, the *hypogeum*, that lay below the lost temple of the Jews, just as Khaled had deduced from the decoded inscription, but they'd found absolutely nothing.

And then another thought struck him as he walked towards the dancing torch beams of the other two men. From what he knew of the building of the Noble Sanctuary, it had been done largely as a single piece of engineering by Herod when he built the four huge retaining walls around the natural rocky outcrop, filled in many of the voids, and then laid a flat artificial surface over the whole area, upon which he then erected the restored Jewish Temple. That implied, at least to Farooq, that the various walls and chambers below the temple would have been inaccessible from that period – from the start of the first millennium onwards. And if that were the case, then how could anyone in the mediaeval period, or in fact at any other time, have got inside to create an inscription?

Suddenly, he was convinced that they were just wasting their time.

'Anything?' he asked as he reached the other two men.

'Nothing at all,' Salim replied. 'We haven't seen a single mark on any of these stones that wasn't made by a stonemason, as far as we can tell. Are you sure we're looking in the right place?'

Farooq smiled in the darkness.

'No, my friend,' he said softly, 'I am not. But we'll finish the job, so that we can report back to Khaled.'

They continued around the southern side of the interior wall, examining every vertical surface, and then the eastern side as well. But it all appeared virtually identical: heavy blocks of plain-dressed stone, devoid of any markings.

'A waste of time,' Mahmoud said, as they slowly retraced their steps.

40

Jerusalem

Chris Bronson didn't speak or understand Arabic beyond a dozen or so words, but as he stood in total blackness just inside the Western Wall Tunnel peering in through the open doorway, he believed that he understood the mood of the two or three men he could hear walking around inside the void.

They didn't sound happy. In fact, they sounded hacked off and frustrated, which almost certainly meant that they hadn't found what they were looking for.

And now they were heading his way. Back towards the open doorway.

Bronson straightened up and began to move backwards and to the side, to get out of view. But as soon as he did so, his left foot kicked one of the padlocks lying on the ground, the noise a dull but entirely audible thud.

Immediately, a torch beam speared through the open

doorway into the Western Wall Tunnel. The light caught Bronson's arm and shoulder as he moved sideways, and almost instantly destroyed his night vision. The light was followed in under a second by two shots – a 'double tap' – the technique used by professional soldiers the world over. The sound of the gunfire was deafening in the confined space.

By the time the shots were fired, Bronson was already out of view of the doorway, but the copper-jacketed bullets slammed into the solid stone wall on the other side of the tunnel and instantly ricocheted, hot shards of lead and copper flying in all directions, one carving a shallow furrow across his forehead.

As he started running, he could hear his feet thudding on the rock floor and his blood pounding in his ears. His torch beam was dancing across the walls and floors because now he absolutely needed to see where he was going. As he ran Bronson wondered if the firing had been a panic reaction to his presence, or if the shooter had expected the bullets to ricochet from the stone and hopefully injure him.

What he needed was somewhere to hide, because if he kept running down the straight section of the tunnel, they'd be able to cut him down the moment they stepped out from the void.

An archway beckoned on the right-hand side, and he dodged through it, swinging the torch beam around to get an idea of where he was, before extinguishing the light. Leaving the torch switched on would simply advertise his presence. He stood as motionless as he could, trying to steady his ragged breathing.

A moment later, the darkness of the tunnel was torn apart by the beams from three powerful torches as his pursuers stepped through the gateway and attempted to seek him out.

Bronson's brief inspection had revealed a space perhaps twenty feet square, with stone walls, ceiling and floor, and entirely empty. As a place to hide, it was far from ideal. But there was nowhere else he could go. He was trapped.

It all depended on what the three men – and he was now certain because of the torch beams that there were at least three of them – decided to do next.

He heard quiet voices echoing along the tunnel, while the three torch beams continued to illuminate the passage outside Bronson's temporary refuge. Suddenly, two of the torches were extinguished. The third continued to shine up the tunnel, but at a slightly changed angle, illuminating the wall closest to his refuge rather than the entire width of the tunnel. By doing that, the man with the torch was ensuring that his two companions, who Bronson guessed would already be making their way silently towards him, would not cast shadows that would give away their position.

He calculated he had perhaps fifteen or twenty seconds before the armed men would reach the entrance to the chamber. But he also realized something else. The moment the men stepped through the doorway, the light from the tunnel would be of no further help to them and they would be effectively blind as they moved towards him. They would have to then use their own torches both to see where they were going and to locate him.

That gave him a tiny window of opportunity – at least a chance to save his life and walk away – and that was a chance he was going to take.

Bronson crouched down and felt around on the floor. In a structure made entirely from stone there must, he rationalized, be the odd pebble or chipping or something. His probing fingers closed around a small piece of stone, about the size of a marble. It wasn't much, but it would have to do.

He heard a faint shuffling sound from somewhere in the tunnel outside, very close. Then another torch beam snapped on, the light shining through the archway, and moving left and right as the man holding it did his best to see inside the chamber.

Then the light was extinguished, leaving only the original torch beam shining. That meant that one or perhaps both of the men outside were about to come in and look for him.

Bronson gripped the length of rebar with his right hand, flattened his back against the wall on the right-hand side of the archway and held the pebble in his left hand, ready to lob it.

He sensed the presence of somebody before the dim light revealed the outline of a man dressed entirely in black and holding a pistol in his right hand.

Bronson knew he had just one chance.

He flicked the pebble into the far corner of the chamber at the precise moment the man stepped inside the room.

The stone clattered on the floor and immediately the intruder turned on his torch, the beam seeking out the source of the sound while he raised his right arm, aiming the pistol towards that corner.

And then Bronson swung the rebar down with all his strength, a short vicious arc that connected with the man's right arm about midway between his wrist and his elbow, instantly breaking both bones.

The man screamed, a high wailing sound that echoed from the walls. He dropped the pistol and the torch, the beam immediately extinguished when it hit the stone floor, his left hand reaching to support his right arm as he bent forward in agony.

But Bronson wasn't finished. He lifted the rebar again, higher this time, and brought it down just as hard on the back of the man's skull. The screaming stopped instantly and the man dropped to the floor and lay still. Dead, dying or just unconscious, Bronson didn't know. Or particularly care. He'd been forced to choose between his life and someone else's. And now he had a proper weapon.

The man outside in the tunnel switched on his torch in panic, obviously having heard the noises but without knowing what had happened. Then the torch beam illuminated the unmoving shape of his companion, and Bronson guessed he'd now be looking for a target.

He reached down and grabbed the pistol the other man had dropped. The weapon felt instantly familiar, and he identified it by touch as a Browning Hi-Power, a pistol he'd used frequently during his Army career. The safety catch was off and the hammer was all the way back, ready to fire.

The man outside must have realized the stupidity of switching on his torch, because doing so had instantly identified his location. As soon as the light appeared it was extinguished. An instant later, the other torch was also switched off.

In the darkness, Bronson crouched down beside the archway, adrenalin pumping through him, aimed the pistol more or less at where he thought the torch had been, and squeezed the trigger once. He didn't want to risk a second shot because he didn't know how many rounds were in the magazine, though from the weight of the weapon he guessed it was at least half full.

He heard a curse, the voice raised in anger rather than pain, and at the same instant two shots rang out, the faint muzzle flashes in the blackness showing that the shooter was already on the move, heading back down the tunnel towards his companion.

Bronson rose slowly to his feet and eased himself through the stone archway until he could look back down the tunnel. About forty yards away, near the open gate, he saw the outline of two figures, the intermittent glow of light from their torches as they flicked them on and off, obviously trying not to become targets, showing that they were heading away from him.

Forty yards is too far for accurate shooting with a pistol, and in any case Bronson would never have shot anybody in the back, so he stepped back inside the chamber and switched on his torch. The man he'd hit was lying in precisely the same position and in the light from the torch Bronson could see the black hair on the back of his head was soaked in blood. He inhaled deeply, steeling himself, and checked the pulse in the man's neck, but found nothing.

He realized his hands were shaking and took a moment to compose himself. Better that the anonymous man – who had after all been carrying a loaded and cocked pistol and presumably had intended to use it – should be lying there dead than Bronson himself.

Very faintly in the distance he thought he heard the sound of approaching sirens, and knew he had to get out as quickly as possible. He placed the pistol on the ground within easy reach and quickly searched the dead man, recovering a handful of nine-millimetre bullets from his pocket and a wallet that only contained cash, and not that much of it. He pocketed the wallet, tucked the pistol into the waistband of his trousers and picked up the length of rebar. His fingerprints were certainly all over it, along with the blood of the dead man, and he couldn't risk leaving it behind.

Then he stepped out of the chamber and back into the tunnel.

41

Jerusalem

Angela had been as good as her word.

She'd waited in the shadows by the entrance to the Western Wall Heritage, doing her best to keep out of sight and listening intently. The sound of the two shots from somewhere deep inside the tunnel complex had both shocked and alarmed her and she'd immediately dialled the Israeli police. But not from her mobile. She'd jogged away from the Kotel Plaza and made the call from the first public phone she'd found, telling the person who responded that she'd heard shots from inside the complex and that the door to the building was open.

The officer or dispatcher or whoever it was had told her firmly to remain exactly where she was, but Angela had replaced the receiver and immediately walked to an entirely different location which gave her a good view of the entrance to the Western Wall Heritage and just waited.

She looked and had sounded calm and in control on the phone, but her mind was in turmoil. Those shots could only have meant one thing: Chris must have been spotted by whoever had entered the complex before they got there. Even while her mind raced, imagining him dying alone and in the dark, lying in a spreading pool of his own blood on the ancient stones of some anonymous chamber or passage, another part of her brain was silently cursing him for his stupidity in going inside the tunnel complex at all, knowing that somebody else was already in there. And perhaps worse than that, for thinking he could take on men armed with guns when all he had with him was a length of steel.

For a few minutes, nothing happened. Then she faintly heard what sounded like another single shot, quickly followed by two more, but she was now so far away from the entrance to the tunnel complex that she couldn't be sure. And moments after that she heard the unmistakable sound of a police siren.

She didn't move, apart from slinking further back into the shadows and making sure that she could not be easily seen. She was determined to hold her position and to wait there until, hopefully, she would see the bulky figure of Bronson emerge from the open gate.

But that didn't happen. Instead, two men stepped out of the gate, glanced in both directions and then exchanged a few brief words. Then they set off, heading away from the Kotel Plaza in opposite directions, not running but moving quickly. In the light from the moon, all she could tell was they had dark hair, and appeared to have swarthy complexions.

Less than two minutes later, four uniformed police officers ran into the square and headed straight for the Western Wall Heritage entrance, briefly examined the lock on the open gate and then vanished inside, pistols drawn and torches in their hands.

At that moment Angela knew that there was no point in waiting where she was any longer. If Bronson was still alive somewhere in the tunnels, the police would arrest him and he'd spend the rest of the night in a police cell, and probably the next several months or years in some Israeli jail. If he was dead, they'd remove the body, and if he was wounded but still alive, they'd take him to hospital.

Those, as far as Angela could see, were the only possible outcomes, and there was nothing she could do to influence or help Bronson with any of them if she stayed where she was. In fact, the longer she remained in the area, the more chance there was of being arrested herself, if only because she was on the spot and might have been the woman who had made the call about the gunshots. If, against all the odds, Bronson had survived and had been arrested, then the best place for her to be was out on the streets so that she could find him a lawyer or talk to the embassy or consulate or whatever British government presence there was in the city.

She took a last lingering glance across the square, emitted a sound that was almost a moan of pain, then turned away and began walking slowly through the streets, heading back towards the hotel because she had no idea where else to go or what else to do.

As she walked, she was aware of more sirens sounding in the streets around the Old City, and a couple of times she ducked out of sight into sheltered doorways when she heard the sound of running feet nearby. She guessed these were people making for the Kotel Plaza and the growing commotion there, but nobody actually passed her as she walked away from the scene, head down.

She walked slowly and appeared calm, but her mind was racing, selecting and discarding possibilities and scenarios. The only glimmer of hope she had was that she had clearly heard two shots and then – she was almost certain of this – a third, and then two more. Bronson didn't have a pistol, and that meant that it had to have been one or both of the two men she'd seen coming out of the Western Wall Heritage who'd been doing the shooting. And the fact that it hadn't just been two quick shots might have meant that the bullets hadn't killed Bronson, otherwise there would have been no point in firing again. So maybe, just maybe, he'd been spotted in the tunnels and they'd shot at him but missed, and then made their escape when they heard the sound of the sirens.

So if her hopeful reconstruction of events was right, it was possible that her ex-husband might still be alive. Wounded, perhaps, and by now in police custody, but alive. She would have to wait until the normal routine of the city had started later in the morning, and then she could start searching by phone, checking the hospitals and of course the local police station.

And then all her tentative plans and schemes vanished completely from her mind as a dark figure stepped out of an alleyway just a few feet in front of her.

Angela gave a gasp of surprise, then a murmur of recognition. She ran the few paces that separated them, wrapped her arms around him and squeezed as if she would never let him go.

'Dear God,' she murmured, her voice muffled by the clothes he was wearing, 'I thought you were dead. When I heard those shots—' She broke off, stifling a sob, and stared into his face. 'You're hurt,' she said.

'Don't worry about it,' Bronson said. 'It's just a scratch. I got hit by a ricochet from one of the first shots they fired.'

'Let me see,' Angela said tenderly, and steered him back into the alleyway from which he had appeared, where the light from her torch would hopefully not attract attention.

She shone the dim beam at his forehead, altered the angle a couple of times to see better, and then nodded.

'It might just be a scratch, but it has bled rather a lot.'

She reached into her pocket, pulled out a packet of tissues and wiped off the blood, which was already starting to clot.

She took out another tissue, folded it to make a pad and then instructed Bronson to spit on it.

'What the hell happened in there?' she asked, ignoring

his quizzical expression. She cleared more blood from Bronson's forehead with the dampened tissue. 'You can't infect yourself,' she added. 'That's why you're spitting on the tissues, not me.'

'There were three of them,' Bronson began, but Angela stopped him almost immediately.

'I only saw two come out.'

Bronson sighed.

'Yes,' he said, in a low voice. 'The third one is still down there in the tunnel.'

'But couldn't he identify you?' Angela began, but then stopped as Bronson gave a small shake of his head. 'Oh . . . You mean he's in no fit state to talk? To ever talk?'

'Let me put it this way: he won't be causing us, or anybody else, any problems in the future. He was about to shoot me so I didn't really have a choice. It was him or me.'

'Are you okay?' she whispered. 'Who was he?'

'I have no idea. I checked his pockets before I left, but all he had were a few spare rounds for his pistol and a wallet containing some cash. I took them both, because he obviously wasn't going to be able to use either. And his pistol as well, just in case we need a bit of firepower before all this is over.'

'You've always told me that professionals never carry ID,' Angela said, a look of worry again crossing her face. 'So do you think that's what he was? A professional, but a professional what? I mean, what did he look like?'

'Black hair, dark skin and fairly pronounced features,

but basically unremarkable. I've never been a believer in coincidence, and in my view the chances of there being another group of people – a group unrelated to those people in Iraq, I mean – exploring the interior of the Temple Mount at the same time as us is nil. I don't know who he was, but I'd bet money that he was a part of the group that hit your camp and destroyed the inscription. So that's another reason why I don't feel too bad about what happened to him.'

Angela didn't respond, and Bronson glanced at her as they walked along the street.

'And are you OK?' he asked.

'No, not really. I had kind of hoped that when we got here we'd be well ahead of our pursuers, so we could find whatever clue there's left under the Temple Mount and then get out of Israel to somewhere a bit safer. But if you're right, that means those people have also cracked the hidden message in the inscription, otherwise they wouldn't be here.'

'Well, the decryption wasn't all that easy, but it also wasn't desperately difficult. I've no doubt that whoever these guys are, they would have done exactly the same thing and reached precisely the same conclusion that we did. And as they're here now, assuming I'm right, it even took them roughly the same length of time to crack it as us.'

'That makes sense,' Angela said, sounding subdued. 'And obviously it's wonderful that you got out of the tunnel before the police arrived, but we can't be too blasé about the fact that you killed a man tonight.

Whether or not he deserved to die doesn't matter, because pretty soon the entire Israeli police force will be looking for his murderer.'

They were silent for a moment.

'And how did you get out?' she asked as another thought struck her. 'I kept watch until the police arrived, and the only people who came out of the entrance were those two men I told you about.'

'I used the other entrance, or rather the exit from the Western Wall Tunnel. Just picked the lock and walked away. I didn't dare risk going out the way I'd come in, just in case one of the men was still waiting for me or – maybe even worse – if the police had got there quicker than I'd expected and found me standing there holding a length of rebar covered in blood and with an unlicensed pistol in my pocket.'

'Where did you put it? The rebar, I mean, because your fingerprints and obviously his blood would be all over it.'

'You don't have to worry about that,' Bronson replied. 'This city is full of holes and crevices because of all the different layers that have been built on it over the centuries. I found a narrow slit between two buildings, wiped the bar and then dropped it down into the opening. It fell quite a long way before I heard a clunk, so I reckon the chances of anybody finding it are pretty much nil.'

'And because you left a dead man down there, I suppose now we have to get out of Jerusalem as quickly as we can. So that's the end of it? The search, I mean?'

Angela sounded resigned more than anything as they continued walking towards the hotel. It wasn't the first time Bronson had inflicted casualties on hostile forces during their searches for relics around the globe, and while she obviously didn't condone what he'd done, she also wouldn't condemn him: sometimes the only way to combat force was to use even greater force.

'Definitely not,' he replied. 'The last thing we should do is leave in a hurry because that might attract unwelcome official attention. Anyway, I think we will be heading somewhere else quite soon, but for a different reason. Because of what was down there, under the Temple Mount.'

'You mean you found something?'

'Well, more didn't find, really. The three men had broken open one of the interior gateways and had gone into the tunnels under the Mount, but when they came back, they saw me and that's when the shooting started. Obviously you'd called the police right after that, which is why they pushed off after I'd killed that man. The problem I had was that I couldn't do a proper search of the chamber they'd opened up because there simply wasn't time. I heard the police sirens and I knew I had to get out almost immediately. But I heard the three of them talking as they headed back towards the main tunnel, and I'm pretty certain that they'd found nothing at all. Certainly not an inscription that could have been this mysterious key.'

'But you don't speak Arabic,' Angela pointed out, 'so how can you be sure?'

'I can't be sure, obviously, but they sounded both resigned and irritated, as if they'd been on a wild-goose chase. I had a very quick look inside the chamber they'd been exploring just before I left the area, and as far as I could see, all the walls were completely devoid of markings of any sort. And, with hindsight, if you look at the history of the Temple Mount, it's difficult to see how anybody would have been able to get inside it, or at least get inside the areas under the old Jewish Temple, to leave a clue or a key.'

'What do you mean?' Angela asked.

'You told me that the Temple Mount was built by Herod in the first century,' Bronson replied. 'And as far as we know, what he did was build retaining walls around the circumference of the Mount and supporting walls at various points on top of the existing hill, and he then laid a flat surface of stone over the top of all that, a level surface on which he was able to reconstruct and enlarge the temple. So around what's known as the Foundation Stone, for example, he built a wall that enclosed the stone completely and once he put the level stonework on top of the walls, the only possible way in to that space would have been by digging down from inside the temple itself or worming your way in from the side and then cutting a hole in that perimeter wall.'

'Okay, I see where you're going with that,' Angela said, nodding.

'So over one millennium later, in the early Middle Ages, realistically there would have been no way that anybody could have got into these chambers undetected.

267

In fact, it's worth saying that the chambers within the Temple Mount, the various rooms that Charles Warren explored when he did his excavations at the end of the nineteenth century, in most cases weren't really rooms at all, but just the voids left between Herod's supporting walls, spaces basically filled up with earth and rubbish.'

At that moment, they reached the hotel, where every room apart from the reception hall was in darkness, and Bronson used his key to open the front door so they could go inside. To avoid waking anybody, people who might possibly be asked questions by the Jerusalem police at a later date, they stopped talking until they were inside their bedroom. And even then, they both made a conscious effort to keep their voices low.

'So what you're saying is that we're in the wrong place altogether,' Angela said, and sighed heavily. 'We've picked the wrong "lost temple", and we've just been wasting our time here.'

42

Jerusalem

In another hotel room not that far away from the one occupied by Bronson and Angela, another debrief – or quite literally and more accurately a post-mortem – was being carried out.

'So who was this man?' Khaled demanded.

'I don't know,' Farooq replied. 'We saw him in the light from our torches for less than a second, and Salim immediately fired at him. That was a mistake, I agree, but it was a reflex action. Obviously we then needed to find him, so we could decide whether or not to kill him, but we never saw him again. At least, neither Mahmoud nor I saw him again.'

'But you did see him, even if it was only for an instant, so what was your impression? Did he look European or Middle Eastern? You must have been able to tell if his skin was white or black at the very least.'

Farooq shut his eyes, trying to visualize the fleeting

image that he had had of the man a little over an hour earlier. Then he nodded, and looked across at Khaled.

'He was definitely white,' he replied. 'My impression is that he was quite heavily built, and he was wearing dark clothing, presumably because, just like us, he was down there for a different purpose. Because of what happened next, I'm quite certain he wasn't just some passer-by who'd found the outer gate of the place unlocked and wandered inside. If that had been the case – or if he had been something to do with the Western Wall Tunnel – then he would have switched on the lights. But this man had obviously been very circumspect in his approach and had probably been observing us in that chamber for quite some time. We were only aware that there was anyone there when we heard a noise from the open doorway.'

'You said he fired at you,' Khaled said. 'Could he have been a policeman, or an army officer, something like that?'

'If he'd been police or army, he would have been armed, he wouldn't have been by himself, and he would almost certainly have returned fire immediately. But he didn't,' Farooq pointed out. 'Instead, he ran off along the tunnel. But what I don't understand is why he only shot the once. He could have stayed within the safety of the chamber, shone his torch into the tunnel and picked off Mahmoud in a matter of seconds. So why didn't he?'

'Is that a rhetorical question,' Khaled asked, 'or are you expecting an answer?'

'It would be good to have your thoughts.'

'If the roles had been reversed, we both know that you would have fired, so that implies that the intruder has a different mindset, and in my opinion that almost certainly means that we know who it was.'

This time Farooq nodded.

'Exactly,' he said, 'it must have been the woman's husband, the man Bronson.'

'And that means she is probably here with him. I know you found nothing under the Temple Mount, and I'm going to have to work out what that means. But in the meantime, I want you and your men to scour the streets and check all the hotels. If that was Bronson in the tunnel, then he and his interfering wife must be staying here in Jerusalem, and it's not that big a place.'

'So you want us to find them?'

'Precisely. I want you to find them and then I want you to kill them.'

43

Jerusalem

'Actually,' Bronson said, 'I still think we're in exactly the *right* place, but I think we're probably misinterpreting the Latin and not looking in the places that we should.'

They were still talking together quietly. When they'd got to the room, Angela had taken Bronson into the bathroom, where he'd washed his face and hands before Angela gently cleaned and dressed the wound on his forehead. They were now lying side by side on the double bed, Angela resting her head on Bronson's chest.

'I thought the Latin was reasonably clear,' she said.

'It is, but "clear" doesn't necessarily mean we're interpreting it correctly. There's a persistent legend that when the Knights Templar arrived in Jerusalem, they spent a long time – most reports say that it was as long as nine years – digging down into the lower levels of the Temple Mount, presumably looking for something. They were accommodated, not in what is now the Dome of the Rock, which is believed to have been the site of both the first and second Jewish temples, but in the present Al Aqsa Mosque. Obviously, nobody knows what they were looking for or whether or not they found it, but roughly nine years after they started digging, they stopped, and then began asking noblemen from around Europe to join the order. And as we know, they were very successful in their recruitment drive.

'Now, the Temple Mount is quite a large area, and despite the fact that the Templars must have been excavating under the Al Aqsa Mosque rather than the Dome of the Rock, in that nine-year period I have no doubt that they could have dug vertical shafts down to the bedrock and then tunnelled sideways to reach the area under the so-called Lost Temple. After all, that was pretty much exactly what Charles Warren did in his excavations. He couldn't get permission to dig on the Mount itself, so he began excavating near it, and when he'd dug down a reasonable distance he told his men to change direction and tunnel horizontally. He managed to get inside the chambers and produce a fairly detailed map of what lay underneath the platform on which the two Islamic shrines now stand.'

'What do you think they were looking for? The Templars, I mean,' Angela asked.

Bronson smiled in the darkness and squeezed her hand.

'That depends entirely upon which particular legend or conspiracy theory you subscribe to,' he replied.

'The suggestions I've read about include the Ark of the Covenant, obviously, because that's the biggie, and it features in just about every story that's even vaguely connected to Jerusalem. Other contenders include the Jewish Menorah, and the True Cross, or at least bits of it, the body of Jesus Christ, and a whole raft of other not particularly believable relics from the earliest days of civilization.

'Obviously these days there's no way of telling what the Templars were digging for, or even if they were digging at all, but they must have been doing something. Those original nine knights arrived in Jerusalem ostensibly to provide protection for pilgrims on the dangerous roads around the city. That was their remit, if you like. But there's no evidence at all that they actually did this, or at least, not as you might have expected. Logically, a force of only nine men, even nine heavily armed and mounted knights, couldn't do much more than provide a token force on the roads. If that really was their objective, you would have expected them to immediately begin recruiting more knights to join them in their mission.

'But they didn't do that. As far as we can tell, they occupied the Al Aqsa Mosque for nine years and apparently did nothing about their principal task. So the idea that they were digging under the building does make a kind of logical sense. And, using the same argument, the suggestion that they then found whatever they were looking for after nine years also has merit, because then everything changed. The order started its recruitment drive, it was recognized suspiciously quickly by the Pope, and immediately began to expand. That could mean that the Templars had found something that gave them considerable religious power, something that could either have impressed the Vatican or – perhaps more likely – have frightened the Pope into recognizing the order so quickly.

'If they had discovered the Ark of the Covenant, to pick the most popular but perhaps the least likely relic, I think the Pope would have run scared. If the Ark really did function as it was supposed to do – basically, to act as a machine for talking to God – then that would have been pretty definitive proof that the Jews were the chosen people, because God would be communicating with the Jews through the Ark and not using it to discuss anything with the leader of the Roman Catholic Church. I think if the Templars had told the Vatican that they'd found the relic and made the implications clear, the Pope would probably have been forced to do more or less whatever they wanted him to. But of course, all of this really is just speculation.'

'But what do you think personally?' Angela asked, sounding sleepy.

Bronson gave a short laugh.

'Me? I have no idea.'

What seemed only minutes later, Bronson's alarm sounded and they both climbed somewhat wearily out of bed.

Breakfast was a kind of buffet affair, and Bronson

made a second visit to the main table, returning with another collection of pastries. Angela looked askance at his choice of food.

'What?' he demanded.

'Full of sugar and empty calories,' she said, pointing.

'I know, but I'm hungry. They're not even particularly nice pastries, but at least the coffee's good.'

Angela watched him take a bite out of the local equivalent of a Danish pastry, then took another sip of her own drink.

'We didn't get to it last night, because I fell asleep,' she said, 'but you said no one had found anything in that place, and you gave the impression that that was a good thing, which I don't understand.'

Bronson glanced round the dining room, and although he didn't think anybody was close enough to overhear their conversation, he was still going to be circumspect in what he said.

'I didn't mean that it was good I couldn't find anything, but it occurred to me while I was down there that it also wasn't entirely bad,' he replied. 'I told you last night that when I was reasonably sure the other two men had gone, I went into the area that they'd opened up and had a very quick look around, maybe only for thirty seconds or perhaps a minute.'

'Not what you might call a comprehensive or exhaustive search, then.'

'No, but I think it was informative. I looked at the inner walls and went across to some of the other structures in there. The one thing I noticed immediately was that, unlike the stones in the Western Wall Tunnel, there were no marks on any of the stones, apart from those that had very obviously been made by masons. No graffiti, no names, no messages. And that makes sense, bearing in mind what you told me about the way Herod had constructed the Temple Mount. It would all have been a new build, probably done fairly quickly, and once the platform had been erected over the top of the bedrock, most of the chambers would have been effectively sealed.'

'But doesn't that kind of give the lie to the idea of the Knights Templars digging there and finding something in one of those chambers?' Angela pointed out.

Bronson shook his head.

'Not necessarily, because if Herod, or more likely the Jewish priesthood, wanted to keep some object or objects safe and securely hidden for all time, concealing them in a chamber that would effectively become part of the foundations of the new Jewish Temple might have seemed like a very good idea. As you've already told me, that was a turbulent time in the history of the city, and perhaps they were worried that some new invader might appear and that would result in the temple being sacked, as it had been in the past. Maybe they looked at their treasures and decided to keep them as close as possible to the new temple, buried in the mount directly beneath it, where their spiritual influence or whatever you want to call it would hopefully be felt by the worshippers, but at the same time they would be completely safe, even if the temple itself were to be totally destroyed. Which is, of course, exactly what happened a few decades later.'

Angela looked at him.

'Now that,' she began, 'is a very interesting idea. Not a new idea, but definitely interesting. It's been claimed, but of course we can't definitively prove it, that the Ark was hidden in a special chamber located deep underneath the temple before Nebuchadnezzar and his Babylonian forces swept through the city back in about 600 BC. Herod's construction of the Temple Mount came much later, of course, but I don't see any reason why they couldn't have made a similar arrangement. The Ark of the Covenant, their most precious relic, could well have been hidden in that way, which could explain why the Arch of Titus in Rome has a very clear carved image on it of the Jewish Menorah, an important part of the spoils of war from the Judaean campaign, but no image at all that could possibly be the Ark itself.'

Bronson inclined his head in an ironic bow.

'It *is* only an idea,' he emphasized, 'a simplistic deduction based on what little I know of this area, and I can't offer you a shred of evidence in support of it.'

'However,' Angela went on, 'if that hypothesis is correct, I don't quite know how it helps us. Your idea, basically, is that the Jewish priests could have hidden treasures within the Temple Mount, and over a millennium later the Knights Templar could have tunnelled inside and dug them up and then, presumably, secreted them somewhere else, possibly to indulge in a little creative blackmail of the Pope, depending on exactly what they'd found. So these two separate events – hiding the treasure or relics or whatever and the Templars discovering them – would have taken place in the first and twelfth centuries respectively. But the Latin translation of the inscription seems to me to refer to the Temple Mount, and the author seems fairly clear that this key – this word or whatever that we need to translate the second half of the text – is inscribed on stone in one of the subterranean chambers. So if the chambers were sealed when Herod built the platform on the Temple Mount, Mount Moriah, how did somebody get inside the structure during – and I'm guessing here – the mediaeval period?'

'It wouldn't have been that difficult,' Bronson said. 'Although the Temple Mount is basically closed and off-limits to everybody today, that wasn't always the case. There's a large vaulted cavern on the south-east side of the Mount that's usually referred to as King Solomon's Stables, though Solomon had nothing to do with it and the chamber was actually built by Herod when he enclosed Mount Moriah. We're almost certain that the Templars used it as stabling for their horses, so obviously access to it was open in that period, which is kind of early mediaeval, I suppose. There are also about half a dozen cisterns within the Temple Mount that were obviously used for water collection, but more importantly there are several gates, all now bricked up but which were open in antiquity. Most of these led into the Mount itself and terminated in sets of steps that gave access to the platform where the two mosques now stand.

Basically, most of these gates and the tunnels and steps inside the Mount simply served as shortcuts for people from Jerusalem who wanted to climb up to the temple to worship.'

'So actually,' Angela said, 'although the chambers in the centre of the Mount were sealed, there were plenty of passageways where our unknown author could have inscribed the key.'

'Exactly. And that's why we need to take another look – a careful look – at the Latin translation.'

44

Jerusalem

Salim's death had been something of a shock to the other members of the group. But they were freedom fighters, battling for Islam and any paymaster who saw fit to use their services, and in that line of work deaths were inevitable. In fact, they all believed – and hoped – that they would die with a weapon in their hands.

Even so, none of them had ever expected to meet their fate in a dark tunnel deep underground, a tunnel under the control of the Jews, and especially not at the hands of an infidel who was actually unarmed. That seemed to all of them to be a shameful death, dishonourable in almost every way, and the best way to avenge their companion was to find the man who had killed him as quickly as possible, and then ensure that his death would take a long time to come.

So when Farooq issued his new orders, there had been no dissenting voices, and a few minutes after dawn the group split up to begin surveillance on the hotels near the Temple Mount. Khaled had been unable to find a decent photograph of Bronson, but he had obtained several good-quality pictures of his former wife. And in a country where almost every woman had brown skin and black hair, Angela Lewis, blonde and with a fair complexion, unmistakably Western European, should stand out.

'If you see her, either by herself or with the man Bronson,' Farooq instructed, 'do not attempt to kill them immediately. Even after we have disposed of these two we will still have things to do here in Jerusalem, and we must not get involved in a firefight on the streets of the Old City. So if you spot them, do two things. First, follow them and do not lose sight of them, otherwise you will answer to me. Second, call me with the exact location, so that I can begin directing your comrades into appropriate positions. There will be a small bonus for the man who locates them.' Farooq paused and smiled at the group. 'This will not necessarily be in the form of money. The woman has to die as well as the man, but her death need not be immediate.'

A couple of minutes later, the five-man group, plus Farooq, slipped out of the café they had selected for their early-morning meeting, each man clutching a street map of the city, a colour photograph of Angela Lewis and a sheet of paper on which Farooq had written the names and addresses of the hotels that they were to check individually, and the streets they were to patrol.

As he stepped out of the building, Farooq glanced up

at the sky. It was a powdery blue, and the first rays of the morning sun were spearing over the buildings and craggy terrain that lay over to the east. It was going to be hot, there was no doubt about that, and already he could smell the streets, that strange mixture of ancient dust and humanity crowded together in one spot, a scent that seemed unique to Jerusalem.

If Khaled solved the problem of the key, and he and his men were able to find and take care of Bronson and Lewis, then they could be heading out of Jerusalem that very same day.

45

Farooq's plan was a good one, but it did rather rely on their quarry making themselves visible, which is what both he and Khaled had expected. Because the spaces under the Temple Mount had not yielded the results they had anticipated, they had assumed that Bronson and Lewis would be back out on the streets, still searching for the key, perhaps at the Wailing Wall or somewhere nearby. Khaled assumed that the English couple must have broken the code and read the first part of the inscription, just as he had done, otherwise they would not be in Jerusalem at all.

What he hadn't anticipated, though, was that Bronson and Angela were one step ahead of him in terms of the trail they were following.

After their breakfast, Angela and Bronson had returned to their room just minutes before Mahmoud, smartly dressed in a dark suit, had walked into the hotel as if he was just another guest, or perhaps a businessman meeting a guest, and had looked at the handful of occupants of all the public rooms. Just as in the previous establishments he'd visited, he had hoped to find a fellow Muslim with whom he could have struck up a conversation and discreetly enquired about the whereabouts of his 'young female English friend'. Farooq had suggested this approach as being less likely to arouse suspicion than a direct approach to a concierge or receptionist. After all, it was just a short step between simple suspicion and contacting the police, especially in a city as laced and riven with racial tension as Jerusalem. And they definitely needed to keep the police out of their business.

But in that hotel dining room, Mahmoud could see that that gambit wasn't going to work. The clientele appeared to be almost exclusively tourists, and European tourists at that.

Mahmoud walked out of the hotel entrance about five minutes after he'd walked in, took a pen from his pocket and made a neat tick beside the hotel name and followed it with a question mark. He glanced back at the building, then made a note on his sheet of paper to ensure that he would visit it again later that morning. So far, he had three hotels in total marked down as possibilities for similar reasons.

Then he opened the tourist map he'd been given by Farooq and on which all of 'his' hotels and streets had been marked, and strode briskly along the pavement towards the next one.

46

Jerusalem

'So what bit of the Latin do you think we got wrong, bearing in mind that these other people have obviously done exactly the same decryption and translation, and you met them right under the Temple Mount, precisely where you were going to search? We all came to the same conclusion, so is it really very likely that we all got it wrong?'

Angela didn't sound at all convinced that Bronson was on the right track.

'It's not so much that we got it wrong,' he replied, 'more that we didn't look at the complete sentence and fully understand what it's actually saying.'

He took the piece of paper that Angela had used to translate the decrypted Latin, and pointed at one particular section of it.

'Here,' he said, 'we decided this meant something like "in the hall under the lost temple where the treasure was concealed the key shall remain for ever". In other words, we assumed that the key was actually in the same place that the hoard or the treasure or whatever it is had been hidden, but when you translated the full sentence, the first few words give it a slightly different slant. Now it reads more like "within the walls around the hall", and that means—'

'I see what you're driving at,' Angela interrupted. 'It doesn't say that the key is in the hall itself but on the walls outside it. But I'm still not sure how that helps us. Surely the walls that it's referring to must be the supporting walls built by Herod around Mount Moriah, the supporting walls for the Temple Mount? And, more significantly, the walls that you looked at for about half a minute or maybe just a little longer and decided were unmarked.'

Bronson nodded.

'You could be right,' he agreed equably, 'and if you are, that's pretty much the end of this search. But usually, where you get one piece of graffiti, even mediaeval graffiti, you get lots, and I saw nothing at all on those stones. But there are lots of marks inside the Western Wall Tunnel, and that would also very obviously be one of the walls that surrounded the inner hall, which means it could fit the description. So maybe that's where the key is actually carved, and we simply missed it when we did the tour. Because of what happened last night, the facility is obviously going to remain closed for a day or two at least so we can't look there again. But I'm hoping that shouldn't matter, because both of us took dozens of photographs of anything that looked even vaguely hopeful. What I mean is that we might already have an image of the clue we're looking for.'

Angela groaned.

'I've only looked at those pictures once but I'm fed up to the back teeth with them already.'

'I know,' Bronson said, with a slight smile, 'but just look on the bright side.'

'There's a bright side?'

'Kind of. This really has to be it. If we don't find anything in those photographs then we give up, get out of here, go home and hope we can keep one step ahead of the bad guys.'

'That doesn't really sound like too much of an option. Or much of a bright side.'

'I'm sorry, but it's the only one I've got,' Bronson said, opening his own netbook and navigating to the pictures folder that he'd used to store the digital photographs that he'd taken.

Angela somewhat reluctantly opened up her laptop to do the same.

'Bearing in mind we've gone through all these once already, what are we looking for this time that's different?' she asked.

'There were certain characteristics in the original inscription,' Bronson replied, 'like the font, if you like, the way the letters themselves were shaped and carved. And that horizontal line of crosses that divided the bit that we could decipher at the top from the bit we couldn't at the bottom. Whoever carved that first inscription must have known about the key, obviously, and there would have been no point in carving the first inscription unless it was intended that the second one, the key, could be found. My guess is he might have included some kind of recognition symbol, maybe like those crosses, or perhaps just the shape and character of the letters themselves, so look at anything that seems even vaguely familiar.'

It took them most of the rest of the morning, but eventually Angela thought she'd found what they were looking for. It wasn't a line of crosses, or even a marked similarity in the style of carving, but it was something she thought she recognized.

'This must be it,' she said, and Bronson immediately stood up and walked over to look at the screen.

'What?' he asked. 'What can you see?'

She traced a more or less vertical oval outline with her finger in the centre of the screen, and suddenly Bronson saw it too.

'The bearded man,' he said. 'Just like the image carved above the altar in your underground temple.'

Angela smiled at him.

'The flash caught it just right,' she said. 'And this shot shows what's been carved below it. The trouble is, I don't really see how it helps us.'

She clicked the left-hand button below the mouse-pad and a different picture replaced it on the screen.

They both stared at it in silence. The carved image of the bearded man had been reproduced almost exactly, although obviously on a much smaller scale. In a horizontal line underneath the image were eight letters, carved into two groups of three and five and separated by a distinct space:

FEI   YBYBY

'Well, that's made everything as clear as mud,' Bronson said. 'What the hell does that mean?'

'What we need,' Angela murmured reflectively, 'assuming that the second part of the inscription was also enciphered using Atbash with the addition of extra words, like the first part, *is* those words. Tacking these collections of letters on to the beginning and end of the alphabet simply wouldn't be enough, not least because it's actually only five new letters. If that were the case, we'd have cracked the decryption using frequency analysis. The only way this could possibly be the key is if both those collections of letters are abbreviations for much longer expressions that would add the right level of complication. And that does kind of make me wonder,' she added.

'Wonder what?' Bronson asked.

'Just give me a minute.' Angela began rooting around among the sheets of paper they'd used when deciphering the first part of the inscription. 'I think it might be instructive to do some reverse engineering.'

'And that means what?'

'If we can find out what words must have been added to the standard alphabet to add the level of complication that we encountered on that first cipher, then maybe that will give us a clue to identify the expressions these letters are meant to represent.'

It didn't take all that long, despite the amount of trial and error involved, and within fifteen minutes Angela wrote two words down on a fresh piece of paper and handed it to Bronson. He looked at it blankly.

YOHANAN MAMDANA

'Now I think we really are getting somewhere,' Angela said, a smile of anticipation on her face.

'You may be getting somewhere, Angela,' Bronson said, 'but you've left me behind choking in the dust. This means nothing to me at all.'

She stood up and stretched, turning her back to the window, the sun pouring through it turning her hair into a halo of gold.

'Then it's just as well that it does to me,' she said.

47

Jerusalem

Mahmoud was taking a break, sipping a coffee at a café a few yards down the street from one of the hotels he had put on to his 'possibles' list, and wondering if he should risk walking through the public rooms in the building again. He had already done it twice before that morning, once during breakfast service and the second time in the middle of the morning when he'd expected coffee to be served. On both occasions he'd seen nobody who resembled his quarry, but the receptionist had stared at him rather longer than made him feel comfortable as he left the second time.

The good news was that he probably didn't need to go in again, because it looked as if many, perhaps even most, of the guests, were heading out, presumably to explore the Old City. But although he never took his eyes off the hotel entrance, he saw nobody who resembled either Bronson or Lewis in the chattering throng.

He was about to try his luck somewhere else when a sudden movement caught his eye. A female figure moved across one of the windows on the upper floor, stood for a few seconds with her back to the glass, and then turned. And in that instant Mahmoud realized that he had found them. He was too far away for her to be aware of his surveillance, and he continued watching her through the glass for a few more seconds, until she moved out of view.

He exhaled deeply, unaware that he'd been holding his breath, then reached inside his jacket pocket and took out his mobile phone.

48

Jerusalem

'So what is "Yohanan Mamdana"?' Bronson asked.
'Some lost city out here in the Holy Land?' he suggested.
'If it is, I've never heard of it.'

Angela shook her head. 'No, it's not a place. It's a person.'

'Well, I've never heard of him. Or her.'

'Actually,' Angela said, 'I can guarantee that you not only have heard of him – because Yohanan Mamdana was a man – but you also know a little bit about his life, and exactly how he died. The manner of his death, in fact, is perhaps better known than much about his life. Any ideas?' she asked.

'Not a glimmer so far.'

'Right. Of course, like all the names from this period that have survived in stories and legends, the spellings have changed, often quite significantly. In this case, "Yohanan" has come down to us as "John", and he was beheaded by—'

'The Baptist,' Bronson interrupted. 'You mean John the Baptist. Herod and Salome and the silver platter.'

'Spot on. Yohanan Mamdana was the original name, or at least the Syriac name, of the man we know as John the Baptist.'

'Syriac? You mean from the Syrian language?'

'No. It was an Aramaic dialect spoken across much of the Middle East.'

'Fine. But what I have no clue about,' Bronson said, 'is why his name should form part of an Atbash cipher used to encrypt an inscription in a temple buried in the deserts of southern Iraq. And, come to that, I've no idea why any of that should have anything to do with the Temple Mount and the Knights Templar.'

'Yes,' Angela replied, 'that bit is pretty obscure, I'll grant you that. But as for the buried temple and the inscription, that does make a kind of sense. You remember when we were talking about it on the way from Kuwait City to the dig, and then when you saw it for yourself. My view was that it was almost certainly a Mandaean temple, because of where it was, that shallow indentation in the floor that could have been intended for baptisms, and even the image of the bearded man. The point that we probably didn't make all that clear to you at the time was that both the ancient Mandaeans and the followers of that religion today all worshipped exactly the same person. And that person wasn't – and isn't – Jesus Christ, but John the Baptist.'

Bronson looked puzzled.

'So was John the Baptist supposed to be another son

295

of God, or someone equally important and unlikely?' he asked.

'Not as far as I know,' Angela replied. 'I think it's generally accepted that he was a prophet of a sort, but in the Christian Bible and the Catholic Church he was seen as very much a bit-part player, somebody who was important for what he did, rather than for who he was. And that, for the Mandaeans, was the problem and the conundrum, because of the obvious logical inconsistency of the biblical tale. If Jesus Christ genuinely was the son of God, then obviously He had to be the most significant and important figure in religious history. But in the view of the Mandaeans, that simply could not be the case, because He was baptized by John the Baptist. No mere mortal could possibly be allowed to anoint the son of God, so very obviously the man who baptized Jesus had to be even more important than Him to be able to carry out that act.

'And the implication, at least as far as the Mandaeans were concerned, was that the Bible and the Church and Christianity as a whole had got everything backwards. Jesus Christ had only been a prophet, one of a long line of such men in those days, and John the Baptist was the individual who deserved to be worshipped. Christ, in fact, was seen as a liar and usurper, a man who had donned the mantle of the son of God without being in any way deserving of the title. As far as the early Church was concerned, of course, this was the wildest and most unforgivable heresy of the lot, because the Mandaeans weren't just guilty of worshipping in the wrong way, like a lot of heretics, but they were worshipping the wrong person and refusing to accept the divinity of Jesus.'

'It's no wonder that temple was buried,' Bronson pointed out. 'The Church had long arms in that period, and could probably have reached out all the way to Iraq – or mediaeval Babylon at that time – to try to stamp out that heresy. Worshipping in secret in a temple that could be completely hidden from view might have been the safest option they had.'

'We thought it might just have been a case of excavating it from the rock underground because it would be permanent and, more importantly, relatively cool, but you could well be right. Anyway, the important thing is that I think we now know how to decipher the rest of the inscription.'

'We do?' Bronson sounded surprised. 'Show me.'

Angela took a fresh sheet of paper and wrote down the two sequences of letters that had been carved into one of the stones in the Western Wall Tunnel.

F E I Y B Y B Y

'If this is meant to be a decode for a kind of extended Atbash,' she said, 'then logically one word group should be written out before the alphabet and the second word group after it.'

'But we still don't know what those word groups are,' Bronson objected.

'Oh, I think we do, now that we've made the connection with John the Baptist. As I said to you before, the names of the characters involved in these events at the start of the first millennium have changed over the centuries, been altered with different spellings and in some cases been changed beyond all recognition. And that applies in particular to the person that we now refer to as Jesus Christ. He was never known as Jesus. In fact, that name is essentially a British invention. His original Hebrew name was believed to be "Yehoshua", which later became "Yeshua" or "Joshua". Later, the name "Yehoshua" was translated from the Hebrew into Greek and then into Latin, where it was rendered as "Iesvs" or "Iesous", and that variant was then changed to "Jesus" in English.

'And the "Christ" is another later addition. According to the Bible, Jesus was believed by some of the people he encountered to have been the Messiah, and that word in Hebrew means "the anointed one". That fact was recognized by the early translators who were rendering the Bible in Greek, and the oil used for that kind of anointing was called *khrisma* in Greek and a person who had been anointed was known as a *khristos*. When the text was then translated from Greek into Latin, the *khristos* was changed into *christus* and, predictably enough, during the translation into English that became "Christ", but it was never a part of Jesus's name when he was alive.'

'Assuming that such a person lived at all,' Bronson interjected.

Angela shook her head.

'Another time, another story,' she said shortly. 'In those very early days, people didn't actually have a second or family name. Instead, Jesus would have been known as "Yeshua bar Yahosef bar Yaqub", or "Joshua, son of Joseph, son of Jacob".' She paused for a moment and pointed at the paper, and at the second group of letters. '"Y B Y B Y",' she said. 'There doesn't seem to me to be any doubt that that refers to "Yeshua bar Yahosef bar Yaqub", the man the Mandaeans saw as the usurper, and if we were in any doubt at all, then the letters "F E I" would seem to confirm it.'

'*Furis et interceptoris*,' Bronson said, remembering their earlier conversation and nodding. '"Thief and usurper". Let's hope that really is it.'

He took another piece of paper, wrote out the three Latin words, then the reversed alphabet, and then Yeshua bar Yahosef bar Yaqub, all without spaces. Then he wrote out the plaintext alphabet below it, repeating it until he had matched each ciphertext letter with its plaintext equivalent. The entire ciphertext string amounted almost to three complete alphabets.

'I've reversed the alphabet this time,' he said, 'but we can always try it the other way round, and I suppose reverse the added bits as well. Ring the changes, as it were. Let's see how it goes.'

As Angela read out the encrypted letters from the temple inscription, Bronson carefully checked the possible plaintext equivalents and wrote each of them down, bracketing each group as he did so.

And slowly, with much trial and frequent error, a kind of message began to emerge from the jumble of letters.

49

Jerusalem

'Where are they?' Farooq demanded, sitting down at the café table next to Mahmoud, who now had a fresh cup of coffee in front of him, a necessary purchase to allow him to retain his seat. 'Don't point,' he added. 'Just tell me.'

'The hotel on the corner to our left. First floor, second window from the right. I saw her for maybe ten seconds.'

'And you're certain it's her?'

Mahmoud nodded. 'I'm quite sure. The photograph you supplied was very clear. It's definitely her.'

'What about the man? Have you seen him?'

'No. I've only seen her, and only for that short period.'

'No other shadows or shapes on the window?' Farooq persisted. 'Nothing that could mean the man Bronson, or anyone else, was in there with her?'

Mahmoud was silent, mentally reliving that brief few seconds when he'd seen their quarry. Then he smiled as realization dawned, and he nodded again.

'I've just thought . . .' he said. 'I was concentrating on making sure it really was her, but there must have been someone else in the room because she was talking. Or at least, her mouth was opening and closing.'

'You've done well, my friend,' Farooq said, and reached across to squeeze Mahmoud's shoulder. Then he took his own mobile from his pocket, dialled a number and held a very brief conversation with Khaled. That completed, he switched to messaging, composed a short text and sent it simultaneously to the mobiles held by the remainder of his men. Then he leaned back in his seat, ordered a coffee from a waiter who'd been waiting expectantly a few feet away and glanced across at Mahmoud.

'The others are on their way,' he said, 'and Khaled will be coming as well. He wants to be here.'

'So now we just wait?'

'We wait,' Farooq confirmed. 'And we watch. If they leave the hotel, we'll follow them to make absolutely sure that they don't manage to slip away.'

'Where are we going to do it? We could take them in the hotel easily enough.'

'We could, and then we'd be shot down like dogs in the street by the Israeli police or the soldiers who would be here within minutes. Like you, my friend, I have no fear of death, but I do want my dying to mean something, something a lot more than that. And don't forget that the man Bronson almost certainly has Salim's pistol. Trying to kill them in the hotel would be too noisy and uncertain. We must wait until they leave and then pick our moment. We'll find somewhere much quieter, a place where they would least expect it.'

Mahmoud nodded, clearly seeing the logic of what his leader was telling him. But then another thought struck him.

'What about Khaled?' he asked. 'He will probably want the job done as quickly as possible. Do you think he will be prepared to wait, as you suggest?'

'Khaled is an administrator, not a man of action. In military matters, or tasks of this sort, I have no doubt he will defer to me.'

50

Jerusalem

Almost two hours after they'd started, Angela finally put down the piece of paper she'd been working on. The writing on it followed a series of wandering lines, the text marked by numerous crossings-out but it did, finally, make some kind of sense.

'Is that it?' Bronson asked.

'Pretty much, yes,' Angela replied. 'There are still one or two words that are a bit ambiguous in translation, but I think it's more or less right. There's no point in reading out the first section of the text, because it's nothing more than a condemnation of the actions of Yeshua bar Yahosef bar Yaqub, Jesus Christ, the usurper. There was obviously no love lost there. It's the next bit that's interesting. Confusing, but interesting.'

'So confuse and interest me at the same time,' Bronson said. 'I'm all ears.'

'Right. The next section makes a reference to the

"brotherhood". That's not an exact translation, but it's as close as I can get. I have the feeling that the Latin word probably had a slightly different meaning at that time, and might well have been rather more specific. But in my opinion the precise meaning is made clear in the very next section, because it states that the members of the brotherhood wear the "splayed cross", and you know as well as I do what that's likely to refer to.'

'The best-known symbol of the Knights Templar,' Bronson replied. 'The *croix pattée*. They wore it from 1147 right up until the day that the order was purged and dissolved.'

'Exactly. So what we have here is an explicit reference to the Knights Templar, and he then goes on to describe the movement of an object, or perhaps more likely a number of objects. I'll come back to that later, because there's another reference that I don't quite understand. But the route or path that these objects followed is perfectly clear, as long as we can identify the various waypoints. The places where the hoard spent various periods of time.'

She glanced at Bronson to make sure that he was still following, which he was.

'There's no information about where the hoard originated, only its movement once it began its travels, I suppose you could say. And that trail leads from "the castle that fell" to "the fortress above the waves". Hopefully, with your knowledge of Templar activities in the Holy Land, you'll be able to identify those two locations, though I'm not sure that it matters too much even if you can't, because I already know where the third place was on the route.'

'Those two are pretty easy,' Bronson replied. 'There were a number of castles and fortifications that were captured by the enemy at various times during the Crusades and the period when the Knights Templar were operating in this area. But putting those two references together almost certainly means that the first castle referred to was the one at Acre. And we know that because pretty much the night before that castle fell to the Mamluks, the treasurer of the order was instructed by the Marshall, a man named Pierre de Sevry, to take the Templar treasure and as many non-combatants as he could fit into his ship, and make his escape north up the coast to Sidon.

'And the point about that, I suppose, is that the fortification at Sidon was known as the "Sea Castle", because it occupied almost the entire land area of a small island just off the mainland and was linked to it by a narrow causeway. If you were going to describe that castle in just a few words, calling it the "fortress above the waves" would be about as accurate a description as you could hope for. So the hoard – and from what I know of Templar history that almost certainly means the order's treasure in Outremer, the land beyond the sea – went from Acre to Sidon. And we even know where it went next, because the Templar Treasurer, a man named Tibauld de Gaudin, got back on his ship a short time after he'd arrived at Sidon, and set sail for Cyprus, intending to raise reinforcements.

'Acre was already lost. De Gaudin would have known that because the Mamluk army that was encircling the city was so huge that even if he had managed to summon ten thousand knights, not even that number would have been enough to make a difference. The next logical target for the Mamluks would probably have been Sidon. Because it was essentially an island fortress approachable only along a narrow causeway, and which might have been able to withstand a prolonged siege, perhaps it was de Gaudin's intention to make a stand there. Maybe he thought that if he could reinforce the garrison at Sidon, the Templars could keep a toehold in the Holy Land and eventually regroup and retake Jerusalem. But that never happened and he was never able to produce any reinforcements at all. Not that long afterwards the Sidon Sea Castle was attacked by the Mamluk army and fell quite quickly because the defenders were hopelessly outnumbered, and that pretty much marked the end of the crusades and the Templar presence there. There were some abortive attempts to re-establish the order at a place called Ruad, but they never came to anything much.'

Angela nodded and traced the remainder of the line on the piece of paper with the tip of her finger.

'This doesn't use the proper name Cyprus, or any proper name, in fact, but it does refer to the hoard being transferred to "the island of copper", and in antiquity Cyprus was famous as a good source of copper, so that seems fairly clear. The historical record that you know about and this translation are in accord with each other, at least so far. What are you smiling about?' she added.

'I was just thinking that on this occasion we might be on the trail of something big, something worthwhile. The Templar treasure of Outremer was never found, was it? Certainly there was no suggestion that it was left in the cellars of the castle at Acre, and de Gaudin's voyage to the Sidon Sea Castle and on to Cyprus is well documented. He was the Treasurer of the order and the obvious man to be entrusted with the wealth of the Templars, and although most experts believe the treasure was carried off to Cyprus, it then simply vanishes from the historical record. This translation of that obscure inscription, as far as I know, is the only documented reference that might possibly show where it ended up.'

'So what was this hoard?' Angela asked. 'Gold bullion or something?'

'It would have been a mixture of a lot of different stuff – most likely gold and silver as bullion or coinage, as well as jewellery of various types. Most of it would have been owned by the Templars, but there would also have been valuables deposited by other people, either for safe keeping or as collateral. The order basically conceived the banking system that we still use today, so a businessman could deposit funds in, say, the Paris Preceptory, receive a coded letter of credit in exchange and take that to the Templar castle at Acre or wherever and withdraw the same funds less a handling charge, so he could travel perfectly safely on his journey, knowing that he could never be robbed. In fact, really, the Templar assets were less a treasure in the conventional sense than simply their working capital. And the other things they would have held were lots of land deeds, because many of their assets were immovable property – castles, houses, farms and estates scattered throughout Europe.'

Angela nodded and turned her attention back to the sheet of paper in front of her.

'Right,' she said, 'the next bit is slightly ambiguous. In fact, I can read what it says but I'm not sure that I know what it means. This next phrase translates as "there was safety in separation", which perhaps suggests that the treasure was divided into two or more smaller units. But I'm not actually sure that that's what it means, because there's another reference here to the "truth", just like there was in the first part of the inscription, and the way it's written could mean that the treasure went one way and this "truth", whatever it is, went somewhere different.'

She paused for a moment and reread the translation of the decrypted text.

'I don't know if I'm reading more into this than is actually there, but the emphasis seems to be that the hoard – presumably the assets of the Knights Templar order in the Holy Land, as you said – is of less importance to the writer, and to the Templars, than the "truth". The text is describing the route the two separate things took from the castle at Acre, but the object the Templars really wanted to save was this "truth", and the treasure was almost of secondary importance, just along for the ride, as it were.'

'So does it say where either object ended up?'

'Yes, but only in the vaguest terms. In fact, although that earlier section describes the separation, the following sentence states that they both ended up in the same place, in "the land from whence came the nine", which I presume means France, as that's where the first Knights Templar originated from. But the text doesn't say where the objects finished up in France, and that's a very big country. It also doesn't state that both the treasure and the truth ended up in the same place in France, and because of that phrase about "separation" I suppose you could reasonably assume that they were taken to different destinations.'

'So that's it,' Bronson said, sounding bitter. 'After all this, all that inscription is actually saying is what we could have probably guessed anyway, that the Templar treasure was sent from Acre to Sidon and then on to Cyprus, and from there it was taken to France when the position of the order in the Holy Land finally became completely untenable. Jacques de Molay, the last Grand Master of the Templars, had accompanied Tibauld de Gaudin in his flight from Acre, and took over from him when the Treasurer died on the island. Most investigators have always assumed that, when de Molay returned to France with the remnants of the order, the treasure went with him, probably to the Paris Preceptory.'

Angela nodded, and Bronson noticed a slight smile playing over her lips.

'What?' he demanded. 'There's something else?'

'I said the text doesn't tell us where in France either

object ended up, but there is one other phrase that I do not understand but which seems to be suggested as able to supply the answer to at least a part of the puzzle.'

She picked up her pencil, turned over the sheet of paper and wrote out a new phrase on it, and then drew a circle around it.

Bronson stared at it for a moment.

Angela had written:

THE TRUTH OF THE TRUTH LIES
IN KRAK DE MONT REAL LXII DOWN

'I don't know about you,' Bronson said, irritation evident in his voice, 'but I'm getting a bit fed up with this. Every time we seem to get close to the answer, we get handed another riddle that doesn't make sense. Is that accurate? And what the hell does it mean?'

'It's as accurate as I can get it, and I have no idea. But I'm going to find out.'

'I presume that's the number sixty-two,' Bronson said, pointing at the 'LXII' notation.

'Yes. But I don't know its significance.'

Angela woke up her laptop, opened the web browser and began typing while Bronson continued staring at the cryptic clue.

'"Mont Real" is French, of course,' he said, after a few moments, 'or probably, anyway, but "Krak" isn't. I think it usually means a castle, like "Krak de Chevaliers".'

'You're right,' Angela replied. 'I don't know the root

of the word, but it does mean a castle. And now I do know where the writer was talking about.'

She turned the computer round so that Bronson could see the screen.

On it was the image of a more or less conical hilltop, similar terrain distantly visible behind it. But the hilltop was far from barren, being dominated by the impressive ruins of a castle, the grey-brown stone walls seeming almost to grow straight out of the bedrock.

'That,' Angela said, 'is Shobak Castle, and it's nowhere near France. It's in Jordan, not far from the old Nabatean city of Petra.'

'I've never heard of it,' Bronson said. 'And we were looking for a place called Krak de Mont Real.'

'That was its old name,' Angela replied. 'Krak de Mont Real or Krak de Montreal. It was never a Templar stronghold, according to this, but it was a Crusader castle. It was built in 1115 by King Baldwin I of Jerusalem, and it was the first of a whole bunch of fortifications he put up to guard the road between Damascus and Egypt. It withstood several sieges, but was finally conquered in 1189 and largely dismantled. When the Mamluks had finished driving the Templars out of the Holy Land in the fourteenth century, this was one of the places that they occupied and restored.'

Bronson nodded.

'That must raise a bit of a question mark,' he said. 'If what you've just found out is correct, then during the time of the Templars the castle must only have been a ruin. So if that were the case, why would whoever

311

authored that inscription have left anything in the building? And if they did, surely the Mamluks would have found whatever it was when they took over the place a century or so later?'

'Good points, but I have a feeling that neither the Mamluks nor anybody else would necessarily recognize the importance or even the meaning of what was in the castle. Let's face it, without having foreknowledge of the inscription from the temple in Iraq, neither of us would have even given that carving of the letters and the face of the bearded man that we found in the Western Wall Tunnel so much as a second glance. We would just have assumed it was a piece of well-carved graffiti. My guess is that whatever was left at Shobak Castle is the same kind of thing. A carving or something of the sort that would be completely meaningless to anyone who hadn't already deciphered the other clues. And at least this time the author of the inscription is pretty much telling us where to look. I'm sure that the number sixty-two will mean something when we get to the castle.'

'So you've made up your mind already?' Bronson asked.

'Not necessarily, but having come this far it seems to me to be stupid not to take that one last step. What do you think? What do you want to do?'

'I'll follow you, Angela, as I always do. Don't worry about that. But if we get absolutely nowhere at this castle, then maybe we should rethink what we do next, because I get the feeling we're being played with, sent from one place to another while we decipher and follow some pretty obscure clues. Really, this is worth doing only because we might have a one per cent chance of tracking down the lost treasure of the Templars, but the last bit that you deciphered suggests to me that maybe we're not following the trail of the treasure but the trail of the "truth", and I have a shrewd suspicion that that might not be an iron-bound box full of bullion but something completely different.'

'So do you want carry on? Yes?'

'Yes, at least for the moment.'

Bronson took his mobile phone out of his pocket.

'Tell me again where this Shobak Castle is,' he said.

Angela referred back to the webpage.

'It's in Jordan,' she confirmed, 'and it's roughly one hundred miles north-east of Aqaba, which is down on the coast, next to Eilat in Israel.'

Bronson found it on the mapping app and zoomed in so that he could see the individual roads.

'Is it way out in the bundu, or is there a town close by?'

'There's a reasonable-sized town called Wadi Musa, which is also on the way to Petra, and there's what looks like a village with the same name – Shobak – fairly close to the castle.'

'Got it,' Bronson said. 'In fact, in a straight line, it's only about a hundred miles from where we're sitting right now. We could drive it in two or three hours.'

Angela looked suddenly doubtful.

'I wonder how easy it is to get across the border into Jordan?' she mused.

'We'll tackle that when we have to,' Bronson said confidently. 'In the meantime, let's get everything packed and then we can see about hiring a car.'

'And you want to do this today?'

'The longer we spend in one place, the more chance there is of being tracked down, so I'm very happy to keep on the move. We probably won't get to Shobak today, but I'm sure we can find somewhere to stay in Jordan, maybe in Wadi Musa, and if we stick to doing everything with cash, we'll be a lot more difficult for anyone to find.'

Fifteen minutes later, they were ready to go. Bronson settled the bill in cash, and obtained the name and address of a car hire company that allowed its vehicles to be taken out of Israel.

Then they stepped out into the street and started walking.

51

Jerusalem

'They've just left the hotel on foot,' Farooq said quietly into his mobile phone.

Just over a hundred yards away, Khaled grunted an acknowledgement, and then stood up to stare down the street.

'Are they leaving? Have they checked out, I mean?' he asked.

'I think so,' Farooq replied. 'They've got bags with them.'

'Good. Tell your men to follow them until you can isolate them somewhere and finish the job.'

Khaled ended the call, tossed a few coins on to the café table to cover the cost of his drink, and then began heading down the street, towards the hotel Farooq and his men had had under surveillance. He didn't want to be seen, but at the same time he definitely wanted to be close enough to make sure the job was done properly.

His mobile rang again and he answered immediately. 'Yes?'

'I had expected them to take a taxi,' Farooq said quietly, 'and I already have one of my men in a cab and another on a motorcycle, but the two targets seem to be heading towards a car hire company.'

'What do you mean by that? Surely they are or they aren't?'

'What I mean is they've turned down a street and the only commercial establishments there, as far as we can see, are two car rental agencies. Do you want us to stop them now? There are about a dozen other people in the street.'

Khaled paused before replying, then shook his head, his action invisible to Farooq.

'No. That's too many witnesses. I want to get out of this alive. Just keep following them, and keep this line open.'

'And if they hire a car and drive away? What then?'

'You have one man in a taxi already. Whichever car hire company the two targets go to, send one of your men into the other one and tell him to rent another vehicle.'

Farooq cleared the line briefly to issue the appropriate orders, then called Khaled back. He was less than happy with the fluidity of the situation, and with having to adjust his plans so quickly and frequently. Now, if Khaled let the situation slide, Farooq knew that they could even end up in some kind of a car chase, and that had definitely never been a part of his plan. But Khaled was the man with the money, so he knew that the final decision rested with him.

Farooq lounged in a shadowed doorway on the opposite side of the road to the two car hire companies and simply watched.

The targets stepped into the car rental office and disappeared from view. Moments later, one of Farooq's men crossed the road from an alleyway and entered the office of the second company just a few doors down.

For what seemed like a very long fifteen minutes, nothing else happened. And then, from the premises of the second company, Farooq's man appeared behind the wheel of a small Ford saloon. Moments later, he pulled the car to a stop right beside where Farooq was standing and pushed open the passenger door.

'I'm now in the hire car,' Farooq reported over the open mobile connection. 'A white Ford Fiesta. There's no sign of the targets yet.' Then he ended the call as he saw Khaled approaching.

Just a few seconds later, the rear door of the Ford opened and the other man sat down on the seat, wiping the perspiration off his brow with a large purple handkerchief.

'The street's quieter now,' Farooq said, gesturing in both directions. 'We can probably take them as soon as they come out. Finish what we came to do.'

'No. We wait. We will follow them until we reach a quiet area where we can take our time with them.'

'I thought you just wanted them dead?' Farooq asked.

'I do. But I don't want to attract attention, and if you're right and Bronson still has the pistol, then we could easily find ourselves involved in a gunfight in the middle of the street. We need to let them get out of Jerusalem and then hit them somewhere where there are no witnesses at all. There are plenty of open stretches of road between here and the airport.'

'Here they come,' Farooq said, watching another vehicle – a white Renault – turn out of the yard beside the car hire company.

He and Khaled immediately ducked down so that they were below the level of the windows of the Ford. The driver, in response to a brief command from Farooq, took his mobile phone out of his pocket and pretended to be having a conversation on it as the Renault drove past. All three of them watched the vehicle as Bronson drove it down the road and made a right turn at the end.

'Keep well back and don't crowd him.'

As the driver accelerated gently to follow the Renault, Farooq used his mobile to call two numbers in quick succession and issued crisp orders.

'The taxi will act as the principal vehicle,' he said to Khaled, 'because the streets are full of cabs, with the motorcycle as the backup. We'll keep out of sight as much as possible, in case we have to take over unexpectedly.'

Farooq's mobile rang and he answered it immediately.

'Good,' he said after a few moments.

'What?' Khaled asked.

'Aziz is on the motorcycle. He'll monitor everything that happens and provide me with a running commentary. At the moment, the targets are heading north, probably intending to pick up one of the main roads to the north of the Old City. That's probably the fastest way to the airport.'

But just a few minutes later something unexpected happened. Farooq listened intently to what Aziz was saying, the purr of the motorcycle's engine a constant background noise behind his words.

'They've turned right, not left,' Farooq said. 'That will take them away from the airport, not towards it. Maybe they've just taken a wrong turning.'

Khaled nodded, but seemed somewhat distracted.

Farooq noticed the change of mood in his companion. 'What is it?' he asked.

For a moment Khaled didn't reply. Then he glanced at Farooq before looking back through the windscreen, just catching sight of the white Renault as it manoeuvred through the traffic perhaps eighty yards in front of them.

'Maybe they haven't taken a wrong turning,' Khaled said finally, a reflective tone to his voice. 'I've been puzzling over the fact that they've hired a car ever since I took your call. You and your men went into the Temple Mount and found absolutely nothing—'

'There was nothing to find,' Farooq retorted, bristling at the implied criticism. 'Mahmoud saw as much as I did, and I even took some photographs. There was nothing there. No carvings, no inscriptions. Not even any graffiti.'

'I'm not saying that there was, Farooq. I have no doubt that you had time to do a thorough search, and I'm quite satisfied that what we expected to find simply wasn't there. And Bronson couldn't have had more than a minute or two to carry out his own search. Realistically, I doubt very much if he would have spotted anything in that time that you hadn't seen.'

Farooq couldn't see where that particular argument was heading, so he didn't reply.

'So if you didn't find anything, and it seems fairly certain that Bronson couldn't have found anything, why is he driving along the road in front of us in a rental car?'

Khaled looked expectantly at Farooq.

'My point is that if Bronson and the woman had come away just as empty-handed as us, why didn't they climb into the back of a taxi and tell the driver to take them to Ben Gurion Airport? Why haven't they just given up?'

Farooq spread his hands in a gesture of helpless ignorance. 'I have no idea. Unless you really think that Bronson *did* see something that we missed, and that they are still following the trail?'

Khaled nodded.

'That would seem to make sense,' he replied. 'My best guess is that we were looking in the wrong place. Somehow, I think Bronson guessed where the right place was and found something: a clue that we don't have and that they're now following.'

'So killing them is a really bad idea?' Farooq suggested.

'No, killing them is a really *good* idea,' Khaled said, 'but only after we've found out where they're heading and why.'

52

Israel and Jordan

'Where are you planning on crossing the border into Jordan?' Angela asked, looking up from a map of Israel she had open on her lap and staring through the windscreen.

'The only obvious junction, as far as I can see, is near Jericho, so we might as well try that first. After all, we're just a couple of tourists, so there shouldn't be a problem. If we can't get across there for some reason, my Plan B is to head south and drive all the way down to Eilat, because I know there's a border post there, and we could cross into Aqaba. Then we'd basically have to do a U-turn and head north again, but this time on the Jordanian side of the border. It'd take us longer to do that, but it would work as an alternative.'

Angela nodded and looked back at the map, tracing the route with the tip of her finger and looking at the roads on the Jordanian side of the border, which were also marked on it.

'Well, I just hope we're right about all this, and there'll be something at Shobak Castle that makes sense. Have you got any idea at all what might be meant by that number sixty-two?'

Bronson shook his head.

'I was rather hoping that inspiration might strike us when we see the place.'

'From what I gathered when I looked on the Internet, there didn't seem to be a huge amount of the structure left. The original castle was about seven storeys high above the top of the hill, and I think that all that's left now are the foundations, then the lowest level, which is more or less intact, and some bits of the level above that.'

'Then we may have to do a bit of lateral thinking to identify the location, and just hope that whoever left the clue there inscribed it in a fairly permanent fashion on a bit of stone that's still in place. I'm assuming that we'll be looking for a carving or an inscription again, because that seems to be the one common feature about the trail that we're following.'

Angela nodded and laced her fingers together on her lap.

'And the other obvious question that we need to answer,' she said, 'is whether or not we're being followed.'

Bronson shrugged, but didn't take his eyes off the road.

'I don't know. I didn't see any sign of anyone behind us when we picked up the hire car. And for anybody to have followed us, they would have had to find out which hotel we were staying in, which we made as difficult as possible.'

He glanced briefly at Angela.

'So far I haven't spotted a tail. There was a taxi a couple of cars behind us for a while, travelling on exactly the same route as us, but he turned off a few minutes ago. The traffic is heavy, though, and there are just too many cars out there for me to keep track of all of them. It'll be a lot easier to see if anyone is following us once we get outside the built-up area.'

A few minutes later the traffic did begin to thin out as they drove along a twisting road that skirted the southern edges of a patch of woodland – according to the map Angela had in front of her, it was called the Hatsofim Forest – and then drove under the 417 dual carriageway to pick up the northbound lane. The road curved around to the north-east, past Mishor Adumim and Mitspe Yeriho, and then continued east as far as Beit HaArava. There, Bronson turned north on route 90, driving past the site of biblical Jericho, and a little under ten miles later turned east again towards the Jordanian border.

He stopped the car a short distance beyond the junction and pulled it off the road.

'We might be stopped and searched at the border,' he explained, 'so I just need to get the pistol out of sight.'

Bronson wasn't certain how thorough any search might be, and in the end opted for wrapping the weapon in a piece of cloth, tucking it under the carpet in the boot of the Renault, putting one of their bags on top of it and hoping for the best.

As it turned out, he needn't have bothered. Because they were leaving the country, the Israeli border guards were indifferent, and as soon as Bronson and Angela showed their British passports and confirmed that they were tourists on holiday, the Jordanians waved them on with a minimum of formalities.

There was still quite a lot of traffic on the road because in a few miles it linked up with one of the main routes leading to Amman, the Jordanian capital. Shortly before they reached a development called Al Khersee, Bronson turned right and then right again, following the signs towards the Dead Sea.

He was still trying to make sure that nobody was following them, but in practice this proved impossible. There was considerable traffic in both directions, making overtaking a risky business that few of the drivers appeared to want to try, with the result that Bronson and Angela's car was just one vehicle in a kind of loose convoy of cars and trucks heading south.

But as they approached the northern end of the Dead Sea, that situation changed when they joined a dual carriageway and the faster drivers were finally able to overtake the slower vehicles. Bronson didn't accelerate, because he thought there was more chance of spotting a vehicle following them if he kept his speed down, although that didn't really work either, because he could still see about a dozen vehicles in his mirrors.

And then they saw the brilliant blue waters of the

Dead Sea over to their right, the cobalt shade a stark contrast to the burnt brown of the desert and low hills that surrounded the landlocked lake, and Bronson involuntarily eased up even more on the accelerator pedal.

'Wow. That really is quite beautiful,' Angela said, staring through the windscreen. 'Beautiful, but implacably hostile to almost all forms of life, apart from a handful of microscopic bugs, which proves that life can and will exist just about anywhere.'

'It's the lowest water surface on Earth,' Bronson said, dredging some obsolete information from his memory banks, 'about fourteen hundred feet below sea level, if my memory serves me correctly, and nine times more salty than any ocean. I remember seeing pictures of people lying on the surface reading newspapers and books because it's so buoyant. Swimming in it, or trying to swim in it, must be a strange sensation – a bit like swimming in soup.'

The road swung gently to the right to follow the shoreline of the Dead Sea.

'According to this map,' Angela said, 'the road stays right beside it pretty much all the way down, and there's no point in us going cross-country until we're a few miles south of it.'

She looked again towards the shimmering waters.

'It's amazing how often the name of this body of poisonous and lifeless water crops up in archaeology,' she said. 'I mean, almost everybody must have heard of the Dead Sea Scrolls that were recovered from Khirbat

Qumrān, and the lake has a very close association with biblical history. Plus, of course, it's also believed to be the location of the cities of Sodom and Gomorrah. They were supposed to have been destroyed by a rain of brimstone and earthquakes, and the remains of both are thought to be at the bottom of the Dead Sea. If you believe that kind of thing, that is.'

The Dead Sea was clearly a popular attraction, because they passed a number of cars parked near the water's edge. Children and adults could be seen in the water itself, and in one or two places men were working in the shallows with shovels and large buckets. Bronson glanced across at them and pointed an interrogative finger.

'What are they doing?' he asked.

'They're probably collecting salt. There's such a high concentration in the water that you can just shovel it up in the shallows. They extract a lot of other stuff from it as well, things like potash, gypsum and bromine, so it's quite an important local resource.'

For about thirty miles the road stayed very close to the edge of the water. Then the body of water began to narrow and for roughly ten miles the road continued south through a harsh desert landscape before once again meeting the eastern shore of the Dead Sea, the part of it that consisted largely of potash solar evaporation pans, before the lake finally disappeared from view.

Without the illusory benefit of the blue waters to the west, the terrain appeared less forgiving and more hostile. The road ran straight for much of the time, but occasionally diverted around a large hill or other feature of the landscape. On either side of the road the ground was largely flat, even in the clefts and valleys that snaked between the craggy hills that bordered the highway.

'You need to look for a left turn,' said Angela. 'The place we have to head towards is called Al Tafile.'

Bronson drove past a settlement on the right and then another on the left called Al Maamura, and then saw the junction right in front of them. The volume of traffic had diminished significantly after they'd cleared the southern edge of the Dead Sea, and there were even fewer vehicles on route 60, the road that they were now on, but there were still at least two trucks and nearly a dozen cars behind the hired Renault. There were so few roads in that part of Jordan, he realized, that there would inevitably be a large volume of traffic on every road, probably for most of the time.

This road was noticeably narrower than the one they had just left, the surface poorer, and the terrain even more unforgiving, the hills and valleys not permitting a straight course to be followed. As it climbed and descended significant heights, there were a few hairpin bends to be carefully negotiated before the road finally straightened out towards a settlement called Arfah.

'Al Tafile is over to the east,' Angela said. 'Just follow this road until you reach a Y-junction, then bear right. It's a new road, the King's Highway, and it's one of the main routes out of Aqaba on the coast up to Amman.

Hopefully it'll be a bit better than that last stretch we were on.'

The road was better, and also much busier, and Bronson again found himself part of a loose convoy of vehicles all heading south at about the same speed. They passed through or close by a number of dusty settlements, while the hills on both sides of the highway were characterized by their rugged and uneven flanks, many of them reaching quite impressive heights.

After a few miles, the road straightened out and they left the small towns and villages behind, the only obvious signs of life then being the occasional Bedouin encampment, the infrequent petrol stations, usually attached to small cafés, and the even less frequent sight of a man on a camel or a shepherd surrounded by the sheep or goats that were in his charge.

The road gradually swung around towards the west, and when Angela spotted a sign for a village called Al Muthallith, she checked the map again.

'We're getting fairly close to the castle now,' she said. 'There's a right turn at the other end of this village.'

The village was busy and the road congested, cars parked somewhat haphazardly and locals wandering about apparently oblivious to the vehicles passing in both directions.

'That's it,' Angela said, pointing straight ahead towards a narrow road that angled off the main street.

Bronson took the turning, and immediately they started to climb, the road rising quickly above the settlement that they had just left.

Within a couple of minutes, Angela pointed over to the east, to where an ancient grey-brown stone structure crowned the crest of a substantial hill.

'There it is,' she said. 'That's Shobak Castle.'

The road didn't really go anywhere else apart from the castle, and as they descended the hill they saw the visitor centre on the left-hand side of the road, where Bronson pulled in and parked the Renault.

There were already half a dozen cars and a coach – all empty – in the parking area, and when they climbed out of the vehicle they could see people milling about in the courtyard of the visitor centre, some holding guidebooks and cameras, others sipping drinks. Beyond the visitor centre, the castle itself and the approach road to it were both clearly visible, as were several groups climbing up to the castle or descending from it.

'Here's where we do our impersonations of tourists, I suppose,' Bronson said, opening the boot of the hire car. 'Just stand in front of me,' he added, 'while I grab the pistol.'

'Is that really necessary?' Angela asked. 'We're just a couple of visitors taking a look at an ancient ruin. Surely you don't think we'll have any problems here? I thought nobody followed us from Jerusalem.'

'I can't see how they can be here already,' he agreed, 'but just because I didn't spot anybody following us, that doesn't mean that they didn't. There was so much traffic behind us on that road that there could have been half a dozen cars tailing us, and I wouldn't necessarily have been able to spot a single one of them. So, yes, I do think taking the pistol with us is a sensible precaution. Let's just hope we don't need it.'

He recovered the weapon from its hiding place and slipped it into the rear waistband of his trousers, ensuring that his light jacket covered it completely. Angela picked up her camera and a spare battery pack, while Bronson took two small but powerful flashlights from his overnight case and half a dozen spare batteries. Then they headed towards the castle.

53

Shobak Castle, Jordan

With the motorbike tailing the car, Farooq hadn't found it a problem to follow Angela and Bronson all the way to the castle.

He was now using a pair of powerful compact binoculars to watch them, and was relaying what he saw to Khaled, sitting beside him.

'He's locked the car,' he said, his voice sounding puzzled, 'and they're walking over to the visitor centre. It looks as if they're going to explore the ruins. But you told me that this wasn't a Templar castle, didn't you?'

'I did and it wasn't,' Khaled snapped. 'It was a Crusader fort, and at no time did any Templar knight even visit the place. But we're not looking for a Templar knight, and whatever clue those two think they might find here must have been left by somebody else. It doesn't matter who was involved back in the Middle Ages. The point is that the only reason Bronson and the woman

could possibly have for being here is because they discovered some pointer or clue that we missed in Jerusalem.
So what we have to do is find it, and the easiest way to
do that is to follow them and see what they look at.'

'So what we do now? Are you sure they're not just
here to look around? As tourists?'

'No. I can promise you this is something more. Tell
the man on the motorcycle to go back down the hill and
to wait in the village, because when they leave that's the
road they'll take. Call the other car, tell them where we
are and have them wait somewhere on this road as
backup. And we'll drive into the visitor centre, park and
then the two of you can buy tickets for the castle and
follow Bronson and the woman wherever they go.
Whatever they stop and look at, you stop and look at,
and take pictures of it as well. They haven't seen either
of your faces, so you shouldn't arouse any suspicion.
You'll just be another couple of tourists wandering
around an ancient monument. I'll stay in the car, for
obvious reasons, and if they do anything that seems
peculiar or out of character, call me immediately.'

Less than five minutes later, their driver stopped the
car on the edge of the parking area, as far away from
the target vehicle as he could get, and he and Farooq
stepped out of the Ford and strode across to the entrance
to the visitor centre. Khaled remained in the car, an
almost invisible shape sitting in the shadows of the back
seat, but with all his attention focused on the visitor
centre and the ruined castle that lay beyond it.

Once they had identified this final clue, he thought

that the desolate countryside they had driven through since entering Jordan would offer an unlimited number of places where they could conclude their business with the English couple in private and without interruption.

Though following the trail to find the relic was still his first priority, Khaled was also keenly looking forward to attending to the two of them. Especially the woman.

54

Shobak Castle, Jordan

Bronson and Angela bought two tickets and a slim guidebook, which explained what was known of the history of the place in multiple languages. The man who sold them the tickets told them in broken English that there were two guides conducting other people around the castle at that moment, and if they went up there straight away, they could probably tag on to the end of one of the tours.

'I wonder how much of it was left when our mysterious mediaeval contact came here to carve his clue,' Bronson mused as they walked down towards the castle.

'That all depends on when he came. The place was built in 1115 and suffered a number of attacks that century and was finally captured in 1189. According to the guidebook, not much happened to it for the next couple of hundred years until the Mamluks decided it would be a useful strategic location for them to occupy, and they restored it during the fourteenth century.

'My guess is that they probably left the castle within a hundred years or so, because their main focus and their power base was Egypt, not Jordan. Once they'd abandoned it, I don't suppose it would have taken long for the local people to recognize that they had a massive supply of cut and shaped stone sitting up here on the top of the hill, just waiting to be carted off and used for other projects. It says here that there was once a large boundary wall surrounding the castle lower down the hill' – Angela pointed over to the right – 'about level with where we are now, in fact, and that's completely disappeared. That would have been the first structure to be dismantled: I'll bet that almost every house in the village at the bottom of the hill is built at least partly with stones that once formed the boundary wall and maybe the upper floors of the castle itself, because there's virtually nothing left of them now.'

'I just hope that the clue is still up here,' Bronson said, 'because if it's on a stone that's now a part of the wall of some village house, that's the end of it.'

'I don't think you need worry. Both the clues we've found so far – the inscription and the letters and carving in the Western Wall Tunnel – were chiselled on to stones that were permanent features of the structures they were a part of. I'd imagine that this clue will be the same – on a foundation stone or something.'

The road led quite steeply down to the bottom of the narrow valley that lay between the visitor centre and the castle itself, and then ascended just as sharply around the left-hand side of the natural hill upon which the fortification had been built.

'This looks to me like the path of the original approach road,' Bronson suggested, 'because there are no gates anywhere in the outer wall that I've seen so far.'

A couple of minutes later he was proved right, because the metalled road terminated in an open area that was more or less level and bounded on two sides by the walls of the castle. In the right-hand wall, close to where the two walls met, was what had clearly originally been the main entrance to the inner part of the fortification. It was a large stone gateway, closed by two heavy wooden doors, but it was immediately obvious to both Bronson and Angela that it was not substantial enough to have resisted a determined siege for any length of time.

'The outer wall, the one that's now vanished, would have been the first line of defence,' Angela said. 'The gateways in that would probably have been about twice the size of this one.'

A heavily built but somewhat sad-looking Jordanian trader had set up a wide stall against the left-hand wall, and regarded the passing visitors with dark eyes from under a flat cap, his heavy black eyebrows complemented by a broad and impressive black moustache. They glanced briefly at the wares on offer, then ignored the trader's eager blandishments and turned right to walk through the open door and into the castle.

The exterior walls near the doorway appeared to be in good order, but when they stepped into the interior of the structure, that impression of solidity was immediately dispelled. It was at once apparent that the walls of the castle were in far better condition than what lay inside them. Most of the structures they saw were incomplete and many were tumbledown.

'This doesn't look good,' Bronson said, glancing round at the disarray that surrounded them. 'I don't know where we'd even start searching.'

'Nor do I,' Angela replied, 'but let's at least try.'

They'd arrived at the castle only a few minutes behind one of the organized tours, and over to their right they could see and hear the guide explaining, in broken but intelligible English, exactly what the members of his group were looking at. They moved up, over the rock-strewn surface, and stood at the back of the dozen or so people who were listening to the Jordanian.

'We can probably learn a lot just by hearing what he has to say,' Angela murmured. 'My guess is that he'll do a circuit of the castle. At the very least that should orient us so that we know which bits are which, and hopefully give us a few pointers about where we should start looking.'

So they followed on, keeping within earshot of every-thing the guide said, and taking their turn to look in various small rooms within the castle and inspecting some of the fortifications that still formed part of the walls. These were generally speaking in good condition, no doubt because the stones that formed them were simply massive, in some cases well over three feet thick. Too massive, far too heavy and simply too inaccessible, in fact, to be attractive to any local Jordanian house-builder.

But what they didn't see was any obvious sign of what they were looking for. There were clearly not hundreds but thousands of stones making up the structure of the castle, and their only clue was the '62 down' notation they'd deciphered. When they discussed it, they'd assumed that it might refer to a particular stone located, for example, as part of the sixty-second course of stones below the battlements. But as soon as they'd seen the castle, they'd realized that that wouldn't work because most of the battlements had been torn down over the centuries.

'I think we're wasting our time here,' Angela said. 'There's been so much damage to the castle, and so much dismantling, that I have no idea what that notation could possibly mean.'

Bronson nodded agreement, his expression grim as he surveyed the piles of old stones and half-listened to the guide explaining the function of each structure when it had been standing.

'I think you're right,' he said. 'I hate to say it, but I think this might be the end of the trail.'

For another few minutes, they continued following the guide and the group of tourists, in the absence of any better ideas, their attention wandering because both of them now believed they were essentially just wasting their time.

'I can't believe we've come all this way only to find that the final link in the chain isn't here – or if it is here, that we can't find it because of the damage the castle has suffered over the centuries. That's just so bloody unfair.'

The frustration in Angela's voice was unmistakable.

Bronson shook his head. 'It is,' he agreed, 'but because of the state this place is in, I just don't think there's any way of even working out where we should be looking.'

But just a few seconds later, he seized Angela's arm and pulled her to a stop.

'Did you hear what he just said? The guide, I mean?' he asked.

Angela shook her head. 'No, not really. I was thinking dark thoughts about the amount of time we've wasted, chasing shadows.'

'Chasing shadows, maybe,' Bronson said, a smile on his face, 'but I think I know exactly where we need to look now that we're here. It's so obvious that I should have guessed it sooner.'

'You know?'

'I think so, yes.'

'So tell me,' Angela demanded.

'I'll do better than that,' Bronson replied. 'I'll show you.'

He led her over to the edge of the path and to the remains of the internal boundary wall, then pointed down into the valley below, to the south of the fortification.

'Do you see that, down there?' he asked.

'I see a lot of stuff. What am I supposed to be looking at?'

'Pretty much at the bottom of the valley. What looks like a very small building or perhaps just a biggish box shape. Made of the same sort of stone as the castle. It's

340

not an old structure, though what's underneath it has been there for millennia.'

Angela kind of sighted down his outstretched arm, then nodded.

'Yes, now I see it,' she said. 'What is it?'

'What every castle needs if it's going to have the slightest hope of surviving a siege.'

For a moment, Angela looked blank, then she smiled and nodded.

'Got it. A cistern, or a spring. Some kind of a source of water, anyway.'

'Precisely,' Bronson said. 'I didn't hear exactly what the guide said it was, but that was where they obtained their water when the place was under siege. And,' he added, turning back and pointing towards an opening in the ground encased by two walls, 'that's the start of the staircase that they had to walk down in order to reach the water. Think it through. That staircase would have been one of the first things the Crusaders constructed when they built this castle, because there would have been no point in erecting any kind of a fortress here without having a water source and a protected access to reach it. And irrespective of what construction and destruction went on here over the centuries, the steps leading down to the well or the cistern would never have altered. So that's where the clue is, on or near the sixty-second step below the entrance – that has to be what the reference to sixty-two down means – and all I have to do now is get down there and find it.'

'Don't you mean *we* have to go down there and find it?'

'I think it's best that I go alone,' Bronson replied. 'That staircase is almost certainly off-limits to visitors, and if both of us vanish somebody might well notice, which would be bad news. In fact, I think the best thing would be if you go back to the visitor centre right now and get in the car ready to leave. That way, if I am spotted and have to make a run for it, you'll be ready and waiting to pick me up.'

Angela glanced at the deep shadow that filled the entrance to the long staircase and shook her head, apprehension washing over her.

'You've got a torch and a camera?' she asked.

'Yes.' Bronson handed her the keys to the hire car and then looked around them.

The party being escorted around the perimeter of the castle walls was virtually out of sight in front of them and, apart from two men who appeared to be examining the stones on the wall about forty yards behind them, there was nobody anywhere near them.

'This is as good a time as any,' Bronson said. 'Go now. I'll be as quick as I can.'

Angela stretched up, gave him a quick kiss on the cheek, then turned and walked away, heading back towards the castle gate and the road that led down to the visitor centre.

After a few seconds, she looked behind her, but Bronson was already out of sight.

55

Shobak Castle, Jordan

Farooq and Amir had entered the castle less than five minutes after their quarry, and had had no difficulty in locating Bronson and the woman. With Khaled's specific instructions fresh in their minds, they had hung well back, making sure that neither of the people they were following realized that they were under surveillance. That wasn't difficult, because there were plenty of visitors wandering around the old stones, looking at the view, taking photographs and examining the tumble-down remains of the fortress.

They'd seen Bronson stop and talk to the woman, and lead her over to the edge of the path to show her something that lay outside the fortress, but a few moments later, something unexpected happened.

The woman had turned and started walking straight towards them. Immediately, both men had turned away, pretending to be engrossed in an examination of a surviving part of the fortress wall, until she walked past them, apparently heading for the castle gate. As she moved away, both men turned to stare at her retreating figure, and when they looked back to where Bronson had been standing, they were stunned by the realization that he had vanished.

For a few seconds, neither man moved, then Farooq roused himself.

'Find him,' he snapped at Amir as he pulled his mobile from his pocket. 'He can't have gone far. I'll tell Khaled what's happened.'

Predictably, Khaled was unhappy at the news.

'Find him as quickly as you can,' he ordered. 'I'm quite certain it's him we need to pursue, not her. He probably sent the woman away while he investigates. I'll watch for her coming back down from the castle. You two find him, and more importantly find whatever it is he's looking at.'

Farooq ended the call just as Amir came trotting up to him.

'He's not with the group they were following before,' Amir said. 'And I went far enough beyond those people to make sure he hadn't overtaken them, and he's nowhere in sight.'

'He didn't pass me heading back to the gate, so he must still be here somewhere,' Farooq said. 'When we last saw him, he was over by that wall, so that's where we'll start looking.'

The two men walked over to the ancient L-shaped wall, and as soon as they reached it they were able to guess precisely where Bronson must have gone.

'There's a staircase going down,' Farooq said, gesturing at the dark opening.

Then he held up his hand for silence, and the two men just listened. Barely audible above the ever-present sighing of the wind, they both heard the sounds of faint movement from somewhere below their feet.

Farooq made an instant decision.

'You don't speak English,' he said to Amir, 'so I'll have to follow him. I'll pretend to be one of the guides, and I'll try to persuade him to come back up here, once I've seen what it is he's looking for. Call Khaled right now and tell him what's happened, and what I'm going to do. And,' he added after a moment's thought, 'if I do manage to discover the clue that Bronson's hoping to find, as soon as he comes back up the staircase, he can have an accident. I think he's going to stumble and fall and pitch himself over the wall. It's a long drop to the rocks underneath.'

Amir made the call while Farooq started to investigate the first few steps of the underground staircase. A few seconds later, he slid his mobile back into his pocket and nodded to Farooq.

'Khaled says you can kill him, but only if you're completely certain that you have identified the clue. And you can kill him down there, underground. It doesn't have to look like an accident. Just get it done.'

'Right,' Farooq said, and promptly disappeared from view down the staircase, his pistol in his right hand.

56

Shobak Castle, Jordan

One of the obvious problems Bronson had was not knowing precisely which step he should use to begin counting. There were about half a dozen steps leading from the level of the path in the castle itself to the entrance to the staircase proper, but he figured that if he started looking for some kind of carving or inscription from about the fiftieth to the seventieth step that ought to cover all possible permutations.

So he included those first six steps in the total number in his mental count as he strode as quickly as he could down the broken and uneven stone stairs that angled away from the castle and towards the location of the cistern or well. The light from his torch illuminated his path well enough. Constructing the tunnel had clearly been a major undertaking, hacking a route through solid rock, and the marks of the picks were still visible on the walls and roof of the narrow passageway. In several places, he had to duck when the roof level was even lower than elsewhere, a reminder that adult males of the twenty-first century were appreciably taller than their mediaeval counterparts.

As well as avoiding cracking his head on the stone, Bronson was also checking for any kind of marks or carvings on the walls, but apart from a handful of initials near the tunnel entrance within the castle itself – and they were most probably comparatively recent judging by the lettering – he saw nothing.

It didn't take long for him to reach the nominal start of his search, the fiftieth step below the level of the path, and immediately he slowed his progress to a virtual standstill, playing the light of his torch over the walls and ceiling in search of whatever it was that the anonymous mediaeval scribe had carved there. He advanced one step at a time, making sure that he looked at every square inch of the walls on both sides, but all appeared to be featureless stone, the only marks those obviously made by the masons when they had first constructed the passageway.

After a few steps, when he assumed he would be getting close to the sixty-second tread on the staircase, he shone his torch further down the passageway, illuminating the wall and ceiling below him. But still he saw nothing – no indication of letters or of a carving or anything else that could possibly be the clue he was seeking.

Bronson's frustration and irritation grew with every step that he took. They had to have been reading this right. The only possible interpretation of the phrase they had deciphered had to apply to this one unique and immovable staircase, the only stones that could not have been moved because both the steps and the walls had been hacked out of the solid rock. There was nothing else at Shobak Castle that fitted.

He carried on for another half-dozen steps, with precisely the same lack of any concrete result.

And then he heard the unmistakable sound of movement in the passageway somewhere above him, and an authoritative-sounding voice called out to him.

'Sir, sir, this area is out of bounds to visitors. You must leave now and return to the castle above. At once, please.'

Two things gave Bronson immediate pause. First, why had the man spoken in English and not Arabic in the first instance, unless he somehow knew Bronson's nationality? And, second, and just as significant, why didn't the man have a torch? Or, if he did, why wasn't he using it? Would a guide really risk his neck by climbing down an uneven staircase in total darkness just to tell a visitor that he was in the wrong place?

Bronson decided to reply, but in French, just to see what would happen.

'*Je suis desolé, mais je ne comprends pas.*'

At the same moment, he swung the beam of his torch around to shine back up the passageway down which he had descended.

And as he did that, he realized exactly why he hadn't found what he had been looking for, because he'd been looking in the wrong place.

Virtually at his eye level, neatly and accurately carved into the riser of a step that simply had to be the sixty-second from the top, was a series of letters.

The second reason for shining his torch up the passageway had obviously been to try to get a look at the man who had called out to him, but the moment Bronson saw the carving he temporarily forgot about him, pulled the digital camera from his pocket, pressed the button on the side of the casing to deploy the flashgun, and then took six shots of the carving in as many seconds, the flash strobing off the old stone walls.

Beyond the flash, in the beam of the torchlight, Bronson saw a dark-skinned man wearing a dark suit and looking straight down at him. He didn't look like a guide, but he could easily have been one of the two men who had been walking round the castle behind him and Angela just a few minutes earlier. Bronson moved the beam of the torch very slightly, and in that same instant, he saw the torch in the man's left hand and the unmistakable shape of a compact semi-automatic pistol in his right.

Bronson slid the camera back into his pocket, reached behind him and took the Browning from the waistband of his trousers. He clicked off the safety catch and, keeping the torch beam focused on the man above him, began silently backing down the staircase, testing each tread as he went.

He could see the indecision on the face of the other man, but then the stranger apparently made up his mind and raised his right hand, the hand holding the pistol.

Bronson made a split-second decision: he switched off his torch, aimed in the general direction of the man above him and squeezed the trigger.

The report of the nine-millimetre bullet firing was utterly deafening in the confined space, the sound echoing off the walls.

But outside the tunnel, almost nobody even noticed the sound, apart from Amir who was waiting by the entrance to the staircase and heard the shot clearly. To everybody else at the site, the noise was muffled by several feet of solid rock. It sounded like a distant thump, perhaps from a piece of heavy machinery like a pile-driver.

Bronson had no idea whether or not his shot had been on target, but a moment later the other man fired his own weapon. Bronson instinctively ducked to the side, though his action would have been far too late if the shot had been accurately aimed, and heard the bullet ricochet off the wall of the tunnel somewhere above his head. Two further shots followed, but both missed.

Bronson aimed his weapon up the staircase, sighting it from memory in the blackness, and fired three times. He dared not use his torch, because that would give the other man an immediate point at which to aim.

Then he crouched down, getting as low as he could to make himself the smallest possible target. He had two choices, and he didn't much like either of them. He could either stay in the tunnel and try to shoot down his opponent or risk ending up like a rat in a trap and carry on down the tunnel, all the way to the end, in the hope that he could force the door on the small building that marked the location of the water source for the Crusader castle.

Bronson flipped a mental coin and, moving as silently as he possibly could, began making his way further and further down the ancient staircase.

He heard the sound of movement somewhere above and stopped, turning round and pointing his pistol back the way he'd come, waiting for a shot or for the beam of the other man's torch to pick him out. But his unidentified opponent clearly knew that switching on his own torch would immediately make him a target, and the passageway remained as dark as the grave.

Every step that Bronson took was hopefully moving him another couple of feet clear of the other man, increasing the distance between them and getting him out of the accurate range of a pistol. And then he received help from an unexpected source. The mediaeval masons who had laboured for months to create the hidden staircase had driven it quite straight down through the bedrock, but as Bronson slowly felt his way along the wall with the outstretched tips of his fingers, he was suddenly aware of a slight bend. The wall turned very slightly to the right, and continued to do so for perhaps another dozen steps.

And he hoped that would be enough.

A quick mental calculation suggested that there should now be solid stone between himself and the man pursuing him, a rock wall created by that gentle curve in the path of the staircase. As long as he stayed close to the right-hand side, anyway.

Bronson took out his torch again and for the briefest of instants flicked it on to show the staircase ahead of him. As he extinguished the light, the sound of another shot crashed against the walls of the tunnel, but the bullet hit somewhere on the left-hand side of the passage. Bronson guessed that the man above him could see the loom of the light from his torch, but couldn't see him.

He switched on the torch again, and left it on, using the sudden flare of brightness to cover the remaining ground as quickly as he could.

Three more shots sounded, but they too hit somewhere on the left-hand wall, and Bronson knew that unless he was unlucky enough to be taken down by a ricochet, he should be safe enough. At least for the moment.

In fact, if the other man continued following him all the way down, at some point Bronson would have all the advantages, because when his opponent reached the bend in the staircase, Bronson could simply switch on his torch and place it well away from him, and then shoot down the other man the moment he stepped into view.

But that didn't sit well with him. It was too much like shooting fish in a barrel. He would far rather just walk away, now that he had – he hoped – the last piece of information that they needed.

Bronson kept the torch switched on as he covered the last few dozen feet to the end of the passageway. There, he found himself in an underground chamber at the bottom of which he could clearly hear the sound of running water. Somewhat incongruously, a modern steel ladder had been bolted to the stone side wall of the ancient chamber.

Bronson checked that the other man wasn't in sight up the staircase, then slid the Browning into his pocket and shimmied up the ladder through a circular opening in a concrete slab. Above was another small square chamber, clearly of fairly recent construction, formed from stone walls and a flat roof, the only opening to the outside world a slightly rusty steel door.

He gave the door a firm push, expecting it to be locked, and he wasn't disappointed. But the pressure he applied showed him where the external lock was positioned, and that was what he really needed to know.

There's a certain amount of science involved in forcing open a locked door, and Bronson knew that the one way that almost never worked, despite being shown on numerous television shows, was to shoulder-charge it. What was needed was a powerful, focused strike as close as possible to the lock.

Bronson stood back, balanced himself on his left leg and kicked the door with all the force he could muster.

The steel door bent, but didn't open, so he repeated the treatment twice more. The third kick slammed the door open, all the way back against its hinges.

Moments later, Bronson climbed out of the opening and looked around. He was on the southern side of the castle, close by the almost unmade road that ran around that part of the base of the hill.

Almost the first thing he saw was the Renault hire car, Angela at the wheel, parked more or less in the middle of the road at the bottom of the valley between the castle and the visitor centre. He could also see what looked like one of the guides walking down towards it, perhaps to remonstrate with her.

Bronson didn't wait, he just ran a few steps along the road towards the car, waving his arms.

Angela spotted him, put the car into gear, turned the wheel hard to the right and accelerated along the road towards him.

Within seconds, they'd changed positions, Bronson in the driving seat and Angela checking the map, and the Renault was travelling quickly along the poor-quality road that led away from the castle.

'What happened in there?' Angela asked. 'Did you get it?'

Bronson looked across at her and smiled.

'After all that,' he said, 'I bloody well hope so.'

57

Shobak Castle, Jordan

Farooq was far from happy. That was the second time he'd encountered the Englishman in an unlit underground tunnel and, once again, Bronson had somehow managed to get away. At least Farooq hadn't been hit by any of the bullets the other man had fired, which was perhaps a surprising bonus in the circumstances, and he assumed that Bronson had also walked out unscathed.

Khaled had immediately issued orders to the men in the second car and to the motorcyclist waiting down in the village below the castle to follow the rental vehicle. But his plan had been thrown by the fact that the car had left the area on an entirely different road. By the time the second car had driven down towards the castle, the Renault had vanished from sight. The only thing they knew for certain was that it had not continued on the main road through the village of Al Muthallith and on towards Aqaba, because if it had, their man on the motorcycle would definitely have seen it.

But at that moment locating and killing Bronson and the woman was less important than identifying whatever clue the Englishman had found in the tunnel.

'He definitely took photographs?' Khaled asked Farooq for the second time.

'Yes, at least half a dozen.'

'You don't think he was just triggering the flashgun on his camera to try to blind you?'

'No, because he'd already destroyed most of my night vision by shining his torch straight at me,' Farooq replied. 'And he would have known that.'

'So he must have found the clue he was looking for at virtually the same moment that you called out to him.'

Five minutes later, Khaled and Farooq retraced Bronson's steps, climbing into the building above the well and walking up the long and narrow staircase towards the castle above, both men now carrying torches.

'How far up was he when you challenged him?' Khaled asked, panting slightly from the steepness of the climb.

'Much closer to the castle. He was probably about a third of the way down the tunnel.'

The beams from their torches played over the solid stone walls as they looked for anything that could possibly have been the clue Bronson had been seeking. They climbed higher and higher until eventually Farooq abruptly stopped, the light from his torch illuminating the stone treads beneath their feet.

'Look,' he said. 'There are two brass cartridge cases on this step. They would have been ejected from the pistol when he fired the weapon for the first time. They may have bounced down a few steps after that, but this must be more or less where he was.'

They resumed their scrutiny of the walls as they continued their slow ascent, but saw nothing at all. No carvings, no inscriptions. Then Farooq had a sudden thought.

'I've just remembered,' he said. 'When he took those photographs, he was pointing the camera more or less straight at me, straight up the staircase. We're looking in the wrong place. Whatever he found must been carved into the stairs themselves.'

They changed their tactics, walked back down the passageway until they reached the spot where Farooq had seen the discarded cartridge cases, then focused their torches on the steps above them and resumed their slow climb.

Two minutes later they were looking at the carving on the stone riser, and Khaled was busy taking a sequence of photographs of it.

'It's just a name,' Farooq said, sounding disappointed. 'Have you any idea what it means?'

'Yes,' Khaled replied, taking another two pictures. 'I know exactly what it means, and where it is. Now we need to move really quickly, because it's essential that we get there before they do.'

58

Jordan

The largely unmade road that Bronson and Angela had followed from the castle took them back to the village of Al Muthallith, but well to the east of the road that led up to the castle.

Knowing that the opposition had clearly been following them, despite Bronson's inability to detect any surveillance, they had decided to take an entirely different route to their new destination, just in case someone was waiting near that road junction. Bronson drove as quickly as he could, trying to put some distance between themselves and any possible pursuit. Once he was sure that no car or motorcycle was following them, he reached into his jacket pocket and handed the camera to Angela.

'I just hope the pictures came out,' he said, 'or it will all have been for nothing.'

Angela switched on the camera, opened up the gallery

and flicked back through the recorded images until she found what looked like the start of the sequence. Then she stared at the screen as she inspected each picture in turn.

'Well,' she said after a few moments, 'I can't pretend that they're the best photographs I've ever seen, but two of them are quite sharp and clear. And that's thanks to the camera, not you, obviously.'

'Bearing in mind the situation I was in I'm delighted any of them came out. So, what does it say?'

'Well, not anything that I would have expected,' Angela said, looking puzzled. 'It's just a name, and a name that I don't recognize. Does "Mont Sanes" – I think it's meant to be two words rather than one – mean anything to you?'

Bronson furrowed his brow in concentration, then shook his head.

'Not immediately, no. Is that all there is?' he asked.

'That's the only lettering, just those two words,' Angela replied, 'but there's what looks like a Templar cross below it, and a Christian cross above it, so perhaps it could be the name of a chapel or a church. I suppose the "Mont" is French, though that doesn't really help us work out where the place is, because Old French was the language of the early Templars and they probably gave French names to most of their important locations, irrespective of where they were located. Just like Krak de Mont Real, in fact. That's only called Shobak Castle now because Shobak or Shaubak is the name of the biggest nearby village.'

Bronson didn't reply for a few moments. The name Angela had read out had sparked some kind of faint recollection, and he was doing his best to remember what the link or reference was. Then it came to him.

'The second word,' he said. 'Can you spell it for me?'

'S A N E S, Sanes,' Angela replied. 'And that doesn't sound very French to me.'

Bronson nodded.

'Okay. Here's a thought. Names change over the years in any language, but there is one place I've heard of which might just fit. If so, it's one word, not two, and in modern French it's Montsaunès.'

'Which is where?'

'In France, oddly enough, in the foothills of the Pyrenees. What's there is probably the most enigmatic of all the known surviving Templar buildings, just as peculiar as Rosslyn Chapel, though of course Rosslyn was built well after the Templars were purged. The village is very small – one of those blink and you've missed it kind of places – but in the mediaeval period it was the site of one of the most important Templar commanderies in the whole of Europe.'

'A what?'

'Commandery – a fortified monastery.'

'And you know this how?'

'I read about it. I've read a lot about the Templars, because they've always fascinated me.'

He paused for a few moments, collecting his thoughts and dredging his memory for what he could remember about the place.

But then Angela held up her hand and stared at the screen of her mobile.

'We have a signal here, believe it or not,' she said, 'and I've just found a website that explains a bit about the village and its history. It was built in the twelfth century,' she continued, 'and it was intended to be a part of a major defensive line on the northern slopes of the Pyrenees, built as a protection against incursions by the Moors who had occupied the whole of the Iberian Peninsula at the height of their powers. By that time, of course, the writing was on the wall and they were being driven slowly to the south as the *Reconquista* gathered pace. The first battle to drive out the Moors took place early in the eighth century, but the process of re-conquest wasn't completed until virtually the end of the fifteenth century, and there were always fears that the Moorish forces might strike back.

'The commandery disappeared centuries ago, after the order was purged at the beginning of the fourteenth century, and the only thing that's now left is the Templar chapel, which is called the *Église Saint-Christophe des Templiers*, and you're right about that. It is a weird place. The website explains that it looks like a chapel from the outside, but the interior is nothing like any other supposedly Christian place of worship. The whole thing is painted inside, but the decoration is really unusual, with a mixture of strange symbols and designs. The author of this website claims that nobody has ever worked out what any of it is supposed to mean, and it's one of the most enduring mysteries that the order left behind it.'

Bronson nodded at her.

'That all strikes a chord,' he said. 'I think the ceiling's painted with stars and things like that. Is there a picture on that website?'

'There is, but on this phone it's so tiny you can't really make out anything clearly.'

Angela glanced down at the roadmap as they passed a signpost, just to confirm that they were still going the right way.

'We're just passing Tamiya,' she said, 'and there's a junction coming up in about half a mile or so. You need to stay on this road and head for a place called Ma'an, where we can pick up the Desert Highway. I presume you still want to head for Aqaba?'

'Yes, because it probably won't take them long to work out what that clue in the tunnel means either. When they do, I've no doubt they'll do exactly what we're doing, and head for France. This has been a race between them and us ever since your archaeological colleagues found that inscription, but this really is the final furlong. Whoever gets there first will find whatever secret is hidden in that chapel, and I've no intention of coming second to those bastards.'

Angela nodded.

'That works for me as well,' she said. 'So where exactly are we heading?'

'For the King Hussein International Airport,' Bronson replied, 'where we're going to buy tickets on the first available flight that will get us to a southern French airport, ideally Toulouse or Carcassonne.'

'But,' he added, 'I definitely want to be standing in the northern foothills of the French Pyrenees before midnight.'

59

Montsaunès, France

Getting out of Jordan and into France proved both easier and faster than Bronson had expected – the flight was on schedule and uneventful – but even so it was still well after ten that evening before he pulled his new hire car, rented at Toulouse's Blagnac Airport, to a stop on the west side of the D117, the Route de Saint-Girons, and stared across the road at the ancient Templar chapel.

'It looks pretty much like any other church,' Angela said.

'I agree,' Bronson replied. 'As you found out from the Internet, it's only the interior that's exceptional. But at least we know we're in the right place,' he added, pointing in the opposite direction.

Screwed to the white stone wall a few feet from where he'd stopped the car was a maroon metal sign with white lettering, the words easily visible in the moonlight.

'"*Place des Templiers*",' Angela read, and nodded. 'Yes, that seems clear enough.'

Bronson looked around, and up and down the road, but apart from a solitary car heading north, possibly intending to join the autoroute just outside the village, the place appeared to be deserted.

He reached up, altered the interior light switch so that the lamp wouldn't come on when he opened the door, then reached for the handle.

'As they say, there's no time like the present. The keys are in the ignition. As soon as I'm outside, get in the driving seat and then just keep your eyes open. I think we're ahead of the game, at least at the moment, but if you see anything you don't like the look of, just start the car and get the hell out of here.'

Angela put her hand on his arm.

'For God's sake be careful, Chris,' she said.

'I will. I'm just going to try the door. If it's locked then we'll have to think of something else.'

Bronson opened the door of the car and stepped out. In seconds, he was invisible, his dark clothes blending seamlessly into the solid black shadow that cloaked the front of the chapel.

The door was set into a fairly ornate arched entrance, flanked by four stone pillars, the whole surmounted by a kind of frieze of carvings that formed a semicircle around the top of the arch. Bronson flicked on his torch and examined the stonework. It was a line of human faces, each different from its neighbour and some apparently in agony, judging by the expressions they were displaying.

He moved the thin beam of the torch around the semicircle, then stopped when he reached the apex to examine another carved image set into the ancient stone directly above the arch. It looked somehow familiar to him. He reached into his pocket, took out his mobile phone, made sure the street was still deserted and then snapped a picture of the carved stone, the explosion of light from the built-in flash bouncing off the old stones.

Then he turned his attention to the door itself. This wasn't, as he had been expecting, a single door, but rather two separate doors hinged at either side of the archway. A printed notice on the left-hand door advised anybody interested that the key was available from the village *Mairie* on four days of the week – including Sunday, predictably enough – but only between the hours of three and five in the afternoon.

He tried the handle anyway, and it was of course locked. He bent to examine the lock, but realized immediately that it was the kind of ancient mechanism that would require a heavy and complex key some six or seven inches long. Bronson's expertise in lock picking was confined to the more modern kinds of devices, and he certainly didn't have the heavy-duty picks and torsion wrenches he would need to try to open it.

And he wasn't even sure that opening it would be a good idea. In order to do any meaningful exploration inside the building, they would need to use torches, and although, like most French villages late in the evening, all the houses in Montsaunès appeared to be shuttered and completely silent, the occupants apparently having retired for the night, he had no doubt that somebody would notice intermittent torchlight inside the old chapel.

Before he returned to the car, Bronson checked both sides of the church. Access to the sides and rear of the building was prevented by a substantial steel fence supported by stone pillars and pierced by locked gates. There were, he noted, at least two other doors into the building, one on each side, and at the right-hand rear of the chapel was what appeared to be a later addition, a single-storey stone structure attached to the church and accessed by a narrow doorway. Bronson guessed it might function as a storeroom or even as a robing room for the local priest. Because the main door of the church was locked, he had no doubt that all the other doors would also be secured.

Even the lowest windows were mounted so high in the walls that a ladder would be needed to reach them, and as far as he could tell by the light of his torch they were all closed. For a few moments he toyed with the idea of clambering over the metal fence and examining the back of the building, but knew he'd be unlikely to achieve anything if he did. And, in fact, he also knew he didn't need to.

By the time he walked back across the street, Angela had already moved over to the front passenger seat of the car.

'It was locked, I presume?' she asked.

'Locked securely,' Bronson replied, 'which at least means that if we can't get in, no one else can either.

All we can do now is wait until tomorrow morning.'

'You took a photograph,' Angela stated.

'Oh, yes.'

He fished his mobile out of his pocket, tapped the screen to open the gallery, then handed it to her.

The picture showed two angelic figures – each had a halo – that appeared to be supporting an ornamented stone circle within which was an unusual symbol, at least to Bronson's eyes. It looked like an enlarged letter X with the elongated shaft of a letter P driven down through the centre point of the X.

'What is it?' Bronson asked.

'It's a Chi Rho,' Angela replied. 'Of a sort, anyway. It's one of the oldest Christian motifs, a monogram that contains the first two letters of the word "Christ" in Greek, the letters *chi* and *rho*.' She pointed at two other symbols, either side of the central motif. 'That's the Greek letter *alpha* on the left and what's left of *omega* on the right, the first and last letters of the Greek alphabet. The beginning and the end, if you like.'

'So it's a common symbol?' Bronson asked.

'Yes. Some Christians still use it, but this particular Chi Rho is a bit different. I'm not sure what this symbol at the top means. It looks like a kind of flattened and elongated letter *omega*, but it's not something I've seen on a Chi Rho before. But perhaps the oddest feature is the snake.'

'Snake? What snake?'

'Here. Entwined around the upright of the letter *rho*.'

'I thought that was the letter "S".'

'That's what it looks like, but it's almost certainly a serpent. There's evidence that the Chi Rho symbol actually existed perhaps half a millennium before the time of Christ, in the writings of Herodotus and Plato, for example. It was known as the Chrestos, and it was kind of backwards, if you like. The Chi Rho was accepted as a religious symbol that was created by combining two Greek letters, but the Chrestos was a symbol from the first. The "X" on the Chrestos is almost certainly a representation of the solar ecliptic path and the celestial equator, not the letter *Chi*, which is why the two straight lines don't cross at right angles.'

Even in the darkness of the hire car Angela could see Bronson's expression starting to glaze.

'Don't worry about it,' she said. 'All it means is that the symbol is a lot older than most people think and originally had nothing to do with Christianity. It probably meant good fortune, and was hijacked by the early Church because the shape of the cross was a visual reminder of the crucifixion.'

'And the snake?' Bronson asked.

'Oh, yes. The snake's been an important symbol for religions and societies for millennia, and most likely that's astrological in origin. It's the sign of *serpens*, the serpent, and referred to the serpent healers of antiquity. So although most people think of the Chi Rho as a Christian symbol of the crucifixion, it actually isn't. It's much older and had a completely different meaning.'

They hadn't seen a hotel in the village, but even if there had been, Bronson wouldn't have wanted to stay that close to their objective. Thinking ahead earlier in the evening, on their way to the village of Montsaunès, they'd pulled off the autoroute at Boussens and picked a hotel at random close to the banks of the River Garonne, checked in, locked their bags in their room and then driven on.

Back in the hotel, they sat side by side on the double bed consuming the sandwiches and soft drinks they'd bought earlier at the airport, while Bronson talked through his plan.

'This really has to be the end of the trail,' he said. 'I can't believe we'll get inside the church and find some other clue intended to send us scampering off to yet another ruin in yet another country. And I've had an idea about where we'll find the relic.'

'Oh, yes?'

Bronson picked up the camera that he'd used in the tunnel under Shobak Castle. He flicked through the pictures he had taken, and selected the one that seemed to him to be the clearest and held the camera in front of Angela.

'Some of the information we've been using has relied upon placement,' he began. 'Things like the positioning of the code words on either side of the alphabet to allow us to decipher the Atbash. I think that the positioning of the symbols on this last clue is just as important. The name is the simple bit, really, because that's brought us to where we are now, or where we will be at dawn tomorrow morning, this tiny village in France. The Christian cross above the name of the village seems to me to be telling us that the place we have to look is the chapel, because that's how you would normally indicate a chapel or a church on a map, and I'm sure the same sort of symbology has probably been used for centuries.

'But note that the Templar cross, the *croix pattée*, is placed under the name. To me, that suggests that the treasure or the relic, whatever it may turn out to be, is somewhere underneath the chapel, in a crypt or cellar or somewhere of that sort.'

'I suppose we'll find out tomorrow,' Angela said, 'but if there's an iron-bound box sitting in a crypt underneath the chapel, why has nobody thought to open it before?'

Bronson shook his head. 'I don't think it'll be anything like as simple as that. The amount of secrecy involved in this and the number of layers of codes and ciphers that we've had to peel away and decrypt suggest that the relic will be extremely well hidden. It won't be a matter of just pushing open the door to a crypt and saying, "Oh yes, there it is." I think there's a good chance that the entrance to the crypt itself will be concealed, and possibly even the existence of the crypt will be unknown to the priest or whoever is in charge of the building. Finding it is not going to be easy, but I suppose the difference is that because of the trail we've been following, at least we know that there is something there to be found. Or at least that something was hidden, and hopefully it's still there.'

'So what do we do? Just march into the building

tomorrow morning and tell the priest that we want to explore his crypt and would he kindly show us the way? Then find the relic and push off with it before the bad guys turn up, guns blazing?'

'Not exactly,' Bronson replied. 'I had to leave the pistol in Jordan, obviously, because there was no way I could get on to the aircraft with it, so we're completely unarmed. The opposition would also have had to fly from Iraq or wherever they're based to Israel, and they would have had the same problem. But within a very short time of them getting there, they were touting pistols, so clearly they have good international connections that allow them access to weapons quickly and easily. It wouldn't surprise me if they'd made arrangements to collect weapons soon after they'd arrived in France. In fact,' he added, 'that's more or less what I'm hoping they've done.'

Angela looked at him quizzically.

'You *hope* they armed themselves? Why?'

'Because we can't handle them by ourselves, and that means we need professional assistance. And the kind of professional assistance I have in mind will only be available if there's a credible opposition force. And,' he added, taking a last swig from his soft drink, 'that means it's time for me to start making a few phone calls.'

Thirty minutes later, Bronson ended his final call, put the mobile on the bedside cabinet and connected the charger.

Angela looked at him and nodded.

'I think I followed most of your French,' she said, 'and

I can see exactly what you've got planned. But it all sounds pretty risky to me. Are you sure this is the only way we can do it?'

'I think so, yes. But if you're not happy to go ahead, you can stay here and I can go it alone.'

Angela shook her head. 'No. I told you before. Where you go, I go,' she said, 'and obviously it'll be more believable if I'm there as well, because they must know who I am. If you're right, I've been their main target ever since the attack in Iraq.'

'Good. Right, now we really do need to get to sleep. I'll set the alarm for five thirty, and we need to be on the road by six at the latest.'

But despite all that had happened, sleep didn't come easily to Bronson. At two o'clock, with Angela's head resting on the crook of his left arm, he was still awake, eyes wide open and staring at the ceiling, wondering if there was anything else he could or should do, or anything he'd forgotten.

And above all, he was supremely conscious of the number of things that could go spectacularly and terminally wrong.

60

Montsaunès, France

In the grey light of early dawn, the *Église Saint-Christophe des Templiers* looked pretty much the same as it had done the previous night. A solid oblong building that almost radiated a sense of impressive age and perhaps even hinted at something of the bloody history of the Order that had created it nearly a millennium earlier.

They'd had to make a brief stop en route to their destination on the outskirts of Saint-Martory, where a dark blue van was parked in a lay-by, a solitary figure, clad entirely in black, standing beside the rear doors. Bronson had pulled in behind the other vehicle and stopped the car, exchanged a few words with the man waiting there, and been given two bulky objects. Immediately afterwards, the van had driven off at speed.

After their short diversion, they'd driven slowly into

Montsaunès down the main road, the Route de Saint-Girons, through the village, and then stopped the car in the same open parking area they'd occupied the previous night, a position from which they both had a clear view of the front of the chapel.

The engine of the hire car made faint ticking noises as it cooled, and in the front seats Bronson and Angela settled down to wait.

At precisely seven o'clock, a tall figure, wearing a long dark coat and a flattish cap and leaning on a cane, walked slowly down the main road. At the chapel, he made his way across to the main doors, pulling an object from the pocket of his coat as he did so.

'So that's the first act of the drama completed,' Angela said, watching as the man turned the key in the heavy lock and then opened both halves of the door. 'Or rather the second act, I suppose,' she added, as he vanished inside the building and the windows of the chapel fronting the road were suddenly illuminated by the flare of electric lights.

'I hope he doesn't hang around,' Bronson remarked. 'This is going to be difficult enough without innocent bystanders getting in the way.'

But it looked as if the old man was following his instructions, because a few seconds later the lights were extinguished and the caretaker re-emerged, closing, but not locking, the door behind him and retracing his steps somewhat hastily along the street.

'That looks like our cue,' Bronson said. 'And even if we've got the timing wrong, I'd still like to get inside the building and have a look at it. Are you okay to do that?'

Angela nodded in a somewhat resigned manner, but immediately opened the door of the car.

'Yes,' she said, adjusting the fit of her light jacket. 'I wish there was another way, but there isn't. And we've come this far, haven't we? Let's get on with it.'

Bronson locked the car and they walked away, crossed the main road and strode over to the looming bulk of the ancient chapel. He turned the handle on the door, opened it and they stepped inside, flicking on the lights as they did so.

It took a few seconds for their eyes to adjust to the sudden brightness, and then they simultaneously looked up to stare at the painted ceiling high above them.

'I see what that website meant,' Angela said in amazement. 'That really is incredible. I've never seen anything like it before.'

Above them, the apex of one brick arch reached to the roof of the chapel, while another arch of similar construction but slightly smaller was surmounted by a vertical wall pierced by three windows. Between those windows was the proof – if any were needed – of the identity of the order that had constructed the building: two very clear blood-red representations of the Templar cross, the *croix pattée*. But that was about the only faintly religious symbol that they could see.

The dominant feature of the hand-painted ceiling was a seemingly infinite number of stars, arranged in a regular pattern of rows and columns, which ran from one end of the ceiling to the other and across it from left to right.

'Could they literally represent the universe?' Angela murmured, craning her head back to try to see them more clearly. 'Could they just be a symbol here in this chapel of what the Knights Templar saw in the night sky around them?'

'Perhaps,' Bronson said, sounding doubtful. 'But if that was the intention, why are they all in straight lines? You would expect them to have made some attempt to represent the constellations that must have been visible to them. No, I don't know what they're supposed to represent, but I don't think it was just the night sky.'

The stars weren't the only oddity, not by a long way. In the central section of the ceiling and bounded by the two archways were two very clear borders, each formed from a double line of alternating black and white squares, while the inside of the border was marked by a double row of semicircles, the ends of these lines making contact with the junctions between the black and white squares. Each row of semicircles was shifted by one space from the other row to create a more complex pattern.

Bronson pointed upwards, towards one of the borders.

'As far as I know,' he said, 'no expert on the Templars has ever visited this chapel and attempted to explain what any of this decoration means. I don't profess to be an expert, but just looking at those borders, it seems clear enough to me that the kind of chequerboard pattern is meant to represent the Templar battle flag, the *Beauseant*, repeated dozens of times. That was one of the simplest flags of all time, just a black oblong above a white oblong. It looks to me as if the semicircular lines are intended to link the flags together, perhaps to emphasize the importance of brotherhood and fraternity to the order, the way that they both lived and died together, on and off the battlefield.'

Angela nodded.

'That does make sense,' she agreed, 'but what about the rest of the symbols?'

For a few moments, they just stared up at the patterns.

Between those two borders were no fewer than twenty-two circles, many enclosing a unique design, though there were also three pairs of identical circles either side of the centreline of the pattern. Along the centreline itself were four unevenly spaced circles with decorated borders, and each appeared to contain another representation of the *Beauseant*. Flanking those were the pairs of matching circles, all containing patterns that could represent the petals of a flower, or possibly a large star. Close to the borders and on opposite sides were two significantly larger circles containing different, though similar, spoked designs. All those symbols were basically laid out in a coherent geometric pattern, but almost all of the other symbols were asymmetric and unique.

On one side were two overlapping circles, each containing a simple star pattern, while on the other was a line of eight circles, one an elaborate design that was twice the size of any of the others, and all slightly different. Most contained the same general type of star or petal pattern, but one held the painted image of the *croix pattée*, while at the opposite end from the large circle was what looked like a random pattern of oval shapes.

But there were two other features that also made no immediate sense to either Bronson or Angela.

'Is that a dagger, or what?' she asked, pointing upwards.

In fact, there were two painted symbols that looked something like daggers on the ceiling, and in both cases the handguard, the metal cross-piece designed to protect the fingers of the user, had a pronounced forward curve so that the ends pointed towards the sharpened tip of the weapon.

'They could be, I suppose,' Bronson replied. 'I think that design of handguard was quite common in the mediaeval period. The idea was that you'd trap the blade of your opponent's sword between the blade and the guard, and you could then twist the dagger to break his blade. What really puzzles me, though, is that pyramid design directly above the middle window.'

'I was looking at that. There's something strangely familiar about it.'

'It would be more familiar to you if you were American,' Bronson said. 'It's very like the pyramid shape that you see on the reverse of every one-dollar bill, under the legend *Annuit Coeptis*, which translates more or less as "He has smiled on our undertakings". What's even weirder is that the decorated circle at the apex of the pyramid up there is very like part of the other symbol that you'll find on the same side of the same American bill. That's a circle filled with stars above the other legend *E pluribus unum.*'

' "From many, one",' Angela translated. 'You're right. Of course, that's also the design of the Great Seal of the United States.' She paused and looked at him. 'I do find it a bit peculiar that we're standing here in a twelfth-century Templar chapel in southern France, and two of the symbols painted on the ceiling bear more than a passing resemblance to the design of a modern American banknote. It's really strange. The whole place feels to me like it's more astrological or qabbalistic than religious, at least in the way that it's been decorated.'

'And this is all original, I suppose?' Bronson asked.

'According to what I read on the Web, this place basically hasn't been touched since the beginning of the fourteenth century.'

They walked further into the chapel, looking up at the ceiling and noting other unusual symbols as they headed towards the altar, which is where they expected to find the entrance to the crypt, assuming Bronson's deduction was correct and there was a chamber underneath the building.

It didn't take a lot of effort to find it. Behind the altar, the stone floor was covered with a faded red carpet, but as they walked over it they both realized at the same moment that the floor was not entirely made of stone.

The feeling under the soles of their shoes was completely different in the central section.

'Bingo,' Bronson said shortly. 'That feels like a trapdoor.'

Quickly, they moved to opposite ends of the carpet and pulled it back to lay it against the wall. Set into the stone floor was a square wooden door, with a recessed metal ring on one side to allow it to be pulled open.

Bronson grabbed the ring and levered it up, pulling the door all the way open so that it lay back against the stone floor. Below the door and descending into the darkness underneath the chapel was a flight of stone stairs, a sight that gave Bronson an immediate and unpleasant sense of déjà vu.

'Shades of Shobak Castle,' he muttered, taking a torch out of his pocket and preparing to descend.

'Surely there must be a light switch somewhere,' Angela said. 'I can't believe the priest or the caretaker would have to use a torch every time he needed to go down there.'

Bronson shone the torch around the perimeter of the hole, then nodded and snapped off the light.

'You're right,' he said, and reached out to flick a switch.

Immediately, the crypt was flooded with light from a couple of fluorescent tubes mounted on the ceiling. The two of them walked down the staircase, stopped at the bottom and stared around them.

As far as Bronson could tell, the crypt was about one third the size of the chapel above it, and was largely empty. In the spaces on both sides of the staircase a number of anonymous cardboard boxes had been stacked, presumably containing materials that would be needed in the chapel above, perhaps candles and the like. The walls on both sides were concealed behind old and faded hanging drapes, possibly in an attempt to provide a degree of insulation, because the crypt felt quite cold.

But the dominant feature of the underground chamber, the one thing that could never be ignored, was the design on the stone wall directly in front of the staircase. In colours that looked as vibrant as if it had only been painted a matter of days ago, the wall boasted a huge *croix pattée*, the most dominant and enduring symbol of the Knights Templar. And, as a further confirmation, suspended from two stone pegs directly below the symbol, an ancient rusted Templar battle sword hung, point downwards.

'Well, that's interesting and impressive,' Bronson said, 'but what I don't see is anywhere that the relic we're searching for could be hidden.'

'That's because you're an amateur meddling in a world that belongs to the professionals,' a cold voice spat from behind them.

Bronson and Angela whirled around to find themselves facing two men who had walked silently down the stairs and now stood just a few feet away, each holding a semi-automatic pistol and giving every impression that he knew how to use it.

It was Angela who reacted first.

'You!' she gasped, with a sharp intake of breath. She was staring at one of the two men. 'I should have guessed.'

61

'Khaled,' she said. Her face was a picture of anger. She looked at Bronson. 'He's the director of the Baghdad Museum. He was basically in overall charge of our expedition. That explains a lot. I always wondered how news of our finding that underground temple got out so quickly, but obviously we were keeping him informed on a daily basis.'

'You talk too much,' the bearded man standing beside Khaled said, his English fluent and almost without an accent. 'Before we leave here I'm going to teach you some manners.'

'Enough, Farooq,' Khaled said. 'First of all, we have to find what we're looking for. These two might be useful for a little while longer.'

'What are you looking for?' Angela asked, ignoring Farooq's warning and immediately deviating from the strategy she and Bronson had discussed earlier that

384

morning. 'And what have the Knights Templar got to do with a Mandaean temple in Iraq?'

Khaled shrugged. 'Everything, and nothing, really,' he replied. 'Both were heretics, and both shared the same gnostic beliefs, at least to some extent. You saw the carved face in the underground temple, and I'm assuming that you are bright enough to know who it was supposed to represent.'

'John the Baptist,' Angela said, after a moment.

'Bravo. Well, the Templars shared that belief.'

Angela shook her head in frustration. 'I know that. But why was it necessary to murder all of my colleagues? What was the point of that? And poor Stephen in Italy. Why did they all have to die? What's so important that you had them all killed?'

'Simple,' Khaled replied. 'They knew too much. I'd been hoping that someone would find that temple for years, and once they did, that knowledge had to die with them.'

'Why?'

'You really don't know?'

'Of course I don't,' Angela almost shouted.

'So what was it?' Bronson demanded. 'Part of some twisted Islamic crusade?'

A smug look passed over Khaled's face, and he shook his head. 'This has nothing to do with religion, except in the most peripheral manner. This was all to do with money and rewards.'

The surprise must have shown on the faces of Bronson and Angela.

'It's really very simple,' Khaled went on. 'The Mandaeans of southern Iraq were nothing to do with the Knights Templar except that they were both heretical groups, both worshipping John the Baptist. That was the Templar heresy, if you like. They were accused of worshipping a disembodied head, of spitting and trampling on the cross, and denying Christ. All of which made perfect sense if they *did* worship John the Baptist, because that would have made Jesus Christ a usurper, somebody who came along after the event, as it were, and stole all of John's glory. They would have reviled and rejected him and everything he stood for.

'Years ago, I discovered a parchment that stated unequivocally that not only were the Templars Johannites, but during their excavations on the Temple Mount they had recovered the head of John the Baptist, placed there for safe keeping and veneration by his followers at some time in the first century AD after he was beheaded. Over the years, John's disciples had established groups in a number of countries – including the Mandaeans of Iraq – to follow what they saw as the only true religion.

'But the really interesting claim made in the parchment was that the head of the Baptist became the "truth" so jealously guarded by the Templars. It became, in fact, the Baphomet idol that they worshipped, perhaps their most sacred treasure. After the order was purged, somebody realized that the Mandaeans were the best hope of keeping the truth alive – the sacred truth about the Baptist, I mean – and stated that in a temple below the sands was a clue to the final resting place of the Templars' Baphomet, the head of John the Baptist.'

Khaled stopped talking, as if that were the entire story, his whole justification for what he and his companions had done.

'But what possible use would it be to you to find the head – and all it would be today is a skull, I presume – of a man who died two thousand years ago?' Angela demanded. 'The skull of a person who may have been John the Baptist, though there's no chance you'd ever be able to prove that.'

'You still don't see it, do you?' Khaled smiled again. 'Despite everything I've told you. Baphomet was the Templars' sacred "truth", the reason why they denied Christ. Even under the most painful and prolonged tortures, no Templar ever revealed its true location or admitted anything about it. When the order was forced out of Outremer, the land beyond the sea, after the fall of Acre, that relic went with the survivors to a place of safety. And,' Khaled paused for emphasis, 'the important thing is that all their other assets went with it, most especially the treasure of the Templars in the Holy Land, the contents of the treasury of Acre that Tibauld de Gaudin took with him when he fled from that doomed castle ahead of the final Mamluk assault. So, find one, and you find the other,' he finished. 'Find the relic and you also find the treasure.'

'So this was just a treasure hunt?' Angela asked, as she realized the essential truth of what he'd just said. 'Nothing to do with a search for historical truth or an important relic, just a grubby little expedition so you could get your hands on something that didn't belong to you.'

'After all these centuries, it doesn't belong to anyone,' Khaled pointed out. 'But, yes, that was the whole purpose of what we've been doing. That was why your companions had to die, and why you, too, won't be walking out of here.'

'I don't know if you've noticed,' Bronson pointed out, 'but there's no treasure down here. Unless somebody's helpfully packed it away in those cardboard boxes for you, which I doubt.'

Khaled's smile didn't waver.

'It's here somewhere,' he said confidently. 'The Templars were hardly going to leave it lying about on the floor of their chapel, were they? Don't forget that as well as being fighting men they were also bankers and engineers. You only have to look at any of their surviving buildings to know that. And perhaps I've already noticed something that you've missed.'

'What?' Angela sounded more annoyed than frightened, despite the death threat the Iraqi had issued just seconds earlier.

Khaled pointed over at the wall behind them, the massive stone wall bearing the red-painted *croix pattée*, and both Bronson and Angela turned to look where he was indicating.

'On the right-hand side, just there, at about shoulder height,' he said. 'There's a circular patch of discoloured stone.'

'So what?'

'So if that wall was actually a door, that's where a man would place his hand to push it open.'

'There could be other reasons for that,' Bronson said.

'Perhaps there are. Let's find out. Go over there and push.'

Khaled gestured to Bronson to start moving, while Farooq herded Angela to the other side of the room.

Bronson placed his hand on the wall where Khaled had indicated, and pushed as hard as he could. Absolutely nothing happened, and after a few seconds he stepped backwards.

'Solid as a rock,' he said. 'Just as I expected.'

Khaled seemed unfazed.

'Then there must be a key or a catch somewhere,' he said, 'something to free it.' He pointed again, at the centre of the wall. 'Remove that sword, and then push the stone pegs upwards.'

Bronson stepped over to the ancient weapon and lifted it down. For the briefest of instants he wondered if it could still be used for its original purpose, but the moment he touched it he realized it was far too fragile. He placed the sword on the floor behind him, then reached up and grasped hold of the two stone pegs.

He had expected them to be completely solid, but the moment he touched the old stone he could feel a very slight movement. He pushed firmly upwards on both of them, as the Iraqi had told him to do, and felt rather than heard a faint click.

'I felt something,' he admitted, unable to hide the trace of excitement in his voice.

'Now push the wall again,' Khaled instructed, his tone noticeably more excited too.

Bronson did so, but again nothing happened.

'It's still solid,' he said, looking round at Khaled.

'Then there must be something else, some other lever that needs to be activated.'

The Iraqi scanned the chamber, but it was Farooq who pointed out what they'd all missed. On both side walls, about two feet from the back wall, were additional stone pegs, each possibly intended to carry another Templar battle sword.

'Maybe you have to move all three sets at the same time,' he suggested. 'And perhaps push on the wall too. That would have been at least a form of protection against the hidden chamber – assuming there is one, of course – ever being opened by a single thief.'

It seemed as good a suggestion as any, and Khaled nodded.

'It's worth trying,' he said.

He told Bronson to push on the wall, waved his pistol at Angela and ordered her to manoeuvre the stone pegs on the side wall directly behind Bronson. Then he stationed himself and Farooq by the other two sets.

'Right, push now,' Khaled instructed, when they were all in position.

Angela knew she had no choice in the matter and, despite herself, she was caught up in the excitement of the discovery, the final revelation that lay at the end of the trail they'd followed across the Middle East and Europe.

This time, the clicks as some ancient hidden mechanism was triggered were quite audible, and almost as soon as Bronson leaned his weight against the side of the back wall, he felt it start to move. Only a fraction of an inch, but enough to show that Khaled had been right: the wall was actually a massive stone door, pivoted in the centre.

For a few seconds, as he continued pushing, nothing else happened. But then, agonizingly slowly and accompanied by a dull rumbling sound as of stone rolling over stone, the entire back wall of the crypt began to rotate, its weight carried on some kind of central hinges located at the top and bottom of the wall.

He continued pushing until the wall would move no further, the openings on both sides now easily wide enough to allow a man to walk through. More obviously, the opening allowed Bronson and the other three people to clearly see what lay inside, beyond the solid stone door.

The fluorescent light from the ceiling of the crypt penetrated deep into the hidden chamber, revealing a room about the same size as the crypt itself, with a solid stone floor and a few rows of simple wooden pews. At the far end an unadorned stone altar had been constructed and on the very centre of it was a small square shape. Apart from that, the newly opened chamber appeared to be completely empty. No chests. No piles of bullion or whatever form the Templar treasure of Outremer might have taken.

Khaled took in the sight and then, with a muttered curse, stepped forward to check for himself. A few moments later, he stepped out again, his face like thunder.

Angela laughed briefly, and he stared straight at her. 'What?'

'You didn't manage to translate the final section of the inscription, did you?' she asked. 'Because you never saw the last clue to the decoding that we needed, the carving that we found on one of the stones in the Western Wall Tunnel. That's why you had to follow us into Jordan, to Shobak Castle.'

'So what?' Khaled's voice betrayed his anger and frustration.

'There was a phrase in that last part of the inscription that didn't make sense to me when we translated it, but it's making perfect sense now. The phrase was "there was safety in separation". We've both followed the same trail all the way from Iraq to Jerusalem, on to Jordan and finally to this place, here in the French Pyrenees. But what you didn't know, because you never decoded the second part of the inscription, was that at some point during the movement of the Templar treasure of Outremer, and the sacred Baphomet relic, the custodians obviously decided to separate them. And because the head of John the Baptist was infinitely more valuable than any kind of worldly possession to the Mandaeans, and maybe also to the Templars, that inscription led us to the location of the relic, but not to where they hid the treasure. That's somewhere else entirely. You've lost,

Khaled,' she finished. 'This is the end of the trail. The treasure isn't here, and all this has been for nothing.'

'Maybe,' the Iraqi snapped, 'but at least I'll still be alive to carry on the quest. For both of you, it's time to die.'

Simultaneously, Khaled and Farooq raised their pistols and aimed them directly at Bronson and Angela.

62

Montsaunès, France

'*Maintenant!*' Bronson shouted. '*Vite!*'

He jumped to the side, putting his body between Angela and the two armed men.

Khaled and Farooq pulled the triggers of their pistols virtually simultaneously, the double report thunderous in the confined space.

Bronson staggered backwards as the two bullets slammed into his chest, knocking him down. His fall took Angela with him. She tumbled on to the stone floor, cracking the back of her head, and lay still as Bronson's dead weight awkwardly covered her body.

Neither Iraqi got a chance to fire a second time. Even as they were shifting the aim of their weapons, two black-clad men stepped down the staircase, silenced sub-machine guns in their hands. When they fired their weapons, the reports sounded like flat metallic slaps, but the effects were devastating. Khaled and Farooq danced briefly and clumsily as the subsonic nine-millimetre bullets slammed into them, before both collapsed to the stone floor.

From the chapel above, similar sounds could be heard, silenced weapons firing followed by the heavy thud of bodies falling to the ground.

One of the newcomers walked over to the splayed bodies of the two Iraqis, the muzzle of his weapon aimed straight at them, while the other one strode across to where Bronson and Angela lay in an untidy tangle of limbs.

His face pinched with concern, he bent over the two silent figures.

'Monsieur Bronson,' he said, and reached out to feel the Englishman's neck, checking for a pulse.

Then he straightened up again, a slight smile crossing his face as Bronson groaned and struggled to move, his hand rubbing his chest. He sat up, clearly trying to catch his breath, then glanced down and behind him at Angela.

'Are you okay?' he asked, panting as he gasped for air, and relief flooded through him when she nodded, before both of them climbed very shakily to their feet.

Bronson grabbed her and held her tight, the sensation spoiled more than somewhat by the bullet-proof Kevlar vests that both were wearing under their outdoor clothes, protective garments that they had donned in the lay-by outside Saint-Martory earlier that morning. The French had insisted on that before agreeing to Bronson's some-what risky scheme.

And in the event, it had been a wise precaution.

Then they turned to look at the slim figure standing beside them, clad all in black with a holstered sidearm and carrying his sub-machine gun.

The man smiled again.

'Was that how you wanted it done, Monsieur Bronson?' he asked.

'*Merci, Capitaine*,' Bronson replied, shaking the gunman's hand, and now speaking almost normally. 'That was exactly how I wanted it done. We – and you, I suppose – really needed to hear those two Iraqis incriminate themselves.'

'Your chest?' the Frenchman asked. 'The vest worked, obviously, but are you okay?'

'It hurts like hell,' Bronson said, 'and I'll be bruised for a month. But that doesn't matter.'

He turned and introduced Angela. 'My former wife, Angela Lewis,' he said. 'Angela, this is Captain Bouvier of the GIGN, the *Groupe d'Intervention de la Gendarmerie Nationale*. The GIGN is a specialist anti-terrorist intervention unit based at Maisons-Alfort, just to the south-east of Paris. He and his men have been in position, hidden here in this chapel and waiting patiently, since before five o'clock this morning.'

Angela shook Bouvier's hand too, trembling a little as she did so, the shock of her own vulnerability and the sudden death of the two Iraqis hitting her.

'Thank you so much, Captain. I only agreed to this madcap scheme because Chris assured me that we would have proper professional help.'

'In my opinion, *madame*, you have had the best professional help available anywhere.' Bouvier was clearly nothing if not proud of his unit's performance. 'And thanks to the questions you asked this man' – he dismissively kicked Khaled's inert body with his left foot – 'we've recorded what amounts to a full admission of what happened at the camp in Iraq and in Milan.'

'Are they all dead?' Bronson asked.

As if in answer to his question, they heard a single thud from the chapel above, the unmistakable sound of a silenced weapon being fired in single-shot mode.

'It would seem so,' Bouvier replied, 'and it's much better that way. No loose ends, no awkward questions, no arguments, and no need for a messy and expensive trial. They were armed and resisted arrest, with this unfortunate but inevitable result. And I'd like to think that the French archaeologists that these animals slaughtered at the dig in Iraq would approve of that decision.'

Bouvier glanced round in satisfaction, and then issued crisp orders to the man standing behind him.

'And now, Monsieur Bronson, it's time for you to leave, so that we can get this mess cleaned up. I don't think you'll want to hang around. Oh, please take off the vests before you go.'

'Could you just give us five minutes, please?' Bronson asked, as he and Angela started to remove the ballistic vests. 'We've followed the trail to this place all the way from the Middle East, and we'd very much like to see exactly what was concealed in that chamber.'

'Take ten minutes,' Bouvier said, 'but then you really will need to leave. And please be careful. Whatever is in that hidden room belongs to France.'

'Of course.'

Bronson and Angela walked forward almost reverently into the chamber – the hidden chapel that had obviously been the Knights Templars' most important place of worship in the long-vanished commandery. As they'd glimpsed earlier, standing in pride of place on the stone altar was a wooden box, perhaps eighteen inches tall, twelve inches wide and about the same deep. It was a very plain and simple design, in keeping with the strict rule by which the Templars had lived, and their vows of poverty and obedience.

The wood was hard and brittle, blackened by the ages. On the front were two small square handles made of gold, and embossed on each was an outline of the Templars' *croix pattée*.

Angela glanced at Bronson, but he gestured for her to go ahead and do the honours. They'd risked their lives for this moment. She grasped each handle and pulled open the door, the unlubricated hinges protesting audibly. And then for a few moments they just looked.

Behind the twin doors was a painting that looked remarkably familiar. A noble, patrician face, marked by a heavy beard and with long hair, stared back at them.

'It's pretty much a dead ringer for the carving in the temple in Iraq,' Angela said quietly.

Bronson pointed at the top of the box, at another

small gold handle, and she carefully lifted that as well, the lid of the box creaking open.

Inside was a complete skull, as far as they could tell without removing it from its resting place, which Angela wasn't prepared to do.

'My God,' she whispered. 'I can't believe it. We shouldn't even be touching this – it will need specialist conservation.'

'So what do you think?' Bronson asked her. 'Is that really the head of John the Baptist?'

'It looks old enough,' she replied, 'and a forensic anthropologist could confirm whether or not the body was decapitated, assuming enough of the neck vertebrae are present, but the reality is that we have no way of knowing if this skull truly belonged to the man known as John the Baptist. But what I can tell you is that the box seems to have been designed so that originally the face of the skull would have been visible behind those two doors. I think the painting was a later addition, added once the flesh on the skull started to really decay, and all that at least implies that the object could have been worshipped. So the short answer is that we're probably looking at the notorious idol, at Baphomet itself, the disembodied head or painted face that was so much venerated and revered by the Templars.'

She looked down at the top of the skull once again.

'But if you want my guess, my gut feeling, then I think the answer's "yes". I think we're looking at the skull of John the Baptist. And there's this as well,' she added, pointing at the wooden face of the box directly below the two doors.

Written in a horizontal line in small but carefully carved letters were two words that they could just barely read.

'Yohanan Mamdana,' Bronson said. 'John the Baptist.'

'That's not proof, of course, but it's indicative. At least the person who carved that had no doubts about the contents of the box. Now let's get out of here.' She closed the wooden doors on the box carefully, leaving it looking exactly the same as when they'd first seen it.

'I'd forgotten about that phrase you quoted at Khaled,' Bronson said as they walked out, 'but it does make sense now. Tibauld de Gaudin, or more likely Jacques de Molay himself, the nobleman who succeeded de Gaudin as the last Grand Master of the Knights Templar, must have decided to send the assets of the order in Outremer somewhere completely different. In fact, bearing in mind that pretty soon after de Molay returned to France he probably found out about the plot Philip the Fair was hatching against the order, he would almost certainly have had the wealth concealed in another country altogether.'

'And you think it's still there, somewhere, just waiting for somebody to stumble across it?'

'Knowing the Templars, I doubt very much if anyone will ever stumble across it, as you put it. Wherever it is, I'm certain it'll be extremely well concealed in a secure location, and it'll only be found by someone who finds a clue somewhere and follows whatever trail has been left.

But, yes, I do think it's still out there, the massive hoard that represents a significant part of the riches of the order, because there's never been any suggestion that it's been found, at any time in history. Maybe we should carry on looking.'

Angela shook her head and gave a small smile.

'Not me, or not right now, anyway. What I want is something to eat and drink, followed by a good long sleep without worrying if some man with a gun is going to try to kill me while I'm in bed. And then I'll be quite happy to go back to my office at the British Museum and get stuck into some really dull and boring, but really, really safe work.'

She paused for a moment as a thought struck her.

'But if you do ever happen to stumble across any kind of clue that might lead you to the treasure of the Templars, just make sure that I'm the first and only person you tell about it. Okay?'

Bronson smiled back at her and nodded.

The café-restaurant a few yards up the road, by the traffic-light controlled junction, was just opening its doors and Angela pointed at it.

'Coffee and a croissant?' she asked. 'It's probably all they'll have available at this time of the morning.'

'Sounds good to me. In fact, that's the best offer I've had in a long time,' Bronson said. He took her firmly by the hand, and led the way across the street and into the early-morning sunshine.

Author's note

I'm a novelist by profession, which means I'm a professional liar – my short job description is that I'm paid to make up stuff – but I have always believed that the best fiction has a grounding in fact. It's far easier to construct a story around real events, though sometimes the truth and the fiction inevitably become somewhat blurred. This short author's note should help separate the one from the other.

Mandaean heresy
In global religious terms, the Mandaean faith is insignificant, with only perhaps 70,000 followers still remaining worldwide, and until the Iraq war of 2003, the vast majority of them lived in southern Iraq. Today this number has dropped to an estimated 5000 in this region of the country, and it is believed that most of the remainder are now living in Iran and northern Iraq.

The Mandaeans followed a Gnostic religion – just like the Greek word *gnosis*, the Aramaic word *manda* translates as 'knowledge' – that would undeniably have been regarded as the wildest heresy by the early Christian church. They believed in the reality of many of the Old Testament figures, people like Adam and Noah, and especially revered John the Baptist, while at the same time utterly rejecting Moses, Abraham and particularly Jesus Christ. They spoke a dialect of Eastern Aramaic known as Mandaic, and were probably of Semitic origin.

Bearing in mind that in mediaeval times a person could be labelled a heretic simply for worshipping God and Jesus in a way that was not approved of by the Church, anyone following the Mandaean religion would have been seen to be completely beyond the pale, and it is therefore unsurprising that they have remained one of the most private and secretive of all religious sects. Virtually all the information about them has been obtained by outsiders.

The concept of baptism was, and is, central to their faith and followers of this belief system are more commonly known in the Middle East as the *Subba*, a name that derives from another Aramaic word that refers to baptism. The place where the Mandaeans worship is known as a *mandī*, and would normally be built beside a river to facilitate baptism (*maṣbattah*), though where this was impossible a ritual bath would be constructed inside the *mandī*.

Knights Templar formation

The description of the formation of the order of the

Knights Templar, the Poor Fellow-Soldiers of Christ and of the Temple of Solomon (the *Pauperes Commilitones Christi Templique Salomonici*) is as accurate as the historical record will permit, bearing in mind that the events described took place almost one millennium ago. As far as can be established, the original nine knights were linked by either blood or marriage, and their ostensible purpose in travelling to Jerusalem was to protect the pilgrims on the roads of the Holy Land, a task that would have been manifestly impossible for such a small number of warrior monks, no matter how well trained, fearless and dedicated they might have been.

And, as far as can be gleaned from the historical record, for the first nine years of the existence of the Order, none of the members made the slightest attempt to do anything of the sort. Instead, having somehow managed to persuade King Baldwin II of Jerusalem to grant them accommodation in the lavish quarters of the Al Aqsa mosque on the Temple Mount in 1120, they apparently rarely ventured outside. This notable absence from their alleged primary purpose led to any number of subsequent conspiracy theories, and it seems to have been generally accepted that they spent most of their time excavating the ground that lay beneath their feet. A number of Templar relics were later found in the hidden rooms below the Temple Mount, and we know for a fact that they made use of some of the chambers that lay within it, most particularly the large space that became known as Solomon's Stables, which they used to accommodate their horses.

In those first years, the Order was notably impoverished – indeed, one of the symbols used to represent the poverty of the Knights Templar was the image of two men riding one horse, the implication being that they could not afford a horse each – and relied upon donations to survive.

However, that changed very quickly once the Order was officially recognized and endorsed by the Roman Catholic Church in about 1129, an endorsement that was gained suspiciously rapidly bearing in mind the tiny size of the Templar organization at that time. This endorsement was followed only ten years later by the proclamation of the *Omne Datum Optimum* papal bull. It exempted the Templars from obeying any local laws, meaning that members of the Order could cross any border into any country, were not required to pay any taxes to anybody, and were subjected only to the authority of the Pope himself.

By any standards, this was an extraordinary piece of legislation, and there appears to have been no particularly obvious reason why it should have been granted by the pontiff. It is therefore not beyond the bounds of possibility that the first members of the Knights Templar did spend years excavating the Temple Mount and in doing so found something, the mere existence of which was sufficient to terrify the Pope into granting whatever the Templars wanted.

Unfortunately, the chances are that we'll never know the truth of this suggestion, or what this powerful object – assuming that they did find something – might have been.

Forewarned is forearmed

The arrests of the Knights Templar in France and other countries, on the instructions of Philip the Fair, took place on 13 October 1307. The claim often made is that these arrests came as a complete surprise to the Order, and that the operation was entirely successful. However even the most cursory examination of the surviving evidence suggests that this was not the case.

The Knights Templar organization was one of the richest and most powerful entities then in existence, far more wealthy than many countries and a majority of European monarchs. But it had a problem – it did not have a secure base, a big enough piece of territory that it could occupy and control and which it could defend against its enemies. Instead, it had a number of small strongholds, like the Paris Preceptory, but every one of these was entirely surrounded by the territory of another nation. The Order was literally surrounded by potential or actual enemies on all sides.

The Templars would have tried to remain as well informed as possible about the intentions of the rulers of these territories. They would have employed spies at court or paid informers. And an operation as big as the arrest of the Templars could never have been kept completely secret. Too many people, in too many different countries, were involved. So almost certainly the arrests did not come as a surprise to the Order, but because of the circumstances, even knowing – perhaps in considerable detail – what was about to happen, there wouldn't been very much that they could have done about it.

In fact, the indications are that they did a fair amount, because the number of Templars arrested in France was only a tiny fraction of the total known complement of the Order in that country. It is also known that when Philip's soldiers opened up the Templars' strong rooms in the Paris Preceptory, the vast quantity of treasure that the king had seen there just a few months earlier had somehow vanished. Some assets were left, obviously, but nothing like the amount of bullion and coin that Philip had counted on finding to clear his own enormous debts.

Exactly where that treasure went, and how it was removed, has never been explained convincingly, and it is quite possible that somewhere in France, or indeed in another country entirely, there may well be a sealed and long-forgotten vault within which the priceless Templar treasure still lies hidden. This is one of the central mysteries about the Knights Templar, which has kept people intrigued about them for centuries.

Baphomet

When the Templar Order was purged and the Knights and Sergeants arrested in 1307, one of the charges brought against them was that of heresy, specifically that they worshipped an idol, apparently a disembodied head, which they referred to as Baphomet.

The name Baphomet predates the Templars by over twenty years. It was referred to in a letter written in 1098 by a Crusader named Anselm of Ribemont, and was used to apparently describe an idol or deity venerated by the Muslim opponents of the Crusaders. The derivation of the name does imply that it was probably both Arabic and Muslim: a chronicler of the First Crusade described the mosques as *Bafumarias*, and there is a suggestion that the word 'Baphomet' was the term used by the often illiterate Crusaders to mean 'Mahomet', more properly known as 'Muhammad'. There are no references to either the word or to any kind of an idol in the Templars' own Rule, the very specific and rigorous code of ethics and behaviour that governed their lives, or in any surviving contemporary documents, and most of the information about the object has been derived from the records of the Inquisition.

These are frequently contradictory and incomplete. The information was obtained from men under the most brutal torture, where they would simply tell their inquisitors what they thought they wanted to hear, irrespective of the veracity or otherwise of what they were saying.

Some accounts described Baphomet as a severed head, others as a cat, and still others as a head with three faces. It has been reasonably well established that the Templars did own a number of relics, and that these included heads of various sorts, some actual skulls apparently having been removed from the bodies of dead saints, one for example was claimed to be that of St Euphemia, and another being the skull of Hugues de Payens, one of the founders of the Templar order. Other heads had apparently been carved out of wood and presumably had a purely symbolic significance.

Were the Knights Templar Christian?

It has been claimed by a number of researchers that the Templars, despite being an order of warrior monks endorsed by the Pope, were not actually Christians, in that they were required to trample and spit upon the cross and to deny Christ during their initiation ceremony. These accusations first saw the light of day after Philip the Fair of France had seized all the members of the Order he could lay his hands on, and had then begun levelling charges against them. However, these were almost precisely the same charges that he had earlier made against Pope Boniface VIII, which gives these accusations very little integrity.

But despite the likelihood that these accusations had no basis whatsoever in reality, it is still probable that the Knights Templar weren't Christian but Johannite – meaning followers of John the Baptist – in their religious beliefs. Though this cannot be absolutely proven, there are a number of pointers.

First, a very large number of churches and chapels known to have been built by the Templars were originally dedicated to John the Baptist, rather than Jesus Christ or one of the Apostles, which was more usually the case. Second, one of the prevalent symbols associated with John the Baptist is the Lamb of God, the *Agnus Dei*, and this image is often found on Templar flags and seals, as well as forming a part of the decoration of Templar buildings, frequently in association with carvings of severed heads.

One of the most convincing pieces of circumstantial

evidence is the seal of the Templar Master of England, which included the *Agnus Dei* image, while the counter-seal displayed the image of the head of John the Baptist together with the legend 'I am the guarantor of the lamb'. If the Order had been a normal Christian organiz-ation, this would have been a most unusual choice of both images and wording.

There is another oblique reference to the Templars and the *Agnus Dei* that can still be seen all over Britain. In 1393, King Richard II passed a law that required all inns and public houses to display a sign identifying themselves to the largely illiterate populace as places where alcohol was sold. One common sign is the 'Lamb and Flag', a direct reference to the Knights Templar, the lamb being their symbol and the flag the *Beauseant*, their *vexillum belli* or battle flag. And, slightly more gruesome, the pub names 'The Saracen's Head' and 'The Turk's Head' are reminders of the likely result of an Islamic warrior encountering the Templars in battle.

And if it is assumed that the Templars did worship John the Baptist, and we take into account the refer-ences to them worshipping a head, it is not too big a leap of conjecture to suggest that they may have possessed – or they may have believed they possessed – the head of the prophet. This may well have been their Baphomet, and it is this assumption which has formed an impor-tant part of the plot of this novel.

Shobak Castle, Jordan, and the Église Saint-Christophe des Templiers, Montsaunès, France
Both of these buildings exist and are exactly as described in the pages of this novel, with two single exceptions.

First, the cistern that supplied drinking water to the defenders of Shobak Castle is located precisely where I described it, as is the access to the underground staircase that leads from the castle down to it. However, actually descending the staircase is not quite as easy as it appears to be in this book, so if you visit Shobak, please don't expect that you'll be able to retrace Bronson's steps!

Second, the location and interior decoration of the Église Saint-Christophe des Templiers is accurate, and it is just as bizarre, mysterious and largely inexplicable as I have suggested. However, the crypt and the concealed doorway that I have described at the end of the book are entirely the products of my own imagination.

The First Apostle

James Becker

An Englishwoman is found dead in a house near Rome.

Her distraught husband enlists the help of his closest friend, Chris Bronson, who discovers an ancient inscription on a slab of stone above their fireplace. It translates as 'Here Lie the Liars'.

But who are the liars? And what is it they are lying to protect?

Pursued across Europe, Bronson uncovers a trail of clues that leads him back to the shadowy beginnings of Christianity; to a chalice decorated with mysterious symbols; to a secret code hidden within a scroll.

And to a deadly conspiracy which – if revealed – will rock the foundations of our modern world.

'Utterly spellbinding. The plot is stunning and breathtaking and leaves you racing to the end . . . A truly amazing book.'
EURO CRIME

'Exciting . . . fast paced and filled with non-stop action.'
GENRE GO ROUND REVIEWS

Crisis

Frank Gardner

In the dank undergrowth of the Colombian jungle, a body is found.

In his pockets are a stained notebook and a British passport. That much the local police know. What they don't know is that Jeremy Benton worked for the British Secret Intelligence Service. That his murder will trigger a crisis. And that soon all hell is going to break loose . . .

MI6 need someone on the scene who can sort out this mess, and quickly. And so Luke Carlton – ex-Special Boat Service commando, now under short-term contract to the SIS – steps out of a plane in Bogotá and into a world of trouble. Hunted down, captured, tortured and on the run from one of South America's most powerful and ruthless drugs cartels, Luke begins to unravel the coils of a plot targeting everything that he holds dear. And now it's a life-or-death race against time to prevent a disaster on a terrifying scale.

'Full of tomorrow's headlines, *Crisis* is a nerve-shredding thriller with an intimate knowledge of the world it portrays.'
TONY PARSONS, BEST-SELLING AUTHOR OF *THE MURDER BAG*

'Written by someone who has been there, done that and knows what it's about, *Crisis* is a thriller you just can't put down.'
SIR ROGER MOORE

Inferno

Dan Brown

Florence: Harvard symbologist Robert Langdon awakes in a hospital bed with no recollection of where he is or how he got there. Nor can he explain the origin of the macabre object that is found hidden in his belongings.

A threat to his life will propel him and a young doctor, Sienna Brooks, into a breakneck chase across the city. Only Langdon's knowledge of the hidden passageways and ancient secrets that lie behind its historic facade can save them from the clutches of their unknown pursuers.

With only a few lines from Dante's *Inferno* to guide them, they must decipher a sequence of codes buried deep within some of the Renaissance's most celebrated artworks to find the answers to a puzzle which may, or may not, help them save the world from a terrifying threat . . .

'Fast, clever, well-informed . . . Dan Brown is the master of the intellectual cliff-hanger.'
WALL STREET JOURNAL

'Jam-packed with tricks . . . A book length scavenger hunt that Mr Brown creates so energetically.'
NEW YORK TIMES

*For everyone who finds a
crime story irresistible.*

Discover the very best **crime and thriller books**
and get tailored recommendations to help you
choose what to read next.

Read **exclusive interviews with top authors** or
join our **live web chats** and speak to them directly.

And it's not just about books. We'll be bringing you
specially commissioned features on everything
criminal, from **TV and film** to **true crime stories**.

We also love a good competition.
Our **monthly contest** offers you the chance to win the
latest thrilling fiction, plus there are DVD box sets
and devices to be won.

**Sign up for our free fortnightly newsletter at
www.deadgoodbooks.co.uk/signup**

Join the conversation on: